The Unidentified redhead

Also by Alice Clayton

Wallbanger
The Redhead Revealed

The Unidentified

redhead

alice Clayton

G

GALLERY BOOKS

New York London Toronto Sydney New Delhi

G

Gallery Books
A Division of Simon & Schuster, Inc.
1230 Avenue of the Americas
New York, NY 10020

Copyright © 2012 by Alice Clayton
Originally published in 2012 by Omnific Publishing.

First Gallery Books paperback edition October 2013

GALLERY BOOKS and colophon are registered trademarks of Simon & Schuster, Inc.

For information about special discounts for bulk purchases, please contact Simon & Schuster Special Sales at 1-866-506-1949 or business@simonandschuster.com.

The Simon & Schuster Speakers Bureau can bring authors to your live event. For more information or to book an event contact the Simon & Schuster Speakers Bureau at 1-866-248-3049 or visit our website at www.simonspeakers.com.

Designed by Aline C. Pace

ISBN 978-1-4767-4122-2
ISBN 978-1-4767-4127-7 (ebook)

For Nancy

acknowledgments

To Elizabeth, for taking a chance on me.

To the online writing community, where I have made so many wonderful friends and gained so much valuable insight.

To my family and friends, who have been so supportive and patient with me while I try on this new hat.

To everyone who has embraced their inner Grace.

And to Peter, who has always been my George.

The
Unidentified
redhead

one

*Y*ou *do* realize I have seen you naked before, right?" Holly shouted through the bedroom door.

"Yes, love, but it's been a while. I don't think you're ready for this."

"Is this an 'I don't think you're ready for this jelly' situation?"

"Did you actually just say that to a half-naked girl? Seriously, you should know better. You'll give me a complex. Asshead."

"You're making this too hard, Grace."

"That's what *she* said," I muttered, and laughed quietly to myself. I was in the process of trying to get my butt into a new pair of low-rise jeans that were so very, very low, they might have been illegal.

"That's it," Holly announced. "I'm coming in. Suck it in, Grace!"

She came barreling through the door, stopping short when she saw me struggling on the bed. I was laid out flat on the sheets in a charming lacy peach bra, halfway in and out

1

of the damn jeans that she had convinced me to buy, even though I knew I was in no way young enough to work them in the way they deserved to be worked. Holly had always had a way of getting me to do things she wanted me to do, under the guise that she knew what was best for me. And, mother-of-pearl, she was almost always right.

"Sweet rack," she said, acknowledging my bra. "Do I need to get a pair of pliers and pull the zipper up myself? Didn't we see that done in a movie once?" she mused.

"Yes, yes we did . . . a little help? I'm giving a full salute here. I'd like to get the girls back under wraps," I answered, struggling to stay on the bed at this odd angle.

"I can see that. Okay, hold your breath," she said, and grabbed the button of my jeans. I pulled with all my might as the zipper finally closed, leaving me breathless.

"Holy Lord. I think my uterus just left. Yep, there she goes," I moaned.

I couldn't believe how tight these jeans were, although I was damn proud to be wearing them. A "you go, girl" thrill rolled through me, but it could have also been the lack of oxygen from the denim restricting my air supply.

Holly helped me climb off the bed, and I turned to admire the way I looked in these badass jeans, thinking that maybe I could actually pull them off. I still caught myself examining the mirror at times and having to look twice to make sure it was really me.

She saw me checking myself out and chuckled. "You're looking sassy there, my friend. I would totally fuck you."

"That's charming, Holly. Thanks." I smiled back at her as I continued to pose in the mirror. I began to vogue and got to giggling.

"Grace, settle down. Vogueing is just wrong." She laughed, giving me one last thumbs-up as she left the room.

I had recently shed quite a bit of weight. In fact, I was in better shape now than when I was in college. Holly was proud of me and made sure to tell me often.

Holly Newman and I met in college. While we both majored in theater, she knew early on that she preferred the behind-the-scenes world, especially the business side, while I was a major drama queen. The entire time we were in school together, we made plans for when we would conquer the entertainment world. She would have her own agency and manage only the best talent, working with artists who shared a similar creative vision. I, however, had stars in my eyes and wanted to be famous, famous, god-*damned* famous.

She made it out to the coast six months before I did, and when I finally got there, she was already working her way up as a junior agent at one of the major firms in town. She had a real knack for artist management, knowing when to be tough and when to coddle. She knew when to really fight for her artists and when to lay the groundwork for future projects. When I arrived, she got me a job temping in the agency, and I watched in awe as she maneuvered in what was still very much a man's world.

With Holly's perfect golden hair, fantastic figure, and stylish sensibility, she was asked all the time why she was working behind the scenes rather than in front of the camera. The girl was a knockout. But she always laughed and said, "It's just not for me," and then worked harder than everyone else.

I loved L.A. I'd moved in with Holly, started taking acting

classes, and worked at the agency with her, while waiting tables at night in a restaurant in Santa Monica. I really felt like I was living the Hollywood lifestyle I'd been dreaming of since I could remember.

After about six months, Holly convinced her boss that I should come in for a reading and be considered for representation. I was prepared, I read well, my headshots were flawless . . . and then I waited. And waited. And then waited some more. Finally, they agreed to take me on if Holly agreed to sign me personally as my sole representation.

She began sending me out on auditions. I auditioned all over that town, and I was damn good. But so was everyone else.

I didn't book a single job.

What they don't tell you when you grow up in the Midwest, light-years away from L.A., is that when you move to Hollywood, everyone is the next Miss Hot Shit. We all think we're the prettiest, we all think we're special, we all think we are the only one who truly has what it takes. We all think our talent is genuine and true, we all think we have something to share with the world, and we all can't understand why we aren't booking jobs all the time.

The thing is, in L.A., you can't just be a pretty face, because you can airbrush that. You can't just have a good bod, because everyone else is nipped and tucked in places you don't even want to dream of. You can't just giggle and toss your hair and be the punch line, because someone else already has that job sewn up.

For all the people who move to L.A. each year, just as many leave, limping back to their hometowns like pretty little sad sacks, telling their "I lived in California" stories over cocktails with their old high school friends.

I became one of those sad sacks—I only lasted in Los Angeles for eighteen months. I limped away, feeling like a failure for the first time in my life. I let the city and the industry beat me.

But now I was back. It had taken me ten years to make it back, and this time I wasn't going anywhere.

☆　☆　☆

Holly was having a party at her house to celebrate the launch of her new management company and had invited her close friends and several of the actors and actresses she represented. She had recently left a very high-profile position with a major agency. A few of her clients had chosen to stay with the other agency, but she was so good at crafting a career, particularly with fresh new talent, that many had followed her.

Since I'd moved back to L.A., I'd been staying with her at her house in the hills. She'd done very well for herself and had a great house off Mulholland Drive with a view of the city below.

Which brings us to the illegal jeans. As a thirty-three-year-old with some preexisting body image issues, I was trying to get into the mind-set I would need to navigate this party in this particular pair of jeans. I had matched the illegal jeans with a fairly conservative turquoise, cowl-neck tank top and slid my feet into some very nice peep-toe slingbacks. I had great toe cleavage.

I was wearing my hair down, which I rarely do, but Holly had banned all my ponytail holders this evening. We had gone that afternoon to get our hair done, and my red hair was a mass of soft curls. That stylist really earned his money, and even *I* had to admit the curls were shampoo-commercial-worthy.

The party was in full swing, and everyone was having a great time. Because Holly only took on talent she truly wanted to invest herself in, they became her close friends as well. They were always at the house, and her circle had become my circle.

"Grace, you can't be serious. Feldman is way hotter than Haim."

I was deep in a discussion with Nick, a screenwriter whom Holly had known for years. He'd become one of my friends and could always be counted on as a good wingman at a party. Tonight we were knee-deep in the dirty martinis. Extra dirty. He was waiting for an actor to arrive whom Holly had recently begun to represent, an actor who apparently was poised to be the next big thing. I had yet to meet him, although Nick had admitted he was, and I quote, "yummy, scrumptious . . . a bit scruffy, but in a totally hot kind of way." Also, his British accent was "lovely," "to die for," and "knock-me-down-and-fuck-me."

"*Fine,*" I said. "I will admit that Corey Feldman was genius in *Goonies,* and even semicute in *Stand by Me.* But no one holds a candle to my Lucas." I was determined to win this round. We had recently gotten into a similar discussion about Steve Carell versus Ricky Gervais, and it didn't end well. Someone got scratched.

I heard a snicker behind me and a British voice said, "I think you've gotta give the edge to Haim, if only for getting to kiss Heather Graham."

I turned to acknowledge the obvious genius of the newcomer who knew *License to Drive.*

"Hey, you're Super-Sexy Scientist Guy!" I cried out, clapping my hands over my mouth as soon as I'd said it. I could feel my face redden instantly.

Holly had a picture of this guy on her computer and had been referring to him as "Super-Sexy Scientist Guy" for the last month. This was her new client—the next big thing. He had the lead in a movie slated for a fall release that was already generating big buzz in town. I didn't know much about the movie, but I knew that Holly was very excited to be representing him.

Super-Sexy Scientist Guy gave me a confused and somewhat sheepish grin. Did he know how hot that grin was?

Oh yeah, he totally knew.

He extended a hand to me and in the queen's English said, "Actually, I'm Super-Sexy Jack Hamilton."

two

I heard Nick's sharp intake of breath as he almost knocked me out of the way to shake Jack's hand.

"Hi, Jack. I'm Nick. I saw you in your movie *Her Better Half. Loved* it! I also saw your pictures in *Entertainment Weekly*. Are you living here in L.A. now? Are you excited for *Time* to come out? Wow, you're pretty." Nick had forgotten to breathe and only stopped talking because he ran out of air.

I watched as Jack's face changed from surprise to confusion, then moved on to wonder and finally barely contained laughter.

I giggled and began to extricate Nick's hand from Jack's. "Settle down, big guy. You can tell Jack he's pretty all night long, but you don't want to shock *and* awe him in the first five minutes." I turned to Jack. "Hi, I'm Grace Sheridan— Super-Sexy Grace Sheridan. It's nice to meet you." I shook his hand while Nick panted next to me. "And you *are* quite pretty," I added as Jack smiled back at me.

Now that my surprised blinders were off, I saw a tall, lean young man who was almost a foot taller than me. He was wearing faded jeans, a black T-shirt with a gray zip-up jacket, and oh my, were those Doc Martens? He had on an old gray baseball cap and a few days' worth of scruff that was definitely working for him. He seemed very comfortable in his skin, which, for a second, I imagined pressed up against mine in a tight embrace.

The guy looks young enough to be your kid, Grace.

Yes, but only if I'd really slutted it up in junior high . . .

I shook my head to clear it a little and saw Holly working her way across the kitchen to greet Jack.

"Hello, sweetness. How're you tonight?" she asked, wrapping an arm around his shoulders and leaning in for a quick peck on the cheek.

"I'm well, thank you. I've just been meeting Grace and, uh, Nick, was it?" Jack smiled again and Nick swooned. I snorted and Jack winked at me mischievously.

"Grace is my girl," Holly said. "We go *way* back. And Nick, well, Nick is necessary," she said teasingly.

Nick feigned annoyance and responded, "Bitch, please. Where are you gonna find another man who will take you to see New Kids on the Block? *And* go along with the lie that it was work related?"

I almost spat out my cocktail, I was laughing so hard. Holly was the biggest closet New Kids fan around. I was one of the very few who knew this secret, maybe because I shared it.

"I don't know why you're laughing, Miss Thing," Nick said, turning his gaze to me. "You still fantasize over Joe McIntyre like you're thirteen years old!"

"Oh, I own my obsession. If Joey Joe were here right now, I'd break him. I have no shame," I said, drinking the rest of my martini.

Jack leaned over and whispered to me loudly enough for

Holly to hear, "Is that why she's been trying to get me an audition for Donnie's next film? Should I be concerned?"

With him this close, I finally noticed his eyes. Wow, they were intense. Dark emerald green with flecks of gold.

This guy must get so much play.

I leaned closer to him and said quietly, "You only need to worry if she asks you to dance for her. Watch out for that."

He gave me a sexy little smile while Holly took him by the hand and began leading him away. "Okay, kids. I need Jack to meet a few people. I'll deal with you two later."

The two of them headed back into the living room as Jack waved over his shoulder, leaving me and Nick to laugh in the kitchen.

"So, you played that real smooth, Nick. Is that the hottie you've been raving about all night?"

"Don't act like you didn't think he was cute. I saw the way you checked him out," he said, fanning himself. "I made such an ass of myself! I wanted to play it cool when I saw him, but I couldn't make myself shut up! Did I actually tell him he was pretty?" A blush stained his cheeks.

"Yeah, you did. But don't worry about it. When I first moved out here, I was convinced I recognized an actor from *Baywatch* in the supermarket. I stalked him from produce all the way to the bakery, and when he finally looked at me, I muttered the word *Hasselhoff* and then ran and hid in the soup aisle. I still get embarrassed when I see a box of Cup Noodles."

"You *should* be embarrassed, because you're still *buying* Cup Noodles, but whatever. Let's get plowed and flirt with pretty boys!" he said, refilling my martini glass, making it extra dirty.

I laughed and ignored the fluttering in my tummy when I heard a British accent floating in from the other room.

☆ ☆ ☆

Later that night, Holly and I were out on the terrace overlooking the city, working our way through our fourth cocktails and toasting her success. Nick came out to say his good-nights and slipped his arm around my waist.

"Okay, bitches, I'm taking off. Be good, and make sure no one goes home with my pretty boy. I need to make sure he stays pure until I can convince him to switch teams," he said teasingly, wagging his finger at Holly.

"How do you know he doesn't already play on your team, Nick?" I asked.

Holly laughed and said, "Oh, sweetie, Jack is the hottest thing to hit this town in a while. He's got girls throwing themselves at him every night. He's discreet, but he is hittin' that shit."

"Oh, God, I can't hear any more. It'll make me too sad. I'm going home to weep over some Manilow," Nick cried as he made his way back into the house. He passed Jack on his way, who was talking to two girls over by the piano, and he winked at Nick. I heard Nick mutter, "Tease," as he walked by, and I could see Jack chuckling.

"So, I get that he's cute," I said, "and what girl doesn't like an accent? But why is he the next big thing? Nick mentioned something about a movie coming out—*Time* or something?" I asked as we watched Jack talk to the two girls, who couldn't stop giggling at everything he said. I noticed he bit down on his lower lip constantly.

11

Was he nervous?

"Grace, are you serious? You can't be serious. *Time*?" Holly looked at me incredulously.

"What? Is this something I would know about?" I wracked my brain trying to remember if I had heard anything about this movie but was drawing a blank.

"You've never read the short stories *Time* is based on? You really don't know anything about them?" she asked, still looking shocked.

"Hey, I've had a lot going on lately. I haven't had a lot of time to read much. Besides, you know I read mostly nonfiction," I answered, looking at Jack through the glass of the French doors.

"It's a series of short stories that were written for a women's magazine, and they have everything you have ever wanted: passion, love, adventure, sex, humor. Practically every woman I know is in love with them! The main character, Joshua—holy hell. He's a sexy scientist man traveling through time, and in each story he's in a different period and with a different woman. This movie is going to be huge!" she squealed.

"Hmm, I'm not usually a romance fan. Too schmaltzy, ya know? Not really a fan of science fiction, either. Gimme a good historical nonfiction, like the new book about Lincoln. They now think that he—"

"Oh, would you shut up?" Holly interrupted. "Honestly, it's like you're sprinting toward the retirement home! And *Time* isn't romance, it's just . . . Gah, I can't describe it! That's why this movie is such a big deal—and why Jack is such a hot commodity right now. Women are losing their minds across this entire country waiting for it to come out, and he's Joshua. Oh man, I can't wait for you to read them! Swear to me right now that you'll read them!"

I had only ever seen her this worked up when Donnie Wahlberg was involved. "Jesus, fine. Calm down. Yes, I will freaking read them," I said, noticing that Jack was coming toward us.

"Jack, listen to this," Holly called. "Grace hasn't read the *Time* short stories. She's never even heard of the movie!" she said as he walked onto the terrace.

He stared at me dramatically and then swept me into a close hug. "Run away with me," he said quietly, pulling back to look at me, placing a hand on each side of my face.

I chuckled nervously and then got control.

"Are you asking random women to run away with you, Jack?" Holly asked, and he dropped his hands from my face, looking at me in mock adoration.

"Random? I meant it!" he said. "I told you before: the next female I met who hasn't heard of this silly little film, I'd run off with and have a tasty little tryst to satisfy the gossip magazines. How lucky am I that she seems normal?" he joked back.

"I really wouldn't rush to judgment on that yet. You don't know how abnormal I am," I stated, placing my hands on my hips.

"I have to tell you, Jack, she's not right in the head," Holly said, warning him. "You don't want any of this. Believe me, I know. I've known Grace since college, and she's insane." She knocked back the last of her cocktail.

"Wait—is this your best *friend* Grace? The one who leaves piles of Chex Mix around the house?" he asked, looking back and forth between us.

"Yep, this is my Gracie. Now ask her *why* she leaves piles of Chex Mix around the house," Holly said teasingly.

I gave her a look. "First of all, thanks for telling my tales all over town, ass. And to clarify, it is not piles all over the house. I happen to not care for the little melba toasts, so whenever I eat Chex Mix, I set them aside. That way, if anyone else wants them, they can have them," I said, showing Holly my middle finger.

"I happen to love the melba toasts," Jack said, laughing at Holly's face when she realized that this seemed to make perfect sense to him.

"Well, next time I have a pile, I'll save them for you. Then if you're ever in some kind of toast emergency—"

"I'll have some on standby. I feel good about this plan," he said.

I noticed the two girls Jack had been talking to inside coming out to join us on the terrace. They approached from both sides as Holly began pulling me into the house.

"I'll see you later, dear. Make sure you come and say good-bye to me before you leave," she said over her shoulder as we walked back across the slate tiles.

"Let me know when you're ready for that tryst," I shot over my shoulder, winking at the girls, who looked a little stunned. I couldn't resist.

"You, me, melba toasts." He grinned back at me.

"Since when do you invite groupies to your house?" I asked once we were inside.

"Groupies? Oh, those two? Sweetie, the blonde is an entertainment lawyer and the brunette is a PR exec. But Brit boy over there turns them all into giggling idiots." She smiled knowingly as I looked back over my shoulder at the three of them on the terrace. Jack was standing between them as they jostled to get closer. He caught my eye and smiled that same sheepish grin.

Wow, a lawyer? Those short stories must be damn good.

An hour later, with the party finally winding down, I was in the kitchen getting some crackers to begin soaking up the five dirty martinis I had sucked down. I was leaning on my elbows on the granite countertop, thinking about how my head was going to hurt tomorrow, when I heard someone come in.

"Hello again," I heard a British voice say.

I looked up, still half-lying on the counter. "Hello yourself. Did you have a good time tonight?" I asked before shoving a saltine in my mouth.

"Oh, no. Crackers—that's never a good sign. Too much?" he asked.

"Maybe, if you consider three more than I usually have too much." I grimaced, remembering the last time I had been hungover. I was really not looking forward to tomorrow.

"I find that the best cure for a hangover is to just keep drinking," he said, smirking. He walked toward the other side of the counter, placing his hands on either side of me.

"Yes, well, that's because you're like seventeen and capable of shit like that. I, on the other hand, will wake up tomorrow feeling like something died in my mouth, with my eyes puffed up like cabbages."

"Wow, that's a really descriptive picture. I'm almost tempted to stick around and see that." He laughed. "And I'm twenty-four, not seventeen, for future reference," he added.

I arched my eyebrow at him. *Young pup.* I used to be able to drink and dance all night, get one hour of sleep, and go to work the next day still looking fabulous. Ah, to be young and foolish again . . .

I stretched my arms over my head and then back behind me, trying to work the kinks out. When I looked at Jack, I realized that I had basically just thrust my chest in his face, and he was letting his eyes linger.

"Are you looking at my boobies?" I asked, doing a little shimmy-shake.

He froze and then burst out laughing. "Yes, yes, I guess I am looking at your boobies. They're quite nice boobies," he managed to choke out between laughs.

"They are quite nice, that's true. And all mine. You probably don't get to touch a lot of bona fide natural boobies here in L.A., but there are still a few of us rocking the real stuff." I laughed along with him.

"I also think you like men looking at your boobies. Why else did you put sparkles on them?" He finally looked me in the eyes again, still chuckling.

"What are you talking about?" I looked down at the girls and noticed that I did have a few sparkles on my cleavage. "Oh yeah, I guess I did. I put on a little shimmer body lotion before I got dressed tonight."

"Girls sure do weird stuff. Especially you American girls. So much shimmer and sparkle. Who told you tits were supposed to sparkle? Sorry, boobies," he said, correcting himself.

"You can say *tits,* although I prefer *boobies.* I also like *ta-tas,*" I said with a straight face.

"How about *love pillows*?" he retorted.

"*Breasticles*?" I said.

"Uhhh, how about *flapjacks*?" he asked, struggling not to laugh.

"Nice, but it doesn't hold a candle to *sweater meat,*" I managed to get out before laughing so hard I sprayed saltines all over the counter. He joined me, and I actually had tears streaming down my face as we started wiping up my cracker spittle.

Holly walked in at that moment, took one look at us, and started shaking her head. "Oh boy, what the hell is going on in here? Never mind. Jack, your ladies are looking for you. They're salivating all over the entryway; it's time to take them back to your place. Grace, why are there cracker crumbs all over your cleavage?" she asked, staring at my saltine-encrusted chest.

We both started laughing again as I extended my hand.

"Jack, it was very nice to meet you. I hope next time I can contain myself a little more. Enjoy your threesome," I said with a wicked smile. This guy was great, and I was excited to have maybe made a new friend.

He took my hand. "Grace, it has been interesting, to say the least. And your sparkly boobies are beautiful. Enjoy your hangover." He shook my hand and laughed again as he left the kitchen, giving Holly a kiss on the cheek as she walked him out.

I watched him leave with his blonde and his brunette, thinking about how much fun this evening had turned out to be.

Holly came back after showing the last of her guests to the door, took one look at the party fouls all over the place, and said, "Clean this shit up in the morning?"

"Or the afternoon?" I asked, holding my head.

"Deal. Let's go to bed," she answered, locking up as I turned out the lights. We trudged upstairs, discussing the evening as we made our way down the hall toward our rooms.

"That was a great party, Holly. I'm really proud of you. You've done everything you set out to do, and nothing has stopped you. You kind of rock." I smiled at her and gave her a hug at her door.

"Yeah, I *have* kicked some ass. Now go vomit. I know you want to," she said, pointing me toward my room.

"I really do. Night," I said over my shoulder as I went to collapse.

"Night, dillweed. Seriously, Grace—five dirty martinis?" was the last thing I heard her say as I shut the door and fell onto my bed.

Right before I slipped into sleep, I thought about my sparkly boobies and laughed.

three

The morning brought hellfire and brimstone, and that was just what I threw up. When I first opened my eyes, which took several minutes of prying through mascara goo, I knew that this was possibly going to be the worst day of my life. I never, repeat *never,* have more than two cocktails. I simply can't handle it anymore. I would love to pretend that I can still hang with the younglings, knocking back cocktail after cocktail and feeling no pain, but that was no longer me. I felt the pain—oh, how I felt the pain.

I attempted to get dressed, but gravity defeated me and I made my way out into the hall in an old button-down shirt, leaving my shorts on the floor of my bedroom, where they had finally given up the fight. After repeated tries at balance, I made it down the hall, hugging the wall and then the banister for support. I could smell coffee, and as if it were a beacon, I was drawn to it. I could hear Holly talking on the phone, and I moaned at her damnable cheeriness. Holly never got a hangover. Bitch.

"Yes, right now you're scheduled to do MTV on the seventh, and then you have an *InStyle* photo shoot on the twelfth of that same month," she said, smiling at me.

I poured myself a cup of coffee, wrapping my hands around the mug and inhaling deeply. I might feel human again in about a day or so. I burped and thought, *Well, maybe a few days.*

"Listen, mister, do you have any idea how hard it was to sync up all the calendars for you guys? Half the cast is going to be there. You have to do the photo shoot on the twelfth. At least it's here in L.A., so there's no travel involved. Yes, I know this fall you'll have plenty of travel. Honestly, Jack, sometimes you sound like such a little bitch." She laughed as she gestured to me to sit down.

Knowing I was on borrowed time with my legs supporting me, I sank into one of the comfy armchairs in her breakfast nook. As I sipped my coffee, I thought about meeting Jack the night before and smiled, thinking of what the other side of this conversation must have sounded like.

"She just woke up. Yes, she appears to be quite hungover. Hold on, let me see," she said, looking carefully at me. "Jack is asking me to inspect your eyes to see if they look like . . . wait, what? To see if they look like cabbages?" She looked at me strangely.

"Tell Hamilton I said to suck it," I groaned, oddly pleased that he remembered our conversation with such clarity— and surprised that I did, as well.

"She said, 'Suck it, Hamilton.' No, she really did say that," she answered back as I laughed quietly to myself. "He wants to know exactly what he is to suck, Sheridan," she responded, rolling her eyes.

"Tell Hamilton that he has it exactly right: he is to suck Sheridan," I yelled, making sure he could hear but splitting my own head open in the process.

"Okay, that's enough of the telephone game. You guys can continue your last-name foreplay another time. Jack, I'll speak to you later. What? Jesus. Fine, I'll ask her. Good-bye—I'm hanging up now." She clicked her phone off and set it on the counter, looking at me carefully.

"What? What are you looking at me like that for?" I asked, grinning.

"You tell me. Why is he asking me about your sparkly boobies?" she asked, raising her eyebrow at me.

I lowered my head to my coffee mug, fighting to not smile wider.

☆ ☆ ☆

Holly took good care of me that day: she left me alone except to bring me Sprite and saltines. I managed to control the crumb fallout this time. I pretty much stayed on the couch. After a day of hangover hell, I must have fallen asleep, because when I woke up, it was dark outside and Holly was gone. She had left me a note and a stack of magazines on the coffee table next to me.

Lush,

Here are the stories you promised you'd read. I'm out for dinner with clients. I shouldn't be home too late. Call me if you

*need anything, and clean yourself up. You
look like shit.*

> *Love you,*
> *H*

Holly was right; I did look pretty sorry. I headed up
to my bathroom to wash my face and brush my teeth. I
needed some energy, so I changed into my bathing suit and
grabbed a towel. As I walked through the house I saw the
stack of magazines marked with Post-its on the table again,
and after rereading her note, I took them with me out to
the pool deck.

High up in the hills, Holly's house had great views from
three sides. It was California modern, with an open floor
plan and lots of natural light. It even had a sound system that
worked throughout the house and on the patio. I plugged my
iPod into it and selected my favorite playlist of quiet-time U2
songs.

The best part of the house was the infinity pool, which
had the nicest view of all: downtown L.A. She even had the
requisite hot tub, which is where I ended up after swimming
laps for about thirty minutes. One of the ways I had gotten
myself back into shape was swimming at least three times a
week.

I relaxed in the hot water, letting the jets massage away
the last remnants of the alcohol and the way it had kicked
my ass today. I took a sip from my water bottle and my gaze
fell on the stack of magazines.

Oh, what the hell. You promised.

As I began to read, I remembered how insane Holly had

looked when she described her reaction to the stories. I had some trepidation, to say the least, as I didn't want to succumb to the madness that so clearly had her in its grip. *Sexy scientist Joshua, huh? We'll see . . .*

I was really getting into it when I heard voices from inside the house. I glanced in and saw Holly and a tall, good-looking man approaching the French doors, making their way outside to where I was. She was dressed in a black wraparound dress with gorgeous snakeskin sandals.

Damn, she looks good. She must have had a date with that tall drink of water . . . Wait, is that Jack?

As they stepped out onto the patio, I realized this wasn't the same guy I'd met last night, and yet it was.

This was not the scruffy Hollywood hipster I had been bantering with in the kitchen. This was a very handsome man dressed in a dark gray suit and tie, clean shaven, with gorgeous shaggy blond curls. The night before, he'd had a baseball cap on and I couldn't see the perfection that was his hair. I had a weakness for curly hair.

Crap, hide the magazines. HIDE THE MAGAZINES!

I quickly threw my shirt over the stack next to me, composing my face in what I hoped was a neutral expression.

"Hey, Gracie. I see you're feeling better!" Holly said as they closed the distance to the hot tub.

"Much better. I took a swim and now I'm just relaxing." I was at a disadvantage, sitting so much lower than them, but Jack squatted down, resting on his heels.

"Hey, Sheridan. This is very Hollywood of you. Hot tub, moonlight, view of the city . . ."

"Strategically placed jets of water for my enjoyment," I retorted.

Holly groaned. "Jesus, Grace, you are too much," she said, laughing.

"That's true; I *am* too much. Now hand me that towel. I'm pruning here," I said. Holly obliged and then sat down in a chair, kicking off her high heels. "So, what are you guys up to tonight?" I asked, taking the hand Jack had offered to help me out of the water.

I noticed him glancing down at my black racing suit. It wasn't as flashy as a bikini, but I wasn't out there for a *Sports Illustrated* cover. The way he was looking at my toned legs, flat stomach, and strong arms, I would say those workouts were paying off. I shook my long hair, squeezing the water out before toweling off my body and slipping into the chair next to Holly. Jack took the seat facing us as we talked.

They had attended a dinner for *People* that night, and Jack was quite a hit. I got the sense that this film was a much bigger deal than I had realized, and he was getting quite a bit of buzz. They had spent most of the night meeting industry people and working the room.

That was what made Holly so good at her job. People forget that it is called show *business* for a reason, and it takes a lot of work to launch a career in the right way. All too often, a young talent gets lost in the shuffle of a hyped movie and then, without the right follow-through, they're last year's news. Holly was great at making sure that the actors she managed worked on projects that challenged them creatively as well as succeeded commercially. To do that you had to work the room sometimes, as they had done tonight.

While Jack joked about some of the funny people they had met and all the *Time* hoopla, I got the sense that he wasn't quite comfortable with it. That was good—too many hot new actors lose perspective, and they burn out fast.

Then Holly started to tell stories about when we first moved out to L.A. so many years ago, and I knew it wasn't going to be long before she embarrassed me.

"So, there was Grace, and she's singing her little heart out for this director. She's convinced she's going to get the part. She's giving it her all, and when she's finished, she stands center stage, looking like she deserves a Tony for this performance." She paused, looking at me.

"Yeah, so there I am, thinking I nailed it. I was finally going to get cast in this new musical! Then I noticed that the director was dressed awfully casually for this audition. Way too casually."

"Like, he was wearing a jumpsuit and had a bucket of cleaning supplies and a mop next to him!" she screamed, collapsing on Jack's shoulder in laughter.

"What? Why was a director dressed like that?" he asked.

"Because he wasn't the director, he was—"

"The janitor," I said, hiding my face in my hands.

"Grace gave the audition of her life for a freaking janitor! She was so mortified, she ran offstage and out to her car and was gone before anyone even knew what happened!"

"But I bet he was thoroughly entertained," I reminded her.

Holly's phone rang and she excused herself to take the call, chuckling. I shivered a little from the night air.

"You should probably go get out of that wet suit. You're going to catch cold. I should get going anyway," Jack said, getting up to hand me another towel.

"Yeah, it *is* getting late. I'll walk you out," I answered, standing up next to him.

He draped the towel around my shoulders and rubbed them a little bit to warm me up.

As we passed Holly on the phone, she gave him a kiss and mouthed, "Call you tomorrow."

"So, Sheridan. Does this mean you're a singer?" he asked.

"Yep, I was singing even before I was acting." I sighed as we walked toward the front door.

"Why do you say it like that, like it makes you sad?" he asked, turning to face me.

"It doesn't make me sad. I just don't sing as often as I used to, and I miss it sometimes. I'm actually going to start singing again at some open-mike nights soon—next week, in fact." I smiled in anticipation.

"Well, be sure to let me know when it is. I would love to come," he said, looking down at me.

Reminded that I was only in a towel and my bathing suit, I decided to mess with him a little. "Hamilton, I would love for you to *come*," I said, implication heavy in the air as I raised my hand and gave him a light slap on the face.

He narrowed his eyes at me. "Hmmm . . . ," he said, and opened the front door.

"What does that mean?" I grinned. *Don't chase him, don't chase him.*

He turned once more, giving me a thoughtful glance. "Hmmm . . ."

"Night," I said as he started to walk away.

"Night, Sheridan," he called over his shoulder. And then he was gone.

I closed the door and leaned against it for a minute, thinking about "Hmmm . . ." When I pushed myself off the door, I was startled by Holly watching me from the other room.

"Hmmm?" She smirked.

"There will be no hmmm-ing going on, I will have you

know. He's my new friend. That's all. He's twenty-four, for Christ's sake," I stated as I walked by her on my way upstairs.

"You could use a good hmmm-ing, ya know!" she called up after me.

That was so true.

four

I woke up feeling strangely disoriented. My back was stiff, and I realized that I had fallen asleep in the big chair by the living room fireplace. I stretched, listening to the tendons in my neck crackle and pop, until I noticed that Holly was sitting across from me with a grin like the Cheshire Cat.

"Hey, what's up?" I asked, snuggling back under the throw I had wrapped up in last night while I was reading.

While I was reading—oh no.

"I told you so. How far did you get?" she asked, looking pointedly at the magazines strewn across the floor next to me.

I held up my hands in surrender. "Okay, okay, I give. It's brilliant and I'm totally sucked in. I'm in *love* with Super-Sexy Scientist Guy!" I blushed as I thought of the passages I'd read the night before. Joshua had arrived in nineteenth-century Paris and was engaged in some rather intense "international relations" with a young woman who worked in a millinery. I didn't know where this story was going to go, but I was totally digging it. I might have also been imagining a certain

Mr. Hamilton in the role of Joshua, which made me blush further.

"Oh, boy," she squealed. "Wait until you get to the part where he picks her up and pushes her up against the—"

"Not fair!" I raised a finger and shook it at her. "Let me read them on my own. At the rate I'm going, I'll be finished by the end of the week."

"I won't tell you anything . . . but promise me you'll keep me posted on what part you're on."

"Agreed," I muttered as she left the room.

Later that day, I was finishing a run at Griffith Park. I'd spent the rest of the morning trying to work but was unable to stay away from the damn short stories. I was well into the third one by now, losing ground fast to this new addiction. By three P.M. it was obvious that I would get no work done, so I decided to go for a run.

I was lucky that my job allowed me a flexible schedule and I mainly worked from home. I had gone back to school after moving back to the Midwest from L.A. and gotten a second degree in instructional design. I created and designed training programs and materials; it was work I enjoyed and was good at, although it wasn't satisfying the way performing was.

As I was running, I reflected on how happy I was here now. The first time, I had been focused only on what I thought fame would bring me. I wanted the attention, the money, the lifestyle—instead of concentrating on the work, on the craft. Back then it was all about the validation, looking out instead of in.

I rarely allowed myself to really let go, to truly trust myself or whoever I was sharing a stage with. I had rare moments of honesty onstage, but they were so powerful and exhilarating that I quickly moved on to surer footing. I would transition into a punch line or camp it up, taking myself out of the moment and back into what I knew. Be funny and beautiful but not real.

And I failed for the first time in my life—really failed. I hated that, but not enough to fight it. After moving back home I gained weight, becoming almost unrecognizable to anyone who'd known me in L.A. It happened over several years, so I didn't notice how unraveled my life and its direction had become. When I went back to school, I was lucky enough to find something that I was good at. Once I was finished with school for the second time, the jobs I was able to get afforded me the luxury of working from home, and I cocooned there.

Holly and I stayed in close contact but rarely saw each other. I had a few friends that I spent time with, and while I went out on dates from time to time, there was no one special. For someone who had partied like a rock star and never lacked male companionship, I had effectively shut down that part of my life. It was as if I was numb down there. I'd had a highly charged sex life and a strong sexual appetite, but once I started to gain weight, I no longer had the desire. Okay, strike that. I had the desire, but I was too reluctant to let anyone touch me. Over time, that part of me just went to sleep. I had become a shell of my former self and didn't even know it.

Everything changed when my friends took me out for my birthday. I had stayed in contact with several of my girl-friends from high school, getting together with them for dinners and cocktails occasionally. They always made me tell them stories about the exciting life I had led in California, all eighteen months of it, and it was fun. There was still a little crazy left in me, and I let it out sometimes, albeit carefully.

For my birthday, they surprised me with tickets to see *Rent.* It had been years since I had seen a play or musical of any kind, and I was touched that they'd remembered how much I had loved the *Rent* soundtrack. I had never seen the show and thought it would be an interesting night. *Interesting* did not even begin to describe it.

From the moment I walked into the theater, from seeing the stage to finding our seats in the mezzanine, my skin was tingling. My senses were heightened, my breath was coming fast, and I actually felt a little dizzy.

Then the lights went out.

There is a feeling, an electricity that happens in live theater. There is a connection between the actors and the audience that is palpable. When the lights came back up, I saw the band onstage and felt the music begin to move across me—I was overwhelmed. When I recognized the opening song, tears formed in my eyes. Before one note was sung, before one word was spoken, I was lost in the moment. And I began to cry.

It was as though everything I had been missing in my life came into focus, and I couldn't hide from it anymore. As silent sobs wracked my body, I was filled with such a sense of joy, of rapture, of belonging. I couldn't stop the smile that was stretching from ear to ear. It was magic. It was the closest to a religious experience that I had ever come. At one point, my friend to my left tried to ask me something, but I just shook my head. I couldn't take my eyes off the stage. I knew that this was what I was supposed to be doing with my life, and I couldn't wait to start living again.

After that night, it was like there was a hand pushing against my back, constantly keeping me moving forward. I went home, looked in the mirror, and cried at what I saw. Not so much about the weight, but because the woman looking back at me had none of the spark, none of the crazy, that I used to love about myself. I cried for the time that I had lost. I cried for letting things go on like this for too long. I cried for the living I had deprived myself of. Then, once I was done crying, I went to work.

I hired a personal trainer the next day and set about changing the outside. I also started speaking to a counselor to change the inside. I took an acting class at the local theater and was insanely happy. I was thrilled to be back in the company of creative people again and threw myself into every scene, every critique, and every exercise as if it were my job.

Then, one evening, I went alone to a club that was sponsoring an open-mike night. I climbed onto the tiny stage with my sheet music, which I gave to the accompanist. I sang my song, hearing my voice ring out strong and clear through the club, and felt whole. I felt like I had come home.

I began to open up and have fun again. As the weight came off, my confidence returned and I became reacquainted with the power that kind of confidence can bring a woman. I went out on dates, and the first time that I invited a man back to my house . . . well, let's just say it was another religious experience. Why the hell did I deprive myself for so long? I rejoiced in my reawakened sexuality, and while I was careful, I certainly enjoyed myself. I was definitely more aggressive than I had been back in the day, and I was pleased to realize that I was still quite good at the sexing.

After almost two years of self-discovery and work, I was ready to make another big change. I visited Holly in L.A., and before the end of the first day, she invited me to move in with her. I thought about her offer for about seven seconds and then agreed. We were both thrilled to be spending time together again. I knew that living with her would be as fun as it was the first time. She was truly my best friend, my sister, and I would do anything for her. She also saw through all my bullshit and never let me get away with it. I had to love her for that.

I stopped reminiscing when I got back to my car and stretched out from my run. After climbing in I put the top down, then took a long pull on my water bottle while I glanced at my cell. I had a few messages, the first of these from Holly, asking me to pick up Mr. Chow for dinner on my way home.

The second was from Nick, asking me if I wanted to go out dancing the following night. His favorite club in West Hollywood played all eighties music on certain nights, and it was the best for shaking your ass.

The third was a text from a number I didn't recognize:

Sheridan, The Lost Boys is on TNT tonight. I know how much you desire Haim.

I laughed when I read it; there was only one unknown number who could have sent me this text. I quickly texted him back:

Hamilton, I already have my DVR set to record it so I can "desire" myself whenever the mood strikes.

I plugged in my iPod and was selecting some driving music when my phone buzzed, alerting me to a new text:

Sheridan, now I am concerned for you . . . I think you need a new celebrity to crush on, someone a little younger, perhaps. More charm, less heroin.

My heart fluttered a little. He was cute *and* funny. *And twenty-four, Grace, twenty-four!*
I thought about his hair then, those gorgeous curls, and his green eyes. I thought about the way he looked when he was biting on his lower lip. *Ah, fuck it.*

Hamilton, I've been thinking about upgrading to some-one new for my "daydreaming." Any thoughts?

I chose my music, and right before I pulled out of the parking lot, I got another text:

Sheridan, I'm having several thoughts . . . One question, though. Still on for the tryst?

I laughed aloud and sent him one more text:

Hamilton, hell yes, although I'll need to be swept off my feet.

He responded in less than a minute:

Here's to getting you off your feet, Grace . . .

Damn it—he'd first-named me.

five

*A*fter getting home, I took a quick shower to wash the canyon off. When I was finished I headed down to the kitchen, where Holly was heating the Mr. Chow I had picked up for dinner.

"How was your day, dear?" I asked in my best 1950s homemaker voice, giving her a peck on the cheek.

"It was busy. I'm glad to be home. I see you had a productive day," she answered, nodding to the magazine that was in the freezer as she removed a bottle of Absolut.

I laughed and said, "I had to hide it. It was making me crazy! I was trying to write training protocols all afternoon and it was calling to me. I finally had to put it away."

I got out the jar of olives and began mixing two dirty martinis.

"How far did you get?" she asked as she gratefully took the cocktail I handed to her.

"Hmm. He was talking with his assistant about making some modifications to the time machine. I really love the character of Isaac."

"Wait until you see the actor they got to play him in the film. Super cute." She grinned, taking a sip of her cocktail and shivering a little.

"How much time until dinner?"

"Oh, I'd say about twenty minutes."

That was just enough time to grab my magazine from the freezer and settle into the living room for a quick predinner read.

It wasn't too long before I shouted, "Wait . . . what? His time machine broke? He's stuck in ancient Egypt! He can't get back?" I jumped up, running into the kitchen with a look of panic on my face.

Holly was placing the food on the table.

"But what about Penelope in the first story? Will he get back to see her? Will he get back to his own time? W-what about . . . ," I stammered, and then realized that I was excessively invested in this story. I attempted to reel it back in a little. "I mean, it just seems that he should have planned ahead for these kinds of mishaps. I don't know. Whatever," I said nonchalantly as I sat down and began nibbling on a spring roll, trying to appear uninterested. "I wonder if, when he gets back, *if* he gets back . . . ," I said, glancing at Holly sideways to see if she was going to give me any information.

"Hell no. I'm not giving it up," she said, rolling her eyes. "You said you didn't want me to give anything away. You'll have to read it and find out."

I sat quietly for a few minutes, sucking on my spring roll, trying to figure out what my next tactic should be.

He couldn't really be stuck there, although the idea of Joshua meeting a pharaoh's daughter had intriguing possibilities. Maybe if I asked nicely, she would at least tell me if—

"You can quit strategizing. I'm not telling you a thing," she said, smiling through a mouthful of garlic noodles.

Busted.

"Man, you suck! I would totally tell you," I retorted.

"Like hell you would! Remember when I was in the hospital with pneumonia and I couldn't see *Sex and the City* until a week after the premiere? I asked you repeatedly whether Carrie and Big got married. Do you remember what you told me?" she said snidely.

"No," I answered, becoming decidedly more interested in my plate of vegetables.

"You said no way in hell would you tell me—you loved me too much to not let me find out for myself. This is the same thing. Sucks for you," she said triumphantly.

"Fine. Whatever. I don't care all that much. I probably won't even finish reading it," I grumbled, sipping my martini.

"Grace, you are *so* Joshua's bitch now. Just like all of us." She chuckled. "Anyway, speaking of Sexy Scientist Guy, did Jack get hold of you today? He asked for your phone number. Care to share?"

"Yeah, we texted. I wondered where he got my number. When did he ask for it?" I said, again trying not to show too much interest.

"He called my office today and charmed my assistant into giving it to him. I swear that guy can get practically anything he wants right now. I have people calling my office constantly to book interviews, to schedule promotions, even club owners wanting him there at night. He's really about to blow up big." She slurped up more noodles.

"Is he ready for all that? I mean, that's a lot for someone so young."

"Yeah, he's ready. As ready as anyone can be. He has such

a good heart, and he's super smart. We're working hard to make sure that this stays manageable and he isn't just being pimped out all around town. Besides, he's having a great time and we're getting offers for some interesting projects. That makes him happy," she replied. "And speaking of having a good time, what's going on with you two? Don't play games with me, missy. I know you way too well for that."

"Holly, I just met him! He seems like a nice kid, and you know I always like meeting the people you represent. He's a funny guy." I pushed back from the table and brought my plate over to the sink.

"Yeah, we'll see," she said teasingly, following me.

"Holly, if what you say is true, this guy can have anyone in this town, and probably has. With all that fine young tail laid out like a banquet before him, why in the world would he want someone like me? I'm enjoying having a new friend; let's just leave it at that. Besides, I think he's a little young for me," I answered, beginning to get a little agitated and not sure why.

Because you do *think he's too young for you and it's driving you crazy.*

"Okay, snark, settle. You're telling me you don't have the tiniest crush on him? Tell the truth, Grace," she said, cornering me by the dishwasher.

"I don't have a crush," I replied. "Well, maybe I have half a crush. I have a 'cruh,'" I admitted, giggling. "But it's strictly Joshua-inspired," I added, knowing that was not entirely true.

"Well, hell—even I have a crush on him that's Joshua-inspired. How could you not?" She sighed, getting a little goo-goo eyed.

With that, I knew that the discussion was over, and I

was anxious to get back to my reading. As we cleaned up the kitchen, we talked about our plans to go dancing with Nick the next night.

Then I grabbed my magazines and took them upstairs with me, telling Holly that I was going to go to bed early. After washing my face, I changed into my favorite old white button-down. I had been sleeping in this shirt since college. I snuggled under my duvet and dove back in, determined to find out what the hell happened to Joshua.

☆　☆　☆

One thirty A.M.

I was still reading.

I only stopped once, to go downstairs and get some coffee, practically running back upstairs to return to the story. I was now solidly into the series and very engaged. So engaged that I was startled by my phone ringing on the bed next to me. It was Jack . . . sigh.

"Seriously?" I grumbled, trying to hide the delight in my voice.

"Sheridan! Are you up?"

"What if I wasn't? Do you know what time it is? Some of us sleep at night," I answered, rolling onto my side.

"You don't sound like you were sleeping. You sound quite alert, actually, almost stirred up. What are you up to?" he asked. I could hear rustling in the background.

"Well, you caught me. I *am* up. And I was reading." I smiled into the phone.

"What are you reading?" he asked.

Shit.

Not wanting to be schooled for reading these stories, my eyes whirled around the room, finally lighting on the other book on my nightstand.

"*The History of Salt,*" I answered.

"*The History of Salt,* Grace? Wow, that sounds . . . dreadful. Why the hell are you reading that?" He laughed.

"Hey, it's really good. Did you know that salt was used as currency throughout history? Many major European cities are founded on or near a salt quarry. This is good information to have," I retorted, settling into my pillow. I could hear more rustling in the background. "What're you doing? What's that sound?" I asked.

"Ever since the other night, I have been craving Chex Mix."

"Well, save me the Wheat Chex. They're my favorites." I giggled, swallowing a yawn.

"So, what should we talk about?" he asked through a mouthful of what I assumed were melba toasts.

"Hey, you initiated this booty call, you tell me. And don't talk with your mouth full, it's rude," I said teasingly.

"Booty call? Is that what you think this is?" he asked with mock outrage.

"Let me clue you in to something, Hamilton. In America, when a guy calls a girl in the middle of the night, *especially* when they've just met, it's most certainly a booty call," I said, deadpan.

"I know what a booty call is, Sheridan, and if I understand the term correctly, I'd be expecting to come over and get some, right?" he asked.

"That's the general idea, yes," I answered, rolling over onto my stomach, in which butterflies had now taken up permanent residence.

"Well, then that is rather presumptuous of you. Who's

being rude now?" he said, teasing me back, leaving me feeling foolish.

"Eh, I . . . um . . ." I struggled to finish a sentence. I had nothing. There was a long pause.

"Maybe I just called to talk *to* your booty," he said finally.

"You are so fucked in the head," I said, having trouble keeping my laughter contained.

We talked for a few more minutes, then I began to yawn, which he noticed.

"What do you have going on tomorrow?" he asked as I put away my magazine and turned out the lamp on the nightstand.

"Um, not too much. I have yoga in the morning and then I'm meeting up with Holly for coffee and to work on the pieces I'm doing in her showcase."

Often agents and managers would host showcases for new talent to introduce them to casting directors. Holly held them about twice a year, depending on how deep she was in new talent. She had agreed to bring me on as a client again, and we were in the process of auditioning scene partners for me to work with.

"Oh, are you in that? She mentioned she had something coming up. What time are you meeting her?" he asked.

"I'm stopping by her offices at eleven thirty," I answered.

"Well, then I'll let you get some sleep, Sheridan. I enjoyed our booty call. Was it good for you?" He chuckled.

"Oh *my,* yes." I laughed. "I don't think I'll be able to walk in the morning. It's a good thing I have yoga. I can work a few things out."

We said good night and hung up, and I snuggled down deeper into my covers, thinking about Jack. He was funny, twisted, and dangerously cute. My hands found their way to the bottom of my button-down and slipped underneath. My fingers ghosted upward across my stomach until they touched the soft swells of my breasts. I thought about Jack's lower lip and the way he bit down on it.

Why do his lips turn you on so much?

My nipples immediately hardened as I thought of what he would look like hovering over me and biting down on that very lip. What his hair would feel like as it brushed across my belly as he pressed tiny kisses on his way toward my . . .

Go to sleep, Grace. This is not helping.

My inner schoolteacher interrupted my daydream just as it was getting good. I placed my hands safely above the covers.

I was going to have to get some. And soon.

six

I woke up early and fixed a quick breakfast for Holly and me while she got ready for work. Since my schedule was much freer than hers, I tried to be a good houseguest and I kept her well fed. I mixed up a berry fruit salad and added it to a parfait glass with vanilla yogurt. As she headed down the stairs, I quickly poured her a cup of French-press coffee, with just the right amount of milk and two sugars—exactly the way she liked it.

"Bitch, you are spoiling me. I think I'll finally need to get a housekeeper when you move out," she said jokingly, sitting down at the breakfast bar and sipping her perfect coffee.

"That, or get yourself a house husband. Then you can get your house cleaned *and* your lady bits pleased all in one fell swoop," I said, beginning to stretch before my yoga class.

"My lady bits wouldn't know what to do if a man came within two feet." She sighed, looking sadly at her fruit salad.

"Have you talked to your contractor lately? Not that I want you to move out. I love having you here."

"Yes, in fact I'm heading over to the house on Friday to check on the progress. Seems like things are moving along as planned. I'll miss being roomies with you, but I'm anxious to be in my own home again," I replied, thinking fondly of my new house.

I had sold my house back home and was in the process of renovating my new home here. Once I'd made the decision to move back to L.A., I flew out at least once a month to go house hunting with Holly. She was a godsend to me then, doing drive-bys on properties I had seen online so we could maximize our time and avoid looking at crap while I was there.

I had saved my money over the years, not having a lot to spend it on. Added to a sudden windfall in the form of an inheritance from a great-aunt I barely knew, I had enough money to brave the L.A. real estate market. I finally found exactly what I was looking for in a smallish California bungalow off Laurel Canyon. It had great bones and a beautiful old garden that needed a lot of work. I couldn't wait to move in. I had a contractor and a team of professionals working 'round the clock trying to get it ready for me. Walls had been removed, trees and shrubs cleared, floors refinished; I loved a fixer-upper. I was hoping to be moved in within the next month or so.

"This is good fruit, by the way—farmer's market?" she asked, spearing a blueberry.

"Yep, I stopped by the other day and stocked up. Speaking of fruit, are we still on for dancing with Nick tonight?" I asked, pulling my hair up into a tight bun on top of my head.

"Oh, yes. I can't wait to shake this ass all over West Holly-wood tonight. I am channeling my inner hag," she answered, shaking her ass right there in the chair.

"It should be fun, although I'm not allowed to have too much to drink tonight. Cut me off after two. Three tops," I said.

"That's a deal. I don't want to have you lying around like third base all day tomorrow," she replied, finishing her coffee and grabbing her bag for work.

"No third base, got it. Love you, bitch. See you at eleven thirty," I said as I put her dishes in the sink.

"You're a dick. I love you, too," she shot back, and off she went to work.

☆ ☆ ☆

After a grueling yoga class, I showered and got ready at the gym. I changed into a clean pair of black yoga pants and a fresh white camisole, then wrapped a hot-pink tracksuit jacket around my waist and called it good. Holly and I were going out for coffee, so I didn't feel the need to get dressed up.

Her offices were in a new space off Wilshire. It was near all the museums and the La Brea Tar Pits, close to where we had shared our first apartment. You could even see the E! building from her window. She said it helped her focus during the day.

After parking, I walked through the lobby and made my way up to the fifteenth floor. She had half of the floor, and when I walked into reception I saw Sara, her assistant, standing at the front desk. She was young and pretty and sweet—a bit fluttery, but nice. Speaking of fluttery, she seemed very on edge this morning.

"Hey, Sara," I said, before she let out a little scream and turned around.

"Oh, Grace! I—I'm *so* sorry. I didn't hear you come in. I'm a little out of it today," she stuttered.

"No problem. What's going on? You look a little crazed."

"Do I? Shit, I was trying to play it so cool." She sighed, sitting down at her desk and then banging her head against it.

"Hey, hey! Stop that! *Who* is *here*?"

Sara had a tendency to get a little starstruck. Once a rather famous movie star had come in to take a meeting with Holly, and she freaked all over reception, making an ass of herself. She actually tripped and went headfirst into a potted fern. Holly had been working with her on her self-control, which she needed if she wanted to continue a career in the industry.

I found it funny watching Holly lecture anyone on control, because I had once seen her chase Donnie Wahlberg across a Carl's Jr. parking lot to get an autograph. New Kids were definitely her Achilles' heel.

"Your new boyfriend, that's who's here! I almost died when he asked for your phone number the other day. How the hell did you land Jack Hamilton?" she asked incredulously.

I groaned. *Damn it, you really have to start wearing nicer clothes when you come in here.*

"First of all, I did not 'land' anything. Nothing has been landed on, no one is landing anything. Second of all, I barely know him." I tried not to look too conspicuous as I ran my hand through my hair, fluffing up my ponytail.

"Sheridan, I'm hurt. Did my booty call mean so little to you?" a ridiculously lovely voice said from behind me.

Sara silently mouthed, "Booty call?" and I shook my head.

"Shut it," I mouthed back, and turned.

Fuck, he's pretty.

Jack was wearing light-colored jeans with the same Doc Martens he'd had on the other night. His white T-shirt and gray sweater were tight enough that I could see his lean yet firm build underneath, but slouchy enough that it didn't look like he was trying. Thankfully, he wasn't wearing the demon ball cap, and those curls were begging me to run my fingers through them. Actually begging.

He grinned at me unabashedly, and I couldn't help but grin back.

"Huh. Fancy meeting you here," I said teasingly. "I recall telling you that I had a meeting with Holly this morning. Co-incidence?"

"Sheridan, that's rubbish. Are you insinuating that I only came here in the hopes of running into you? I happen to have had an appointment as well," he said, taunting me.

"That's crap, you stalker," I said, deadpan, moving in closer to him.

"Really, I have an appointment. Ask Sara to check her book."

I looked to Sara, who was watching this little exchange with the same interest she usually reserved for reality TV.

"It's true, Grace. He had the appointment right before you," she replied, trying not to get worked up again with him so close to her.

I knew the feeling. Jack shot me a cocky half grin, thinking he'd won this round.

"Sara, when did he book this appointment?" I asked, not taking my eyes off Jack, who suddenly looked at Sara in conspiratorial panic.

"Um, let's see. There was an e-mail from him this morning when I turned on my computer," she answered, still looking dazed.

"What time was that e-mail sent?" I asked with my own cocky grin beginning to form across my face.

Sara clicked around a few times and then said, "Two-oh-seven A.M."

"Shit," Jack said quietly while I laughed aloud.

"I knew it! You are *so* busted, Hamilton!" I cried, inwardly dancing like an imbecile.

He totally came up here to see you. Girl, you are on.

He laughed and ran his hands through his hair, biting down on that damnable lower lip as I heard Sara gasp audibly. I had trouble controlling myself as well. He was that hot.

He grinned sheepishly and said, "Okay, you caught me. I wanted to see you. Is that so terrible? I'm bored, and you're fascinating." He was smiling, but I swear I saw a look of nervousness flit across his face.

"Well, I'm glad I can amuse you. You're mildly entertaining to me, as well. Although, as Holly can attest, I can become a lot to take," I replied, suddenly becoming shy. Sara had answered a phone call during our latest round of banter, and I found myself alone with him.

I was very aware that our only physical contact so far had been two handshakes and a perfunctory rubdown through a towel when he was helping me to dry off. I wanted *contact.*

"I somehow doubt that, Sheridan. In any case, I'm quite sure I can handle it," he said, moving slightly closer.

If I weren't so conscious of where he was in relation to me, I probably wouldn't have noticed it. Nevertheless, every single molecule, every particle, every speck of matter between us had begun to hum, and I was aware of everything. I knew exactly where he was.

Keep moving over here, sweetie, keep moving.

"I don't think you realize how nuts I actually am. And no one 'handles' me, Hamilton," I said tauntingly, creeping infinitesimally closer to him. Now I was the one on the move.

"I think you're the right kind of nuts. I like girls who are nuts."

I could literally feel his eyes on me. I could feel them moving across my body. I watched as his lips pushed his words out, watched the tip of his tongue slide gently across his lower lip as he punctuated his sentence. He cocked his head slightly to the side and as he raised his right hand to his head to run his fingers through his hair, I finally noticed his hands, his fingers.

Holy Lord, look at his hands. Good. Night. Nurse.

The tension was so thick in the room, it was too much. *He* was too much. I couldn't take the pressure, so I panicked. Sexy and in-control Grace left, and twelve-year-old-dork Grace took her place.

"Heh heh, you said *nuts*." It burst out of me. My self-edit button was now turned off for good.

I began to giggle uncontrollably as I watched his face scrunch up. My giggles turned into chortles, then guffaws, and finally full-on belly laughs—the kind where you look more in pain than anything else. I was completely into the ugly-laugh stage. Thankfully, he joined in.

I grabbed on to him, almost losing my balance. I was

laughing so hard I was seeing stars, and about the same time Jack started wiping tears away from his face, I could feel mine fall as well.

When we finally began to settle down, I noticed he was staring at me with a look of contentment. The kind you only get after a truly great laugh.

"Oh man, you really are nuts." He sighed.

"Don't start. I can't handle another fit like that." I began to giggle again and then squelched it down. We stared at each other for a long moment, our breath still coming fast from the insanity of what had just happened. And not just the laughing.

Sara came out from the inner offices and said, "Grace, Holly is just finishing up on a call, but she said to come on back."

Holly? Who's Holly? Oh, right . . .

I turned back to Jack. "Well, it's been—" I'd started to say when he interrupted me.

"Huh-uh. You have a meeting with Holly for coffee right?" he asked.

"Yeah, why?"

"I'm staying right here, and when you're done, you and I are going for a drive," he stated, rather than asked.

"Yes," I answered, not even bothering to try to come up with something witty. I started for Holly's office but then stopped to look back. Jack was settling himself down on the couch, getting out his iPod.

"I'm not going anywhere, Sheridan. Now, get your ass in there and take your meeting," he commanded with that sexy half grin. He was serious.

"Okay," was all I could come up with as I continued toward Holly's office, totally dazed and confused.

You are so *in over your head.*

☆ ☆ ☆

I walked down the hall, trying to regain my focus. Holly knew me too well, and if she saw me at all flustered, she would give me hell. I composed my face and pushed the office door open.

"So, are you two fucking yet?" she asked, a telltale grin on her face.

Heat burned across me with the image of Jack underneath me, face flushed with passion, that same sexy grin on his lips as he said my name. I quickly recovered and sat down.

"Who am I allegedly fucking?" I asked, trying to play it off.

"Please, who do you think you're talking to? I just spent thirty minutes with him, dancing around the issue of Grace Sheridan. He's so transparent. He likes you. He thinks you're 'cool,'" she answered, using air quotes.

"I *am* cool, but that's beside the point. Did he say anything else?"

"No, except that when I mentioned that I had a meeting with you today he seemed to already know about it. Now, how would he know that, Grace?" she said teasingly.

"He might have called me last night," I answered.

"And what time did he call?" she asked, eyeing me carefully.

"Um, it was about one thirty this morning," I said, almost under my breath.

"No way! That's a booty call. I knew it!" she yelled as I attempted to shush her.

"Shut up! He'll hear you," I whispered.

Her eyes got wide. "He's still here? Why?"

"He asked me if I wanted to go for a drive after I was

done with you, and I said yes," I said quietly, wishing I were anywhere but there. She was going to tease me mercilessly about this. My new friend and me. My much younger new friend. She didn't tease, though.

"I think that's great, Grace. Have fun . . . just be careful. The press is starting to really ramp up lately with him, and his fans are beginning to seek him out. You'll see," she said, warning me. "Enough of that. Let's order up some coffee and get started on your showcase piece."

She pushed the speaker button on the office intercom and we could hear Sara giggling. "Hey, Sara, can you make a run to Starbucks for us?" she asked, rolling her eyes kindly at the giggles.

"Sure, Holly, what did you want?" she asked, her voice high. She was obviously still losing her mind out there over Mr. Hamilton.

You might be losing your mind, too.

"Grande soy caramel macchiato for me. What do you want, Grace?" she asked.

"Tall nonfat, no-whip iced mocha with three sugars please," I shouted over the intercom.

"Doesn't anyone just get regular coffee anymore?" I heard Jack grumble in the background.

"Quiet, Brit boy," Holly said, "or I will make sure you get cast in *High School Musical 4: Electric Boogaloo.*"

I laughed loudly and then heard Jack say, "I might need to rethink my representation."

We worked for about an hour, planning which scenes I was going to do. My scene partner would be another actor she was representing, and we were doing a scene from a film that hadn't even been released yet, where the two characters kiss for the first time and change the trajectory of their relationship forever. It was intense and sweet, and I thought we would do it justice. The second scene was between a couple going through a messy divorce, and it was full of tension and drama. The two scenes did exactly what a showcase should do, highlighting the emotional range that an actor was capable of.

We had yet to choose the songs, but I had a few in mind. Holly and I agreed to discuss it again later that night after I had narrowed my choices down. As we finished up I was reminded of the treat that was waiting for me out in reception, and my heart sped up a little. We walked out toward where we could hear Sara, who was still giggling, for God's sake, and I looked at Jack. He was still sitting on the couch, listening to his music, exactly where I had left him. He looked up as we walked out and he smiled at me, standing to walk over.

"Gee, Jack, what are you still doing here?" Holly asked him directly as I blushed behind her.

"I'm trying to chat up your friend here. And don't pretend you don't know everything already. I could hear you two cackling in there," he said, placing an arm around my shoulders and pulling me toward the door.

"See you at home!" I said to Holly as we walked out, leaving Sara and her wide eyes behind. She had finally stopped giggling.

"Don't forget we have a date with our gay tonight, Grace!" Holly called after me as the door swung shut.

Once we were in the elevator lobby, he dropped his arm and leaned against the wall, looking at me. "So, what do you feel like doing?"

"Hey, man, this was your idea. I thought we were going

for a drive," I said as we entered the elevator. He pushed the button for the ground floor and turned to me. We were alone in the elevator and I began to feel the tension from earlier building again.

"Well, we can, but I have to warn you. I have kind of a shit car. I only bought it because you can't *not* have a car in L.A. We should probably take yours," he said, smiling slightly.

"You asked *me* to go for a drive and now you want to take my car? What the hell, Hamilton?" I laughed as the elevator dinged open. "Come on," I said, walking in the direction of my car. My black convertible was parked at the end of the row and we walked toward it.

"Did you have a place in mind where you wanted to go?" I asked, tossing him the keys.

"You want me to drive?"

"Yep, this is your party. Where are we going?"

"Santa Barbara?" He grinned back.

"Nope, I can't leave the greater Los Angeles area." I laughed, thinking there was nothing in the world I would have liked more than to drive to Santa Barbara with him.

"Well, how about we drive Sunset to PCH and then grab some lunch? Sound good?" he asked, starting the car.

"Yes, I love driving Sunset, especially once we get past Hollywood. Top up or down?" I asked, my finger on the button. He looked at me, turning the full force of his green eyes on me.

"Top definitely down," he said as his eyes left mine, moving lower across my body and then finally back up to mine. I let my breath out in a slow whoosh.

Damn.

"Whatever you want, Hamilton," I said quietly, my heart struggling to return to normal. This guy had yet to hug me, hold my hand, even touch me, really, and with his eyes alone he had me coming apart at the seams.

"I'll remember that, Grace." He smiled sexily.

Double damn.

☆ ☆ ☆

As Jack and I rode through the streets of L.A., we began the process of actually getting to know each other past all the banter. We talked about how long he had been in California and whether he preferred it to London. He didn't. I asked him about the film that was coming out in just a few months, pretending that I still knew nothing about the story. He gave me the CliffsNotes version. I prayed silently that he wouldn't reveal anything that happened late in the series, as I was only about halfway done. I'd have to get on that.

Jack had been working in the industry for just a few years, having been spotted in London one day by a casting director. He auditioned for a small role in a movie for the BBC and then began working in independent films. After he landed some breakout roles in a few high-profile films, Hollywood had come calling. Being cast as the lead in *Time* had quickly made him an official "star on the rise" and "one to watch." He called it all "rubbish." He loved acting, but I got the sense that he could have walked away from it all and been happy working on a set somewhere in London's West End.

As Sunset wound through Brentwood toward the Pacific Palisades, we moved on to other matters. I learned he had two older brothers and that he had lost his mom to cancer when he was only sixteen. His father was still in London, but one of his brothers was now living here in the States, work-ing for the embassy in Washington, DC.

We both liked dogs and cats equally. We discussed the last few movies we had seen and whether we liked the cur-rent president, and I discovered that we shared a mutual love of Tina Fey. We laughed as we talked about our favorite sitcoms and argued about whether the UK or U.S. version of *The Office* was better. I thought he secretly preferred the U.S. cast, but being a proud Londoner, he could never admit that.

As we talked, I found him to be delightful. He was charming and funny, yes, but he was also very intelligent. He seemed interested in what I had to say as well, and I couldn't remember the last time I'd enjoyed talking to a guy more.

I had plugged my iPod in when we first took off, and we'd been so busy talking that I hadn't even turned it on. I selected my favorite "driving" playlist and turned up the ste-reo. When the first song came on, he looked at me curiously.

"What made you turn this song on?" he asked, moving his eyes back to the road, which was beginning to get curvier as we got closer to the mountains.

"Oh, this is one of my all-time favorites. This is my driv-ing playlist, for when I just want to relax. Do you like it?" I asked, tucking my feet underneath me on the seat as I set-tled back.

He didn't answer but smiled at me.

I pulled on my ponytail, letting my hair spill out behind me and get picked up by the breeze. I could feel myself begin to relax further and a slow grin spread across my face.

"This song never ceases to make me happy. If I had a top-five song list, this would be on it." I leaned my head back against the leather seat and let "Into the Mystic" pour over me.

I began to sing as we drove. I could never resist this song. I sang along, keeping my eyes closed as I let my hand trail along in the wind. The sun was shining perfectly, warming my skin and making little patterns on the insides of my eyelids. It was one of those moments when you find yourself and your own little world in perfect harmony. I was content.

I could feel Jack's eyes on me, and when the song was over, I looked at him. The sunlight had caught his hair and was bouncing shades of blond, wheat, toffee, and vanilla around him. His eyes were burning green as he watched me. He hadn't spoken since the song came on. He looked at me for so long that I began to get a little self-conscious about my singing. Not everyone was a sing-along-in-the-car kind of person.

"Sorry, I tend to get a little carried away," I said.

He took his right hand off the steering wheel and placed it on my arm. "Shh," he said softly. "That was lovely, Grace." He smiled sweetly as he lightly traced shapes on my skin.

Okay, look. Whenever I hear people say that they felt "sparks," I usually think it's a load of poo. I mean, I've felt attraction to people, sure, and I've even felt some instant lust. But sparks? Please.

Then he touched my skin. Purposefully. Pointedly. Nowhere near platonically.

Sparks. Sparks. Sparks. Hot sparks. Flashing sparks. Lightning-bolt sparks. Hal Sparks? Jesus, Mary, and Joseph, *sparks.*

We were at the end of Sunset Boulevard where it meets the Pacific Coast Highway. I pulled my gaze away from his and looked across to the Pacific crashing against the sand.

"End of the road, Grace. Where do we go from here?" he asked gently, still touching my arm.

"Gladstones," I croaked out, my breath catching in my throat.

"Where?" he asked, snapping out of his own reverie.

"Gladstones," I said again, pointing to the restaurant on the other side of the PCH. "I need to eat."

My breathing was finally coming under control again, and he chuckled a little as he followed my finger. "Well, then, let's get you fed."

seven

*G*ladstones is one of my favorite restaurants, and although it's a little touristy, it is perfectly so. It's an indoor/outdoor restaurant, with a worn plank floor and concrete benches to sit on outside. We chose to do just that and had the entire Pacific Ocean as our backdrop. I ordered a beer immediately, which Jack joined me in as we continued to smile at each other. I know I must have looked like I had fallen asleep with a hanger in my mouth. I could still feel his hand on my arm, as if it had burned an impression there.

Our server came back with our beers and we ordered our lunch. As it was a seafood restaurant, I always got the she-crab soup and the coconut shrimp. I'd been ordering the exact same meal for years. Even when I came back to visit, I'd always made Holly bring me here.

After the waitress finished taking our order, Jack raised his glass of Killian's Irish Red to me and said, "To Van Morrison, and the sexiest version of 'Into the Mystic' I've ever heard."

I blushed a little. "Well, thank you, sir. But you're really in for it if a U2 song ever comes on the radio. I *really* lose control when I'm subjected to the Edge," I admitted.

"Then here's to me finding more ways to make you lose control," he said with a wink.

Before I had a chance to respond to that little nugget, I saw his eyes flick up behind me. I turned and noticed two women, a little older than I was.

They wore the same expression Sara had had on that morning. They began to approach us, both giggling, neither wanting to be the first to say something. Finally the bolder of the two stepped forward and said, "Hi, are you Joshua—I mean, Jack Hamilton?"

Jack began to blush. "Yes, how are you? What's your name?"

"Wow, I'm Claudia and this is Michelle. Can we take your picture?" she said, the words rushing out.

"Sure, of course." He smiled as they clicked away merrily.

The two women paid no attention to me. They were caught up with their Super-Sexy Scientist Guy.

He chatted with them for a moment and then the forward one said, "Okay, enough. We'll let you eat your lunch now. Thank you so much. You don't know how much we, uh, I mean, uh, bye!" she said, turning quickly and then marching them away. They had barely made it twenty feet before the screaming started.

"Oh, man, you really are a hit with the womenfolk, huh?" I said teasingly, taking a sip of my beer. When it was just us, it was easy to forget that all signs were pointing toward his becoming a major Hollywood player by the end of the year.

"Yeah, yeah. The ladies, they love me. What can I say?" He shrugged.

"Ass," I stated as the server brought our lunch. Then we

slipped back into our comfortable conversation; the fans had broken the tension that had been building all day.

☆ ☆ ☆

After sitting and watching the waves for a while, we decided to take a walk before heading back into town. Malibu was always beautiful, and this day was no exception. I held my sneakers in my hand as we walked along the water.

"This is really a Hallmark moment, Hamilton. Walking on the beach, sunshine, seagulls. It's freaking perfect," I said, glancing at him sideways. He was silhouetted against the horizon, the sun highlighting the exquisite planes of his face.

"If it was perfect, we'd be rolling around on the sand together, kissing like mad."

I stopped walking and looked him straight in the eye. Then I lay down on the sand and began to roll myself back and forth.

He closed his eyes and tilted his face to the sky. "Fucking nuts girl." He sighed.

"Come on, big boy, get down here and roll with me. I can't do this alone. Someone will call *Baywatch* and tell them there's a girl on the beach having some kind of fit." I snickered, getting covered in sand.

He laughed and joined me, wordlessly rolling back and forth, making me laugh harder. It was so easy, so authentic, being with him. We both stopped and lay on our backs next to each other, looking up at the sky. The sun was out over the ocean, and I raised my legs. Pointing my toes, I covered up the sun with my feet and then moved them apart to reveal it again. I did this several times; then I noticed that Jack was staring at my legs. My yoga pants had slid down toward my thighs, revealing the skin above my knees.

Thank you, God, for the shaving reminder this morning.

He rolled onto his side, propping his head up on his arm. I looked at him but kept my legs in the air, toes pointed toward the sky.

"See something you like, Hamilton?" I retorted, waiting for his witty response.

"You have no idea," he answered softly, his tone making my legs stop in midair. I brought them back down and rolled onto my side as well, facing him.

"I have some idea," I said, dragging my fingers through the soft sand between us. His hand began to creep toward mine. My heart stopped, then started up again, crazy fast.

"I was wondering about something," he said.

"Yes?"

"Did you know that U2 is one of my favorite bands? I mean, like, my absolute favorite band?" His hand was dangerously close to mine.

"How would I know that? I just met you." I picked up a shell to examine it, then put it down, my hand landing closer to his.

"There's all kinds of stuff on the Internet about me lately. You could've Googled it." He moved his hand closer still. I could feel the energy between us begin to hum again.

"I think that you should go Google your*self,* Brit boy. I'm not interested in Googling you." I frowned, moving my hand back toward me slightly.

"Are you intrigued by film stars?"

"Not particularly," I lied. *Only one . . .*

"Are you intrigued by romantic beachside gestures?" he asked, moving his fingers an inch away from mine.

"Nope," I said, barely breathing. His eyes were actually smoldering as they looked deeply into mine. A lock of hair had fallen over his forehead, and I was aching to sweep it back.

"Would you be intrigued by a film star who wanted to kiss you?" he breathed, his fingers finally touching mine.

I paused as I looked back at him, almost panting. "Mm-hmm," I whispered.

Holy shit. Holy shit. Holy shit.

His eyes were heavy as he gazed into mine. He closed the distance between us and his hand came up to my cheek. I could feel the sand clinging to his fingers graze my skin, and it was cool. I was not.

As he cupped my face gently all I could focus on were the perfect, soft-looking lips that were about to touch mine. I moved in to meet him and then closed my eyes. I knew if I had to look at him right now, I would lose my nerve.

I felt him even before I felt his lips. The energy between us shifted, and I knew exactly where he was. The instant before his lips met mine, I could tell that he was about to deliver a kiss that would stun me stupid.

It was soft and sweet. It was tentative and deliberate all at the same time. He kissed me once, then again, and then a third time, with a little more *grrr* behind it. His scent, which up until now I had somehow overlooked, filled my nostrils. He smelled like sand and sun and sweat, mixed with chocolate and smoke. Not icky cigarette smoke, but warm pipe tobacco and chimney smoke all rolled into one.

Sweet Jesus, he's like your own personal s'more.

The combination was seriously messing with my head, as well as making my pants feel excessively confining. We broke apart and just looked at each other. I inclined my forehead to rest against his. Frankly, I needed the prop—I was spinning.

He smiled first, and I answered back with my own.

"Did you feel that?" he asked, concern crossing his face.

"Yeah, I felt it. You too?" I answered, flirting back.

"No. I mean, yes, obviously I felt that—but didn't you feel *that* hit your head?" He began to grin broadly.

"What are you talking about?" I asked, raising my hand up to my hair.

"Grace, a seagull just shit on your head," he stated, beginning to shake.

"*What?*" I shouted, springing up to run in circles.

Of course *a seagull shit on my head*.

His laughter rang out down the beach.

eight

$\mathcal{R}$ epeated rinses in the Gladstones bathroom and a roll of paper towels later, I emerged ready to face whatever was coming, and I knew there would be no mercy shown.

Jack's face lit up when he saw me. "Nice do, Sheridan," he said jokingly.

I had attempted to dry it with the hand blower, resulting in sticky strands radiating outward from my mortified face.

"Keep your fucking mouth shut, or I will kick you next time I'm wearing pointy shoes," I said, noticing how the waitstaff was struggling not to laugh. Obviously, Jack had clued them in to what had happened with the seagull. And I knew then that he would never let this go.

I had started walking toward the parking lot when I heard one of the waiters say, "Miss? You forgot your doggy bag!"

Don't forget your leftover coconut shrimp. You'll want that tonight at about midnight.

Never one to pass on food, I turned back around—and noticed that it was wrapped not in the traditional aluminum swan shape but in the shape of a mother-loving seagull.

Blast it.

The entire staff started laughing aloud while Jack laughed harder. I sweetly smiled and took my shrimp, then informed him where he could stick his seagull. He shook his head and walked with me out to the car; he was heading toward the driver's side when I stopped him.

"Oh, no, fucko. Driving privileges are revoked. Keys, please." I motioned with my hand as he withdrew them from his pocket.

"Oh, come *on*, Sheridan. That was hilarious! You'll tell that story for the rest of your life. That was pure comedy. You can't write shit like that!" He pleaded with me, handing me my keys and sinking into the passenger seat. "I can't believe you're pouting. You know bloody well if this happened to someone else, you'd be in hysterics on the floor."

"Listen, Johnny Bite-Down." I turned to him. "While I admit it would be slightly funny if it was someone else, it wasn't. It was me. And until I have showered or removed my head from my body, or both, let's not discuss it." I peeled out of the parking lot and headed back toward Sunset.

We were both quiet for a moment, then I added, "Well, maybe it's more than *slightly* funny. But now I am gross and defiled. I feel violated."

"Hell, if it's defilement and violation you want, I can think of a few things—wait, what did you call me? Johnny Bite-Down?" He turned to look at me.

"Please, like you don't know how hot it makes you look! You with your biting down on your lower lip, and your accent and your curly hair. You look like you're gonna throw me up against the wall and make me scream your name!" I shouted, all the adrenaline from the day pumping through me and flying out of my mouth.

Too much, too much! Man down, man down!

He sat there looking stunned at my outburst. I fumbled with the stereo, trying to plug my iPod back in, while I chanced another look at him. He looked confused now but was smiling.

"That might have been the hottest thing anyone has ever said to me," he stated.

"Well, I say hot things when I have poo hair," I replied with a smile, trying to defuse the situation. I was still struggling with my iPod.

"Can I help you with that?" he asked.

"I can't get this into the little hole," I answered.

"That's what she said," we said at the same time, then stared at each other.

"You might be the most perfect girl I have ever met!" He looked at me in amazement.

"Perfection will cost you, pretty boy," I said brightly as I sped back into the city.

He selected a song, and we danced in our seats the rest of the way home.

When we got back to Holly's office I turned into the garage.

"Aren't you glad we took your car?" he asked, nodding toward his car. The old MG looked like it was held together with string.

"Well, I suppose. Although, other than the seagull poo, this was a great day. Whose car we took wouldn't have changed that," I replied, allowing myself a small moment of honesty.

He turned his entire body toward me. "It *was* a great day. I'm so glad we did this . . . no jokes. It was great."

The structured walls of our banter were coming down, and the deafening roar of pheromones was beginning to seep through. You can't fight chemistry.

"So, you have a date with your gay, if I heard Holly correctly?" he asked.

I shook my head for a moment, trying to remember. "Oh, my gay! Yes, we're going out dancing with Nick. You remember him from the other night, right? He's head of your West Hollywood fan base. You *know* you're hot when you cross over into that crowd," I said teasingly.

"Yes, that's what I hear." He laughed.

We were quiet for a moment. I was thinking of that kiss and whether I had the right to ask for another one. I needed another hit of Hamilton. I didn't want him to go, and he didn't seem to want to, either. However, I knew I needed to get home and get ready for tonight.

"Call me tomorrow?" I asked tentatively. His fingers came up to brush my cheek, and I leaned into his hand without knowing I would do it, until I did.

"You can count on that, Grace," he answered, his fingers sweeping softly over my lips.

I kissed his fingertips lightly and then smiled. "Okay, now get out of my car, Johnny Bite-Down," I joked.

His face fell. "You will be the death of me, Sheridan. I can already tell." He sighed, unfolding his long legs to get out.

"Yes, but it will be a good death. I'll be gentle. You won't even know I'm coming."

He turned back and grinned. "That's what she said."

Perfection.

"Oh, and Grace?" he said, walking toward his car. He stopped when he reached it and leaned back against the door. "I will *definitely* know when you're coming. And so will you," he said, biting down on that lower lip.

Fucking perfection.

I found my chin somewhere in my lap and attempted to drive home. I ran two stop signs and almost hit a Pomeranian.

☆　☆　☆

When I arrived at Holly's house it was almost six, and I wanted to make us some dinner before going out for our ass-shakery. She had a fantastic kitchen, with a professional range and Sub-Zero fridge. I indulged my inner chef whenever possible.

Since Holly wasn't home yet I put two glasses in the freezer to chill for cocktails, then paced between the pantry and the fridge, taking out everything I needed. Opening a can of San Marzano tomatoes, I drained them in a colander and then put a pot of water on the stove to boil. Then I rinsed off some fresh spinach and dumped it into the salad spinner to dry while I sliced and grilled some good Italian bread, rubbing it with garlic for crostini.

When Holly walked in, I was frantically chopping onions on the cutting board with tears streaming down my face.

69

"Grace, it's fine. Don't get all choked up. I'm home now," she stated dramatically.

"Funny, Holls, funny. Cocktail?" I asked, gesturing toward the fridge.

"Are you offering or asking me to make one?" she asked, already on her way.

"Asking, obviously. Extra dirty please," I replied as she grabbed the vodka and olives.

"Something smells good—what the hell happened to your hair?" she inquired, stopping to take a closer look. I hadn't had time to shower yet, and my hair was still in orbit from the beach/poo incident.

"You don't want to know, but I'll tell you later." I sighed, thinking about the heaven that had been happening right before the shit hit the fan.

Are you technically a fan? Hi-yo! Bah-dum-bum.

"Never mind, I'll let it remain a mystery," she replied, sitting down across from me at the counter. "So, how is the British invasion going? Has he invaded your hoo-ha yet?"

Sweet lord.

"How long have you been waiting to use that one?" I asked, staring at her.

"Just since this afternoon, I swear," she said. "Things went well, though, I take it?"

"Yeah, it was good. And no hoo-ha has been invaded." I gestured with my knife, pointing it at her.

"Really? You're losing your touch, missy."

"If I may remind you, Slutty Slutterson, I only met him a few days ago. That's hardly enough time to let anyone invade anything," I scolded her, dropping the pasta in the pot with a big handful of kosher salt. Giada would have been proud.

"And if *I* may remind *you* of a certain night in New York City—New Year's Eve, I believe it was . . . ," she said, scolding me back.

"No, you may not remind me. That was a long time ago."

"Really, Grace, in a bathroom at the Marriott Marquis . . . for shame." She shook her finger at me.

"Enough! You wanna go? You wanna go?" I said. "Graduation? Nicholas Rabinowitz . . . *and* his girlfriend?"

That shut her up fast.

"Truce?" she huffed, eyeing me warily.

"Truce," I said in agreement, offering her my olive.

"Olive juice," she said.

"Olive juice, too, ya little fruitcake," I said, adding oil to the pan and lightly browning some garlic.

"Hmm, so no invasion yet. But how did the afternoon go?" she asked, stealing a tomato out of the bowl.

"Hey, you'll spoil your dinner! And today was . . . wow," I said, closing my eyes briefly.

"That good, huh? Where did you go?" she asked, taking the opportunity to grab another tomato, as I noticed when my eyes opened again.

"We drove Sunset all the way to the beach and then had lunch at Gladstones. I saw that, by the way," I said, chiding her for her tomato thievery.

"And then what happened?" She leaned forward on her stool.

"Then we walked on the beach and we talked and laughed and lay on the sand, andthenhekissedmeandaseagullshiton-myhead." I rushed through the last part, holding my breath to see which admission would get the loudest scream.

I was surprised when I heard, "He kissed you! Fuck me, Grace, you just made out on a freaking beach with Super-Sexy

Scientist Guy!" She launched herself across the cooktop and hugged me, coming dangerously close to lighting herself on fire.

"Hey, *hey,* watch yourself! Be careful, please. I want to go dancing tonight, not to the burn unit!" I shouted, untangling her arms from around my neck and scooting her safely back across to her side of the counter. "He's *not* Joshua. He's Jack. And he's damn fine," I said, pressing my lips together, trying not to scream myself. "And we didn't technically make out. We kissed."

"Tongue?"

"No tongue . . . not yet." I waggled my eyebrows at her. She continued to watch me in amazement. I could tell she was beside herself that her best friend was getting some play.

"The thing is, though, I don't get it. I mean, I'm nine years older than he is," I grumbled.

Yep, I had done the math.

"So? He clearly doesn't care about you being an old bag," she said teasingly.

"No, seriously. He's cool and all, and we have a good time together. And fuck, there are some powerful sex vibes being thrown back and forth, but come on! He's going to realize any second that this is crazy." I stirred the sauce vigorously, finally giving voice to my concerns.

"He seems to like crazy, and you definitely fit that bill. Besides, I don't know who you think you're convincing here. I've seen some of the guys you were dating before you moved back out here. They were all younger than you," she said, challenging me.

"That wasn't dating, that was eight years of sexual frustration exploding and landing on pretty boys." I smiled, thinking about Trevor, my trainer at the gym.

Mmm, remember when he had you work on your core strength by making you balance on the exercise ball, while his mouth worked on your—

"Grace, the pasta is done," she said, interrupting my thoughts. "Take it out before it gets soft."

"That's what she said," I muttered, smiling to myself. Maybe I could handle this after all.

"Wait a minute! You just cooked me dinner with bird shit in your hair?"

Oops.

☆　☆　☆

After dinner, I let Holly clean up the kitchen while I went to take a shower. After washing my hair three times in scalding water, I exfoliated myself in all the places that needed exfoliating and was shaving my armpits when I heard Holly come into my bathroom.

I peered through the frosted glass at her. "What the hell? You here for a peep show?"

"I couldn't wait to show you this. Look what's on the Internet," she said, mischief in her voice. I opened the door slightly and looked at her laptop. It was on the TMZ home page.

It was Jack and me at lunch. He was laughing, hand in his hair and leaning toward me. I was glaring at him, pointing with a shrimp.

I remembered this moment. He had just told me I had a bat in the cave.

The caption below the picture said: "New heartthrob Jack Hamilton, caught at the beach with an unidentified red-head. Is this the new lady in his life?"

73

The next few pictures were of Jack and the two women who had approached him. Those bitches sold his pictures to make a buck!

"Are you kidding me?" I said angrily, rinsing off my razor and attacking my underarm.

Mistake!

"Hey, what did you expect? I told you, he's getting more and more popular by the day. You should see all the websites devoted to him. This is nothing," she said, pulling her phone out of her pocket.

"Who are you calling? Shit," I moaned, shampoo running in my eye.

"Who do you think? It's time to call the Brit," she answered.

"Wait, wait! Don't call him!" I pleaded, trying to stop the flow of blood from my underarm and the flow of bubbles directly into my eyeball. Not my prettiest moment.

"Too late . . . Hi, Jack! It's Holly. Listen, just had to let you know you're on TMZ again . . . Yep, I'm looking at it right now. Yep, it's you and Grace at the beach . . . No, you're not rolling in the sand, you're eating lunch. Wait, when were you rolling in the sand? I didn't hear about that part." She moved the phone away from her mouth and yelled, "You didn't tell me about the rolling in the sand, Grace. I'm hurt you skipped over that. All I heard about was the kiss!" She loved her life right now.

Mortified, I slid down the wall of the shower and let the water beat down on me. I was an unidentified redhead with a British addiction. Moreover, my best friend was delighting in it.

"Yeah, she's right here. She's in the shower, in fact . . . Oh,

Jack! I told Grace the funniest joke about the British invading her hoo—Wait, what? . . . Hold on . . . Grace, Jack would like you to know that he's seen the pictures, and he thinks you were pointing that shrimp at him far too aggressively . . . No, she isn't acknowledging you. She's now banging her head against the shower tiles . . . Oops, now she's glaring at me . . . she's turning off the shower, Jack . . . she's coming toward me . . . she's naked, Jack . . . and angry . . . she's naked and angry, Jack . . . you would probably love angry, naked Grace. It's something to see. She's hitting me, Jack . . . I think she's going to take the phone away from—"

Silence.

I stood over Holly, one hand holding the phone and the other over her mouth.

"You will be quiet, starting now," I stated in a low voice.

She nodded her head, her eyes wide. Then she licked my hand in an attempt to throw me off.

I could hear Jack laughing maniacally over the phone.

"Hi, Jack. Things are under control here now. Can I call you back in a few minutes?" I asked, tightening my grip on Holly's mouth.

"Are you really naked? Like, all kinds of naked?" he asked in between wheezes.

"All kinds of naked. And wet. That should be enough to tide you over for a few minutes. I'll call you right back."

"Jesus, wet? Wait, Sheridan, wait!" I heard him say as I hung up the phone.

"Nice touch with the naked and wet," Holly mumbled through my hand.

"Yeah, I thought so, too," I answered, smacking her with my loofah.

☆ ☆ ☆

A little while later I sat on my bed in my robe, looking at my laptop. I had seen the pictures several times now. I looked sassy. I looked sexy.

You looked gooood.

I did look good. I dialed the phone.

"I can't believe you hung up on me after giving me that kind of visual. You little cock tease," he grumbled. His voice was low and thick.

If I could have heard Jack Hamilton say one word for the rest of my life, it would have been *cock*.

"I had an ass to kick. I saw the pictures. Sorry about that," I said.

"Why are you apologizing? I should've warned you about that. That isn't the first time this has happened."

"Yeah, Holly mentioned that things were beginning to get a little crazy for you. You okay with that?" I asked, leaning back onto the pillows.

"It's not too bad. I mean, meeting people who are fans of the stories is actually cool. It's weird, though. If they only knew how boring I actually am, they wouldn't be interested."

"I don't think you're boring. I find you quite . . . stimulating, in fact," I answered.

"Really? What exactly do you find stimulating?" he inquired.

"Well, right now it's your voice. That damn accent is driving me crazy," I breathed into the phone. This had gone from innocent to sexpot fast.

"It's always the accent that drives you American women crazy. I'd no idea you fancied it, too."

"Oooh, 'fancied it.' Say more like that," I begged, smiling.

"Like what, Grace?"

"Talk British to me," I whispered, only half joking.

"Dustbins."

"More," I said encouragingly.

"Crumpets."

"More!" I demanded.

"Knickers."

If I could have heard Jack Hamilton say a second word for the rest of my life, it would have been *knickers*.

"Say 'put another shrimp on the barbie'!" I cried.

"Grace, that's Australian," he said chidingly.

"Say it!"

"Fine. Put another shrimp on the barbie. Bloody hell," he muttered.

"Aaaahhhhhhh!" I screamed into the phone. Holly was passing by my room and rolled her eyes. I grinned at her.

"Are you quite finished now?" he asked.

"Oh, *my,* yes. That was great. Thank you for that," I giggled.

"Anything for my unidentified redhead."

His unidentified redhead? Damn skippy.

"So, what do you have planned for the evening?" I asked.

"I'm going to a club opening, somewhere off Robertson," he said, not sounding that excited about it.

"Well, be careful. And you're not allowed to sleep with anyone from any reality show on MTV," I said.

"Oh, laying claims now, are we?" he said teasingly, making me realize what I had just said.

Too early, Grace.

"Then I want to lay some claims, too," he said.

Maybe not too early . . .

"None of my claims are getting laid tonight, but go ahead."

"You're not allowed to sleep with anyone who has ever watched a reality show on MTV," he said in a silky voice.

"So is there an after-midnight clause?" I said teasingly.

"Don't tempt me, Grace, or I'll comb every club in West Hollywood looking for you, starting at the stroke of midnight," he said matter-of-factly.

My toes curled. I still needed that second shot of Hamilton. "Heh heh, you said—"

"*Stroke.* I know, I said *stroke.* I'm onto you, Sheridan."

Please, be onto me . . . at least on me.

"Okay, Holly's wearing a hole in the carpet outside my door. I need to get going. I'll speak to you soon?" I hated to get off the phone, but I couldn't take much more of this.

"Yes, I need to meet up with my mates, too. I'll call you tomorrow. Don't put too much sparkle on your boobies. They look great, by the way. Nice robe." He chuckled.

"Thanks. I— Wait, how did you know I'm wearing a—"

"Night, Grace," he whispered.

I sat there. What the fudge?

I heard a snicker and looked toward the door. There was Holly with her camera phone, and on the screen was a picture of me from a few minutes ago. My robe had fallen open just enough that you could see the tops of my girls, to say nothing of how high it was open on my legs.

The worst part was that she had taken it when I was screaming after he said "shrimp on the barbie." I looked like I was in a porno.

She danced away from my lunge and said, "Never smack me with your loofah again. I know where it's been."

Bloody hell.

nine

*T*he night was fun. Holly and I met up with Nick at a club in West Hollywood. They were having "decades" night, and we danced all night in the eighties room. I didn't mention to Nick the fact that I had been engaged in a back-and-forth with Jack. First, I knew how big a crush he really did have. Second, he worked in the industry too, and that was just too tempting a rumor.

After the hangover from the other day, I restricted myself to a two-drink maximum, despite Nick's best attempts to get me wasted and onstage with a drag queen. It was not going to happen—the getting-wasted part. I *did* dance on the stage.

I packed my tired ass into bed sometime after three— well past my bedtime—and was asleep almost instantly, although not so instantly that I didn't spare a thought for the Brit and wonder whether he was home yet or not.

Only a few hours later, after some much-needed power sleeping, I decided to go for another run in Griffith Park. As I drove through the canyons on the way, my phone rang. It was the Brit.

"Hey there," I chirped merrily into the phone. I was happier than I wanted to be to talk to him.

"Hey, Nuts Girl. What are you up to?" he asked, his voice deliciously thick. He sounded like he'd just woken up.

"I'm going for a run. You?"

"I'm still in bed, trying to decide if I can talk the girl at Starbucks into making a home delivery. Is it too pretentious to ask if she's a *Time* fan?" he asked, already knowing my answer.

"Yes, it is. Don't you dare," I said, chiding him.

"Where are you going for your run?" he inquired, setting me up.

I let him. "Griffith Park, why?"

"Oh, that's really close to my place. Pity I don't know who that unidentified redhead was. I bet she'd get me some coffee."

"Maybe if you ask really nice and then you kiss on her for a while, she might consider it." I loved where this was leading.

"That's a deal. When I see her, I'll kiss on her until she tells me to stop."

"Who says she'll tell you to stop?"

"Then you better get your sweet ass over here so I can begin the kissing," he said.

You're going to let him touch your boobies, aren't you?
Maybe. Probably.

"Okay, I'm going for my run, and then I'll be by with your coffee. Did you need a muffin, too? Or am I just your java wench for now?" I said, sassing him back.

"Ha ha! Just the coffee, but skip the run. I'm lonely."

"No, I need to run. Besides, that will give you time to clean up your place."

"How do you know if I need to clean up my place or not? You've never been here."

"You're twenty-four, right? I'm going to guess that your boxers are on the coffee table, there are pizza boxes on the floor, and the bong is on the back of the toilet. Yes?"

He was quiet for a moment, and then he burst out laughing. "Go for your run, I'll see you soon. And the bong isn't in the bathroom."

"Kitchen?"

"Maybe."

I pressed. "Has it ever been in the bathroom?"

"Damn it, yes."

"I am the master! Text me your order and your address and I'll be along soon. I'm warning you, though: I'll be all hot and sweaty from my run. You may not want to kiss me."

"Not possible. I'm looking forward to the hot and sweaty. And, Grace?"

"Yes?"

"Run fast," he said darkly.

"No problem. See you soon," I replied.

I ran like my ass was on fire.

I made it to his apartment in less than sixty minutes, forgoing my usual longer run in favor of a more Jack-friendly workout. I had picked up his coffee, a grande espresso, and my iced mocha as well. I climbed the stairs to his door and knocked carefully, balancing the two cups.

When he opened the door, my breath drew in with a hiss. He was wearing a white T-shirt and low-slung jeans and was barefoot. The hair was curly perfection, and he hadn't shaved for a few days. The roughness of his beard accented his jaw-bones, making him look virile and angelic at the same time. He was smiling at me while looking devilish. I said hello to him, walked past him into the hallway, and continued into what I assumed was the living room. He said nothing, just followed me in. I could hear the soft slap of his bare feet on the wood floors. I turned around to hand him his coffee and he was right behind me. He took both cups and set them on the table.

"I got it with two sugars, just the way you—" I was silenced by his stare.

He slid his hands around my waist and pulled me into him. His green eyes were blazing, and his jaw set as his fingers touched the skin between my tank top and my track pants.

"Sorry, I told you I was going to be sweaty. Do you want me to—"

"Grace?" he said, interrupting me.

"Yes?"

"Shut the fuck up and enjoy this," he whispered as he bent his head to mine.

He's right, Grace. Shut the fuck up.

His lips touched mine, and where yesterday's kiss had been sweet and amazing, today's was serious. His mouth moved over mine urgently. I'd been dying to touch his hair since the first day I saw it, and now I dug in. I felt the silk and the softness of every strand as I wound my fingers through, drawing him closer to me. I sucked lightly on that damn lower lip, and when his tongue met mine I . . . thought . . . I . . . would *explode*.

His hands were rough on my hips, tugging me closer, and I could feel each fingerprint pressing into my skin. My senses were so heightened that I could even feel slight calluses on his left hand as they dragged toward my belly. I moaned into his mouth, feeling my skin pebble and shiver. He pulled back for a nanosecond and inhaled, gazing at me through heavy eyes, and then leaned in for more.

His lips trailed down my jaw toward my neck, and I turned my head to give it all to him. It was my sweet spot, the one that made my toes point . . . yep, they were pointing. He used his tongue to tickle his way from my collarbone up to my ear, stopping to nibble and nip here and there. I pulled my right hand away from his hair and began running my fingertips up and down his back, feeling his strong muscles through his thin shirt. His hands returned to my hips, pushing me backward until I felt my legs hit the table. He stopped then and lifted his head from my neck to look at me. I took the opportunity to snake my hands around to the front, slipping them under his shirt and letting them feather across his stomach. He closed his eyes.

"You're driving me crazy, Sheridan," he groaned, pushing me back onto the table.

"You like crazy, remember?" I quipped, scrambling up so that I was sitting with him in between my legs. "Now, come get your crazy," I whispered, grabbing his shirt and pulling him back down to me.

It was hot.

He was hot.

I was hot. I was really hot. I was almost . . . *uncomfortably* hot. I was . . . burning?

"Ow ow ow!" I shouted, pushing him off me and springing off the table. "What the what?" I cried, feeling my back. I had lain right on his espresso and knocked it over, and it was now all over my back and sweet mother-of-*pearl* it was hot! It was dripping off the side of the table and onto the floor.

"Are you okay?" he exclaimed, unsticking my shirt from my back and holding it away from my body so I could get a little airflow.

"Yes! Goddamn it, that hurts!" I cried. And what the hell, who makes out with someone as hot as this guy and then lies in hot coffee?

You do, Grace.

"You'd better take that off. It's cooling now," he observed, staring at the coffee destruction that I had inflicted on my shirt.

"Ya think?" I asked, more frustrated that the kissing had stopped than that my back was probably blistering. I could tell he was concerned that I'd really hurt myself, but there was also a twinkle beginning to build in his eye. He was trying not to laugh as he continued to hold my shirt away from my back.

"If I take this shirt off, I'll be topless. No bra, mister, can you handle that?" I inquired.

"Why don't we just take a look at your back first, make sure you're okay? Then I'll see about handling you," he said teasingly, still trying not to laugh.

I turned around and grasped my tank top, pulling it slowly up toward my shoulders. As I revealed my back to him, I heard him gasp.

"Yeah, that's right. Liking the view?" I asked, swaying

my hips suggestively. I peered over my shoulder in what I thought was a seductive gaze.

He was frowning. "Settle down, Crazy Girl, you're really red back here. Let me get you some ice. Stay here."

He walked into the kitchen and I could hear him puttering about. He came back in a minute, holding a Ziploc bag filled with ice and wrapping a kitchen towel around it. He took my elbow and began leading me into his bedroom. I still had my shirt pulled up around my chin, trying to keep the girls under cover in front. I saw him sneak a glance down and then shake his head. He was smiling that sexy little half grin.

"You're in quite the compromising position."

"Compromise this," I shot back as we walked into his bedroom. It smelled like Febreze. I could tell he had just straightened up right before I got there, and I was touched.

He guided me over to the bed. "Right then, you lie down, and I'm gonna put this on your back. It should feel better. I promise I won't peek," he stated as I stood in front of him. I stretched up on my tiptoes to place a soft kiss on his neck and then kicked off my sneakers.

"Close your eyes," I whispered.

He grinned and his eyes slammed shut dramatically.

I lifted my shirt off over my head and dropped it on the floor. As it hit the tops of his feet, he smiled again.

"You promised, no peeking," I said, moving over to his bed.

"I know. I'm trying. You're kind of killin' me here. Let me know when you're settled," he said softly.

"All right, I'm good. You can open now." I had settled myself on the middle of his bed, lying on my tummy, facing him. I had grabbed a pillow and placed it below me, and it was keeping me covered. Mostly. I might have arranged my cleavage a little.

He opened his eyes and took me in. "Why the hell couldn't you have spilled some on your pants, too, Grace?" he said jokingly, sitting next to me. "Hold still, here comes the ice." He gently placed the towel-wrapped ice bag on the place where it was the most red, and I hissed involuntarily.

"Does that hurt much?" he asked, his other hand running up and down my arm soothingly.

"No, not too much. It's just the cold."

I looked around his room and noticed a guitar in the corner. I'd have to remember to ask him about that.

I sighed dramatically.

"What's that about?" he asked.

"It's nothing. When I imagined me being topless in your bedroom, there wasn't an ice pack involved," I said.

"You are not the only one who's imagined you topless in here. Who knew you'd sustain an injury, though?" he answered.

"Well, I'm here. And I *am* topless."

"Yes, and still burned. I wouldn't want you to injure yourself further," he said firmly.

I looked at him. He was sitting cross-legged on the bed next to me with the ice bag in one hand, holding it to my back. His other hand was still on my arm. He looked like a piece of heaven and I couldn't resist him. He was too delicious.

I sat up, with my hands still covering me. He slid the ice off my back. I reached out my hands to him, leaving me open to his gaze. His eyes widened and a slow grin spread across his face. I pushed him back onto the pillows and swung one leg over.

"It's okay, Hamilton. I'll just have to be on top."

"Beautiful," he breathed.

Nice move, Grace. Now go get yours.

☆　☆　☆

We did not do the deed. That would have been too easy, too soon. It would've been amazing, but amazing too soon. As I drove home, my mind kept flashing on images that were particularly pleasant.

His eyes, staring up at me as I straddled him, running my hands through my hair, smirking down at him . . .

His hands, when he touched me for the first time. He'd run them slowly from my hips to my belly and then proceeded with agonizing slowness to my breasts. He watched my face for approval as he circled them, caressing the sides of each before gently kneading my skin. I had moaned when his fingertips brushed against my nipples, which hardened instantly.

His soft smile, as he watched me begin to come undone . . .

His strength, as he sat up underneath me, nuzzling at my neck. He'd been so careful not to touch my back, using my hips to guide me closer to him. I only cringed slightly when he grasped me there; I wasn't quite as self-conscious as I had once been. I had lost my hands in his hair again. His breath had gotten heavier and more uneven as I pressed my hips downward onto him, eliciting a groan that made my blood boil and my tummy flip.

His lips, as he pressed them farther down my neck toward my breasts. I had arched backward to get better leverage, and he kissed down between them. He had planted soft kisses all over, between, below, and around.

His tongue, when he finally took my right nipple into his mouth. He had sucked torturously, running his tongue back and forth before releasing it with a nibble. He grinned wickedly at me as he watched my reaction.

It had been unreal. There were truly no words.

When we'd finally broken apart, panting heavily, we'd just stared at each other with lust. My lips were swollen from his more passionate kisses and his stubble. I was still sitting on his lap, my legs wrapped around him. He laid his head on my chest, nudging my head back so he could snuggle into the nook between my shoulder and breast. His strong arms encircled me, making sure there was no space between our skin. I trailed my hands gently through his hair again, using my fingernails to massage his scalp. This was something I'd quickly discovered that he loved.

He had sighed contentedly and asked, "How is it possible that I have only known you a few days?"

"I know. I know," I said soothingly, pulling him even closer to me. The franticness of earlier had segued into smooth, easy touching and feeling and comforting and closeness. It was sweet.

"How's your back?" he asked, cuddling closer to me. I felt his warm breath on my chest.

"It's better. Thanks for the distraction," I replied, kissing his forehead, his temples, his nose, his eyelids, his eyebrows. He sighed again, making a light humming sound in the back of his throat that I'd filed away as "Jack's Happy Sound."

A horn honking brought me back down to earth, snapping me out of my memory. I brushed my fingertips over my still-swollen lips and grinned. My shirt had still been wet with espresso when I left, so I was wearing one of his shirts. The long-sleeved white thermal would have fit him snugly, but I was swimming in it. He'd taken the time to roll up my sleeves for me at his front door, and I noticed again how much taller he was than me. He was easily over six feet, and he gazed down at me adoringly. We had made out all morning, hardly joking at all, and I wondered if things would change now. Would we be friends? Would we be mushy? Would we be anything now?

He leaned to kiss me good-bye and whispered in my ear, "In case I didn't tell you, you have gorgeous tits."

I grinned inwardly, then placed my mouth right next to his ear. "I know. Wait until you see the rest of me."

We both cracked huge smiles and I trotted away toward my car. When I got there, I looked back and saw him still standing there, watching me.

"See ya, Hamilton!"

"Later, Sheridan."

Yeah, things will be just fine.

☆ ☆ ☆

Jack and I had agreed that for the rest of the day, I was working. He was between jobs right now, although he was doing more and more press for the film. Holly also had him taking meetings all over town, making sure that the doors would be open when this movie premiered. All the industry trackers were predicting a commercial success, possibly even forty million plus on opening weekend. If all went well, Jack would have significant bargaining power when choosing his next few jobs. Holly was determined to use his new power position to secure his career, rather than capitalize on just the next eighteen months while he was the new "it boy."

Because he wasn't technically working right now, he was enjoying his last few months of relaxation in relative anonymity, although even that was no longer guaranteed. I thought about the pictures from yesterday, and I thought about how a picture of me leaving his apartment in what was obviously his shirt could affect him.

It would have looked like we were indulging in a little morning delight, to which I was no longer opposed.

But I was behind on my work with my scene partner, not to mention almost overdue on a project that I was working on for a client. I told Jack emphatically that he was not allowed to call me, e-mail me, or send me texts until I reached out to him. He was so charming that he would pull my focus from whatever task I was trying to complete—not that I was complaining. The time we'd spent together that morning was crazy-town good. I needed to keep both feet planted firmly on the ground, however. It would be so easy to get carried away with all things Hamilton. Besides, I had another motive for spending the afternoon alone.

I wanted to Google him.

Ever since he'd mentioned it at the beach, I'd been considering it. I mean, really, it wasn't too stalkerish, was it? If I was dating any other guy and I knew there was oodles of information available, just waiting for me, wouldn't I take advantage of it? Was this creepy?

Hell's bells, Loretta, just Google him for fuck's sake.

I made myself work for a few hours when I got home, after I took a peek at my back. It was still red, but not too bad. I thought I might milk it a little next time I saw him, score some sympathy points. Maybe even a back rub. Yeah, a back rub. His hands would trail lightly down my back, farther still to my panties, and then . . .

Focus up, Grace.

I did work for a few hours, and then I switched over to the open-mike night I had planned for the following week. I strummed my guitar, practicing the songs I'd chosen. I'd recently begun to write some of my own songs, but I wasn't quite confident enough about them yet to sing them in public.

I was still singing when I noticed it was almost dinnertime and Holly would be home soon. I'd have to Google later. I raced through the shower and was just getting dressed when she called to let me know she was about five minutes away. She was bringing Thai home for dinner.

I was slipping into a white linen shift when she poked her head into my room.

"Hey, dinner's downstairs and you've got a package waiting for you on the front porch."

"I do?"

"Yeah, it's right outside. Go get your package." I walked past her, raising an eyebrow. She just shrugged and pointed down toward the front door.

Outside, I saw a white envelope on the front step. I opened it and found a Starbucks gift card. The note attached said:

> *Sheridan,*
>
> *You didn't say anything about handwritten delivery when you cut off all forms of communication.*

"Oh man, Hamilton, are you here?" I called out as I looked around.

He caught me up into a close hug, pulling back to kiss my forehead. "I brought you this since you didn't really get your money's worth this morning."

"You're silly, and I told you *no* communication. Obviously this would include face-to face." I pouted, relaxing a little into him.

"Why are you so serious about this no-communication thing?" he inquired, beginning to sweep gentle kisses from my ear down to my neck.

"*This* is why. Because I can't focus when you do that." I sighed, leaning fully into him against my better judgment.

"Huh. So, I shouldn't do this?" he asked innocently, brushing his fingertips down my bare arms. He slid his hand along my shoulder, then inside the linen dress, and began to move toward my breast.

"No, you shouldn't," I protested weakly. I was beginning to get worked up and could feel my breasts tighten as he moved closer.

"I like this dress, Grace. I've never seen you in a dress."

"No kidding—we've just met! So far you've seen me in workout clothes, a racing swimsuit, and a slutty pair of jeans. And a saltine shower."

He laughed, clearly remembering the saltines. "Well, they were all memorable. But the dress? My favorite so far." He continued his assault on my senses, running his hands farther down my sides and starting to gather handfuls of linen, lifting my dress high on my thighs.

"For fuck's sake, we can't do this here! This is so inappropriate. This is . . . Oh, God . . ."

He'd allowed his fingertips to slide all the way up my legs, stopping only when he reached my lacy panties. He traced the edge of the lace, starting at my hip and moving down, then covering me with his hand. I couldn't help the moan that escaped me.

"Are you focusing right now, Grace?" he breathed into my ear.

"Um, yes? But you don't affect me as much as you think you do." I tried feebly to keep control of the conversation, since I was losing control of the lower half of my body.

"I don't think that's true." He frowned at me, pulling the lace aside, his fingers hovering just above me. Like before, even though he wasn't actually touching me, I could feel him. I could feel where he was, and I knew he knew exactly what this was doing to me. "In fact, I would say you are very affected by this," he whispered hotly, his piercing eyes not allowing me to look away.

Then his fingers touched me.

I have never in my life felt so aroused. It was magic. His fingers fluttered along, grazing me lightly, and I almost came right then. I shuddered.

"Mmm, Grace. You sure this isn't affecting you?" he said, pressing down on me. I almost lost my balance. He pushed me back up against the doorbell and I heard it ring.

"Coming!" Holly said as she clicked across the floor inside.

"Not quite, but she's close." He chuckled, removing his hand and leaving me breathless and rosy cheeked. "I'll just let you get back to focusing. Call me when you're ready to finish this," he said, laughing lightly at my frustrated, confused look.

"Guh," I mumbled. He slipped into the darkness, but I could hear him. I amused him.

Holly opened the door and took one look at me. I was still against the door with my dress bunched up around my hips. I was shaking my head in wonderment, looking frazzled and thrilled all at the same time.

"Oh, God, the British have landed, haven't they?" she asked.

I looked up at her, incapable of speech.

I distinctly heard Jack's laughter as his car started up.

"You better not have fucked her up against my front door, Jack!" she called after him.

As his car went down the driveway, he yelled, "Not yet, Holly!"

Holly shook her finger at me in a tsk-tsk fashion and went inside. Seconds later, she turned the porch light out on me.

ten

*T*hough we had only known each other for a few days, that night was a turning point in our "relationship." It was on. I knew that we were stupid attracted to each other. I knew that it made no sense at all that we were engaging in what was now beyond a mild flirtation. I knew that the nine-year age difference was huge and that whether I wanted to or not, it would eventually be something that I'd have to deal with. I knew that he was already Mr. Hot Shit, UK version, and about to blow up into a huge star. I knew that there was little to no chance that we would both make it out of this okay.

I knew that he was going to fuck me like it was his job.

And I knew that I was going to let him.

I was beyond the point of being able to resist. I was going to let my body take over and my brain worry about something else. All the mental junk got pushed into a box titled "Grace Will Deal with You Later, She Is Now Being Run by Her Oonie."

The rest of that week we talked on the phone, we e-mailed, we texted, and we even made Holly our go-between. She was forced to relay messages over the phone, like "Tell Sheridan I saw a seagull this morning that needed a soft place to land" and "Tell Hamilton there is a sale on ChapStick if he needs to stock up. That bottom lip is looking a little ragged" and "Tell Sheridan that she should use Bengay if her joints are acting up. That's what my dad uses" and "Tell Hamilton that the meter-reader guy put some on me last night, and it felt gooood."

Eventually Holly refused to continue this telephone game, shouting, "Would you two just fuck and get it over with?"

We didn't see each other until the following week. I really was behind on work. I was getting ready for the showcase and that night I was finally testing out my two songs at open-mike night. Holly and Nick were meeting me at a club off Fairfax. I was a little nervous but mostly excited. I needed to practice, and I was just becoming comfortable performing in front of an audience again.

I was also still working my way through the *Time* series. I was hooked. Was I reading erotica? Time-traveling erotica? Perhaps . . .

I had talked to Jack in the late afternoon. He'd been on set all day, doing reshoots at a studio in the valley, and was going to try to make it to the club in time.

"I'm not sure what time I'll be done. They tell me I should be out of here by eightish, but that's usually rubbish." He sighed.

"Well, if you get here, you get here. If not, no big deal. I might be doing another open mike next week, too," I answered, picking at a nonexistent piece of lint on my jeans. I was getting more nervous about tonight than I'd expected. This was good, though—good energy to have.

"Actually, I'm not sure if I'll be here next week," he said. "Holly said I have to start doing some more press. They've got interviews lined up for me all next week, and at some point I have to head up to Santa Barbara for a photo shoot."

"Oh, okay. Well, whatever. It's just an open-mike night. I understand," I replied, shocked that this affected me so. I could feel my stomach tightening up as I realized that I had really been looking forward to having him hear me sing.

Grace, this isn't your boyfriend. This is someone who hasn't even seen you naked yet.

That wasn't for lack of trying, though. Although I'd kept him away all week while I was working, he'd tried almost every night to talk me into going out, or at least letting him come over. After his front-door performance, I was sorely tempted. Nevertheless, I was being an adult and getting my work done first.

Was I maybe also playing a little hard to get? Hell yes.

"Grace, you know I'll be there if I'm in town, right? You're not going to get rid of me that easily," he said. Then I heard someone talking in the background. "Right, then. They need me back on set. I'll ring you if I can't make it. Otherwise, I'll see you soon."

"I'll talk to you later. Hey, one more thing."

"Yes?"

"If I do see you tonight, you're going to finish what you started," I said teasingly, remembering what he'd promised the last time we were together.

He was quiet, and I thought he'd hung up until he said, almost in a whisper, "Grace, I will focus on nothing else in life until you come. I will start it and I will fucking finish it."

Oh. My. God. The Brit was a little dirty birdie. I scraped

myself off the floor and tried to start breathing again. "Hamilton, I have no words for you."

"Good. I like you speechless. Now, let me go work so I can get to you faster." He hung up.

Christ on a crutch . . .

☆ ☆ ☆

I arrived at the club early. Sitting at the bar to wait for my friends, I nursed a hot tea, trying to get my mind off Jack's words. I was getting warm for his form just thinking about him, and I found myself wishing that the night was over so we could be together.

Girl, you got it bad.

Yes, but I was hoping to get it good.

I felt a pair of hands on my waist and smiled as I turned around. But it wasn't Jack.

"Bitch, this redhead has been identified!" Nick was holding a copy of the TMZ picture from the beach, and he was not pleased. "Tell me you are not fucking him. *Please,* God, tell me you haven't hit this."

"Why would you assume that just by looking at this picture? Maybe we were just sharing a harmless lunch," I said, protesting innocently.

"So, you haven't slept with him? Oh, thank you, Lord. I was going to smash my head through a plate-glass window if you stole my British dreamboat before he knew he was secretly gay. I need some more time to convince him." He laughed.

"No, Nick, I haven't slept with him," I answered truthfully, wondering how I was going to dodge this particular bullet.

"Not yet," Holly piped up, sneaking around me to steal a cherry from behind the bar. "I give it another week before penetration happens."

Nick's face moved through all shades of red and on toward purple. "How *could* you? My dreamboat, my British hotness, my steak-and-kidney pie, my, my . . . ," he stuttered.

I struggled not to laugh. "Nick, I *am* sorry for your loss, but he's thoroughly, completely straight. If there were a chance that he wasn't, I never would've kissed him. And that's all I've done."

"He felt you up the other day. Oh, and almost made you scream up against my doorbell," Holly added gleefully.

"Not helping." I seethed through my teeth.

"Well, at least he's putting it to someone I know," Nick said. "That makes me a little happy, and no one needs it more than you. Except maybe you, dear," he said, suddenly turning on Holly.

She gulped, swallowing her cherry. "When did this become about me? I'm fine," she said in protest, turning her own shade of red.

"Oh, please, it's been months since you had sex with someone else in the room. And don't try to lie. I am in tune," he said fiercely, placing his fingertips to his temple in an attempt to divine the last time Holly had gotten some.

I pulled myself away from the conversation as they bickered back and forth, smoothing down my outfit. I'd settled on a tight, fitted black linen button-down, strategically leaving the top few buttons undone. I'd paired it with black swingy pants, finishing off with the Urban Shoe Myth: black patent-leather Mary Janes. My hair was down, and I didn't even pretend to fool myself that it wasn't for Jack. He'd told me on the phone one night that he loved my hair, especially when it was curly.

Yes, I was now analyzing what he said as if I were in junior high—which I practically was, when he was born . . . oh, man.

Grace, settle. You've been over this. Jack is just Jack. Forget the age difference. Focus on the prize. The package is the prize.

The package was indeed the prize. I'd been dying to peek at that package ever since the day I was straddling him on his bed. The boy was excited, and I had taken notice.

I kibitzed with Nick and Holly for a bit, and when performers started taking the stage, I scanned the crowd for Jack. It was almost nine thirty, and no sign of the Brit. Ah well, reshoots must have run longer than he'd anticipated.

When the host called my name, I climbed onstage with my guitar. I had picked two different songs, and I was happy with my choices. Watching Holly and Nick applaud for me, I let the familiar feeling that I got from performing take me. It always made me a little high. I closed my eyes, found my center, and when I finished the intro, I opened my eyes to sing.

Jack was by the bar, several feet away from Holly and Nick, and he was staring at me, smiling. I sucked in my breath with a whoosh and grinned back at him, feeling my tummy flip. I was so knocked out by this guy—it was seriously twisted, how into him I was.

As I began to sing, I couldn't tear my eyes away from his. They penetrated me all the way down to my tingling tiptoes, and it was all I could do to get through the song. I'd chosen "Strong Enough" by Sheryl Crow, which was perfect for tonight.

I focused on the lyrics, asking with my eyes if he was up for this, for all of it, for all of me. He nodded his head as the lyrics asked him all the questions that it was way too soon to actually ask. When it was over, he applauded louder and longer than everyone else did, adding a few wolf whistles.

I thanked the audience and strode purposefully through the crowd. I was taking what I now considered mine, and damn the consequences.

"Grace, that was amazing—" I silenced him with my mouth, grabbing the back of his neck and pulling his face to mine, forcefully meeting his lips with my own. With my other hand I grasped his wrist, placed his hand on my ass, and then pushed him against the bar. His eyes were wide with surprise but quickly mirrored back my own growing need.

I couldn't think, I couldn't hear, I couldn't focus on anything except him and the fact that if I couldn't feel him very soon, I would literally burst. As I pressed my tongue against his frantically, his hands grew urgent, pulling me closer against him, and I was ready to mount him on the freaking bar. Luckily there was enough of my brain working and enough of his British manners to prevent this, and as we became aware that the clapping had shifted from my singing to our very public groping, we reluctantly separated.

I looked at him, his blond curls messy and sexy, and nearly lunged again. As it was, I had already started trying to kiss his neck when I felt Holly's hand on me.

"Grace, there's a lot of people watching. And there are at least ten girls who recognize Jack. Settle," she said, warning me, attempting to step between us.

Jack wasn't having any of it and kept me tucked against his side. "Fuck all that. I don't care who they recognize," he said, his hands working their way up and down my back.

Holly exhaled, and I dragged my eyes away from Jack's

long enough to look around. She was right. There were at least three groups of girls staring at us, and one was pulling out her phone.

"Shit," I swore, backing away from him. He grimaced and tried to pull me back.

"Hold on. Just wait a minute. Holly's right," I said. He tried to interrupt, and I placed a finger over his lips. I heard the fangirl posse closest to us collectively hiss.

I removed the offending finger, so as not to antagonize the seething posse, then I continued. "Holly's right. And I think Holly would also like to remind me at this time that she and Nick are going out for a late dinner—isn't that right, Holly?" I turned to look at her as a slow grin began to creep across the Brit's face.

"We are?" Holly asked, looking confused. Nick just looked happy to be standing so close to Jack and was trying to acci-dentally-on-purpose touch Jack's elbow with his own. None of this was lost on Jack, by the way.

"Yes, I believe you are. And I also believe that you'll be gone for at least two hours," I added.

"Two hours?" Jack interrupted, looking insulted. "A really good, thorough *dinner* will take at least three to four hours, maybe even longer. It depends on how hungry you are and how satisfied you want to be. When I have *dinner* I usually can't stop at just one course. I practically insist on multi-ples," he said, snaking his arm around my waist and pulling me back against him. His eyes were on fire as he looked at me, and I could no longer feel my legs. What was directly above my legs, however, I could feel intensely.

Nick had begun to breathe rather heavily during this last speech and was leaning on the bar, fanning himself. Even Holly's eyes got a little glazed over, to say nothing of the bartender, who was now leaning across the bar, looking quite beside herself.

I peeled myself off the Brit, looked at Holly, and said, "Okay, you heard the man. Dinner right now, you two—and at least three hours. If you come home before that, I make no guarantees that you won't see a little ass." Then I turned back to Jack. "You and me, let's roll."

He grabbed my hand and started to pull me toward the front door.

Holly stepped in front of him. "Hey, can I be your manager for just a minute? It's not a good idea for you to be photographed with anyone, and there could be cameras out there. Not to mention, you know, those girls are all watching you like a hawk. It'll be all over the Internet tonight if you leave with Grace, especially holding her hand—which I personally think is sweet." She flashed a quick smile at me. "You should stay here for a few minutes, talk to them, let Grace get out of here. You can meet her at my house in just a little while."

Jack thought for a minute and glanced at me. I shrugged. I didn't care. I just needed the man so badly at this point, it didn't much matter how it happened.

"I'll do this your way, but then you have to do something for me," he told Holly.

"What's that?"

He pressed something into her hand. "Get dessert, too. It's on me." With that, he tapped on his watch and held up ten fingers, smiling devilishly at me. He bit down on that perfect lower lip, and as I felt my tummy go silly, he walked over to the first group of girls, who began to squeal as he started to sign autographs.

I ran to my car. *Thank God I waxed!*

As I drove home, I began checking off what I'd need for my British tryst.

Sexy lingerie? Already wearing it.

Hot music for the background? Got it covered.

Clean sheets? April fresh.

Condoms? Yep, and the pill too.

Wait, condoms? That was a trick question . . . are you sleeping with him tonight?

I put that question in the "Grace Will Make That Decision Later" box and focused back on the fact that yoga had made me very flexible, and I knew he was going to be very pleased. Then *I* would most likely be very pleased.

He would be all about pleasing me.

I let out a hyperactive little squeal as I thought about how thoroughly I was about to be worked. I had the top down and the stereo loud as I drove through the streets of L.A. on my way to Mulholland, singing Dramarama at the top of my lungs. I was driving up Coldwater Canyon when I saw headlights behind me.

They came up fast and didn't back off. I could see a car swerving in my rearview mirror and could hear the engine revving. I pressed my foot on the accelerator as I drove higher up the mountain. When I took a tight curve, I saw the car get even closer and I realized that it was an old, beat-up MG. It was Jack, driving like a bat out of hell . . . and gaining.

He was pushing me to drive faster.

I smirked and put my left hand out of the window, motioning for him to bring it. Then I shook my hair out of the ponytail I usually wear when I drive with the top down and heard him honk in appreciation.

He was chasing me like Kelly McGillis chased Tom Cruise in *Top Gun*. Tires were squealing, brakes were being stomped, other drivers were yelling and pissed. I was already breathing heavily in anticipation of what was waiting for me when we finally got home.

When I got closer to Holly's driveway he swerved up next to me and sped ahead, getting into the spot first. He had parked, jumped out, and was halfway to my car before I had even killed my engine. Music from my stereo screamed into the night as he stalked over to the car.

"You're fucking nuts!" I yelled, watching him walk toward me.

"I thought you needed a little push." He closed the distance in three quick strides and then had his hands in my hair, running through it.

I turned my car off and the music cut off sharply.

Silence.

"Get out of the car, Grace," he commanded quietly, holding my face between his fingers, pressing the tips to my lips. I kissed them gently and slid from the car.

When I turned to shut the car door, he was on me. Arms slid around my waist, hands slipped under my shirt, lips pushed against my neck, hips pressed against my own. The breath was forced out of me with a rush, quickly followed by a moan. He was everywhere all at once.

My hands found his hair and I tugged his mouth toward mine, greedily kissing him with everything I'd worked up since I'd left the bar, my hands wild, in his hair, on his face, gripping the back of his neck as he assaulted my own with his kisses. His hands moved to the front of my shirt, popping two buttons almost instantly.

I was suddenly reminded of where we were and pulled back a little. "Hey, let's take this inside, Hamilton."

"That's the plan, Sheridan," he whispered hotly against my neck, moving his hand down and applying pressure against my center. "I'm trying to get *inside*."

"Oh. My. God," I moaned, my eyes rolling back in my head. I pressed into his touch, deliciously increasing the friction. I was literally panting and beginning to see stars. He continued to move his fingertips, finding more and more ways to make me moan.

I was a screamer when it was done right, and this man was going to make me lose my voice for *days*.

I could feel myself beginning to build already, and I didn't want the first time Jack made me lose my mind to be in the driveway.

"Hey, mister, come on. Let's go in the house," I said, continuing to kiss whatever was closest to me. In this case, his ear.

"If you insist, but then you're all mine," he snarled, pulling me off the car and toward the house.

There was a frantic moment at the front door when I couldn't find my key, and once inside, we raced toward the stairs. As we climbed our kisses slowed a little, becoming more and more tender, less frenzied. I walked him down the hall to my room and we stood in the doorway, hesitating. Things were about to change—for the better, hopefully, but definitely change.

"This is my room," I said quietly, almost shyly. I motioned for him to enter and he did. He looked around, checking the pictures on the dresser, the books on the shelf, the CDs by the stereo, finally settling on my iPod in its docking station.

"I'm dying to know what you have cued up." He laughed, pressing play.

"No, wait, don't!" I started across the room, cringing at the inevitable.

Jack burst out laughing as old-school gangster rap screamed into the room, and he sank onto the bed. The mood had shifted. There was still that smolder, that burn, but this was us. There would be laughing along with the loving.

I stood in front of him, letting his hands slink up around me to hold my bottom as he nestled his face against my stomach. I could feel his hot breath on my skin and it tickled, pleasantly.

"Ah, jeez, Grace, you kill me. Only you would have this in your iPod."

"Hey, man, I'm old-school. Don't make me bust out the Eazy-E and the NWA. I will go straight-up gangsta on your ass. No one is more hard-core than a rich, suburban white girl," I teased, pressing his face closer to me, running my fingers through his hair the way I knew he liked and scratching my nails through from the top to the bottom.

He made my new favorite sound, the "Jack's Happy Sound" that I'd been replaying in my head for the last week. He smelled amazing, again that mix of sun, chocolate, pipe tobacco, and pure unadulterated Hamilton.

He kissed my tummy, turning his face up toward mine as he sighed again, seeming completely at peace. I loved that I could do that for him—make him look so peaceful and content.

But hello, what was this? He was unbuttoning my shirt

from the bottom up, gently pulling it apart. Taking in my black lace bra peeking through the linen, he sighed again.

"Grace," he whispered, kissing me through my bra, bringing me to attention immediately.

I laughed when I realized a fabulous but not very mood-appropriate song was still playing.

"Hey, I'm just going to go freshen up a minute. Why don't you find something else for us to listen to? Your choice." I pulled away quickly when he frowned, clearly not pleased about letting me go even for a minute.

"You're already fresh. Cheeky even," he said teasingly, giving me a playful swat on the butt as I turned to walk toward my bathroom.

"Cheeky? Oooooh, are you going to say more British words to me tonight?" I said, teasing him back, only half joking.

"Nope, not until you come back," he said, leaning on his elbows, looking for all the world like a sex god.

"That's a deal. Now, pick some music, Hamilton." I swished across the room and had just made it behind the door when he playfully grabbed me.

"You have only as much time as it takes me to pick something out, and you better have some good shagging music on this thing," he said as I shook my head in amusement.

I looked at my reflection. My hair was crazy and full, blown out by the wind from the drive. My lips were kiss-swollen and rosy. My shirt was open, and I looked good. Good enough to seduce a twenty-four-year-old? Oh hell, I sure was going to try. I wanted to make this last.

I quickly checked my breath, ran my fingers through my hair once more, and readjusted the girls, cinching my cleavage up just a little more. I felt confident in saying that Jack was a boob man, and I really wanted to make sure that he was happy. So, I began to formulate a plan in my head on how to make sure that he, um, well, that he ... first ... oh hell.

Just say it, Grace.

I was dying to get him off.

Even thinking this thought brought color to my cheeks as I imagined what he would look like when I brought him to where I was craving to bring him.

Maybe I should just go for it. Yeah, guys like aggressive women. I'd go out there, get control of the situation, and then . . . Wait a minute. What song was he playing? Was that . . .

He'd chosen one of my favorite, most infinitely sexy songs from the iPod.

All thoughts of his "going" first left my head as I opened the door to see him standing there, smiling and waiting for me. The Psychedelic Furs filled the room, and the first words of "Until She Comes" rang out.

"Nice choice," I said, leaning against the door frame.

"I thought you would approve," he answered, holding out his hand to me and winking.

I went to him. Willingly. Wantonly. Wickedly.

Prepare yourself, Grace. This will likely be earth-shattering.

eleven

*J*ack gazed at me as he slowly slipped my shirt from my shoulders, letting it drop to the floor. He ran his hands down the length of my arms, his fingers entwining with mine. Then he crossed our hands behind me as he kissed me long and deep, pressed so tightly against me, I almost couldn't breathe. In a really good way.

As soon as he released my hands, they found their way to their new home, tangled in his hair. He feathered kisses down my neck to my collarbone, and my breath caught in my throat. Jack smiled against my skin, knowing this was my sweet spot. I felt his hands as they unclasped my bra, adding it to the pile at my feet. He bent his head and left a trail of kisses across the tops of my breasts, his hands traveling up to cup them gently. His thumbs grazed my nipples and I almost came out of my skin.

"That feels amazing." I sighed, watching him attend to me. "Oh my" left my mouth as I dropped my head back to enjoy. His tongue flickered across my right nipple and his mouth zeroed in, taking me between his lips. His teeth softly encircled me, biting gently. I cried out, letting him know that this was exactly what I needed. His teeth nibbled more insistently and his left hand began to move toward my legs. I ran my hands up and down his back, beginning to feel the slow build that was going to quite possibly bring down this mountain.

We moved together across the room while I struggled to remove his shirt. When I took my first look at him shirtless, it was a good thing he was holding on to me so tightly, as I felt my knees shake.

He was so mother-flipping beautiful. I pushed him away just far enough to take him in, my gaze traveling up and down. He was long and lean, strong and handsome. He had a scattering of pale, almost strawberry-blond hair on his chest that gathered into a happy trail low on his tummy. I planned to take that trail as far as I could.

He noticed me staring and he grinned. "What are you staring at?"

"You. You're beautiful." I ran my fingertips lightly across his chest, lower onto his stomach, and he groaned.

"Nuts Girl, you're the beautiful one in this room," he answered, echoing my movements with his own. We stood about a foot apart, and I felt a sudden burst of shyness as I realized my much older body was being scrutinized. I tried to cross my arms over my chest but he caught them, holding them out to the sides so he could continue to let his eyes roam across my skin.

"Beautiful," he breathed again, returning his hands to my body. I returned mine to his. As my fingertips slipped into the waistband of his jeans, he raised an eyebrow.

"You first," he said, scolding me lightly, reminding me of his intentions. He began walking me backward toward the bed and our hands and kisses became urgent again. I knew I only had seconds left before I was going to be powerless, and I wanted him significantly more naked than he was now.

I expertly snapped open his button and unzipped him before he knew what I was doing. As his eyes widened, I slipped one hand inside, found what I was looking for, and gave him a gentle but insistent squeeze.

"Fuck, Grace . . . ," he moaned, buying me a few more seconds, which was all I needed.

I slipped his jeans down his legs. He gave in, kicking off his shoes and allowing me to continue to slide them off. I knelt in front of him before he could stop me, and as I finished removing them, I chanced a quick look up. He was staring down at me with such a look of lust and want, it almost made me rock back on my heels.

His dark gray boxer-briefs were molded to his body as if they were made to be there. I could see his excitement underneath and my fingertips gently teased, fluttering and massaging him through the fabric. His hands wound in my hair and I pressed my face against him, feathering kisses on him, running my nails up the insides of his thighs.

"Sweet Grace, you are trying to distract me. It won't work," he said, warning me.

Is that a challenge?

I looked up at him, running my hands up along his bottom, grasping the back of his boxers firmly.

"You sure about that?" Before he had a chance to answer, I pulled them completely down, grasped him in my hand, and took him into my mouth . . . fully.

"Oh, God, Grace . . . Jesus," he groaned, his hands tightening in my hair, reflexively bringing him deeper into me.

Hearing that gorgeous voice, that unfettered British accent—oh my God. I let him fill me, feeling the hardness of him at the back of my throat, and I inwardly smiled. This was exactly where I wanted him. He was perfect and huge and smooth and rock hard.

I was in penis heaven.

I pulled back slightly, placing both hands on his length, and decided to mess with him a little. As I admired his perfection, I looked up at him. "Would you call this a distraction?" I asked innocently, letting my tongue lick him from base to tip, playing it up as he watched me.

"Grace, what are you doing to me?" He moaned quietly, tracing his fingers lovingly around my face.

And in a voice that would have made a porn star proud, I answered back naughtily, "Sucking your cock." I even shocked myself a little.

There was silence. Jack stopped moving—fingers stopped, hands stopped, hips even stopped rocking.

I closed my eyes in embarrassment. *Oh, God, why did you say that? Too soon!*

Which is why I was so surprised when I suddenly landed on the bed with such force that pillows were thrown all over the room.

Jack had picked me up, thrown me on the bed, and was now attacking me vigorously. My pants were unceremoniously yanked down and tossed aside. All that was left between this now-crazed Brit and me was a tiny pair of black lace panties—oops, I'd spoken too soon.

He tore, actually *tore,* my panties from my body, leaving me naked and in shock. Who knew the word *cock* would do all this? I'd have to remember that.

The sweet, sensual music of the Psychedelic Furs ended,

and loud, aggressive industrial music filled the room. The Prodigy's "Firestarter."

Oh my.

Jack looked at me with crazy in his eyes, stopping where my legs met and licking his lips.

"Fucking brilliant," he growled, and pulled my hips toward the edge of the bed, sinking down so that his face was level with them.

Then he bent his head to me and began to give me the most earth-shattering series of orgasms I had ever experienced in my entire life.

When his tongue touched me, I arched off the bed so violently that he had to hold me down. "No, love, you aren't going anywhere," he said, admonishing me, and the feel of his hot breath against me almost made me come again instantly. His hands gripped my hips, angling me so that I was completely vulnerable to whatever he wished to do to me. I shivered in anticipation.

Oh, sweet lord.

His tongue made another pass, dragging all the way up, stopping just below where I needed him, circling, and then pulling back again. I gave a passionate groan, knowing that he would tease me as long as he thought I could handle it. I didn't know how long I could last. My hands buried themselves in my pillows as I gave myself over to the sensations that were coursing through me. The mix of the loud, crazy music and the feeling of Jack's hair as it tickled my tummy was an amazing combination.

The music seemed to drive him on, setting a pace to his tongue. He began again, starting at the bottom and licking me, gathering me, never quite touching me where I wanted him, but dancing around it and over it, making me begin to moan and groan and thrash about on the bed. He did this for what seemed like hours, building me up and then letting me back down. It was maddening. It was intoxicating.

It was not to be believed.

"Oh, God, that's so good!" I cried, and I could feel him smile against me as he moaned back, his lips vibrating slightly.

Holy Lord, Jack Hamilton is going down on you. And the Brit has mad skills.

"Grace, you taste unbelievable," he murmured, letting his nose graze me. Then his fingers finally began pushing into me. I cried out from the sudden pleasure; feeling him inside of me was almost more than I could bear. I clenched down around him, unable to stop the good orgasm that was soon to rip through me.

"God, you're beautiful," he moaned, watching me react to his every touch, every stroke. His hands, his fingers, were genius.

I suddenly remembered the guitar in his bedroom. Guitar players always have the best hands.

I moaned again, beginning to lose it. He filled me up, pressing and twisting, searching for . . . fuck me, there it was. When he hit that, all my breath whooshed out of me in a rush. He had found what would forever be known as my J-spot.

I knew I was so close and I moved my hand from his hair, seeking his hand. His right hand let go of my hip and entwined with mine, and I began to see points of light dance across my eyes.

As he continued to apply pressure, stroking me from the inside, his tongue finally, thankfully, caressed me at the center of my world. He pressed it against me, not moving, not licking, not sliding, just holding me down and anchoring me with that one constant, perfect pressure.

And I came undone.

I chanted his name repeatedly as wave after wave crashed through me, my hands tight in his hair as my back arched and I screamed lustily, the insides of my eyelids a mix of exploding colors.

☆　☆　☆

I lost track of all time. All I know is that in the space of several Prodigy songs, he made me come again and again. I was like a rag doll by the end, limp and limbless. He had taken me with his tongue and his fingers and his hands all over that bed. I was on the edge of the bed, and then I was flipped over on the bed. I was up against the headboard, spread-eagled, while he worked me from below. There was a particularly intense moment when he had me above him, my hands gripping the headboard for balance while he worked his magical fingers and his super-magical tongue inside me.

And he had marked me.

Just before he dragged his body back up mine, he'd nibbled lightly on the inside of my right thigh. I sighed his name once more and he actually bit down, piercing the skin and making me shiver delightfully. He had flashed me a triumphant grin— there is nothing like a proud, proud man. A man *should* feel pride in his work, and making me come was now his job.

I had never been given it so good in my life. My throat was hoarse, my legs were on permanent shimmy-shake, and I couldn't wipe the grin from my tired face.

And I was still wearing my heels. Slut.

I was lying on my back with Jack snuggled up against me, his head pressed into the nook between my neck and my shoulders. His hand absently continued to caress my breasts, traveling from one to the other while I breathed contentedly beneath him. I had no energy to speak with, but I did channel a little strength into making my fingers scratch his head, granting me a peaceful sigh back. It was the least I could do. He had earned it.

"Grace?" he whispered long after the music had switched to something softer.

"Hmm?" was all I could manage.

"I love that you called out my name when you came," he said quietly.

"I did?" I asked incredulously.

"You don't remember?"

"Sweet Nuts, I don't remember anything after you ripped my panties off. I think I may have blacked out." I sighed.

He laughed and continued to stroke my breasts. It was more than pleasant.

"I'll tell you what, though. You give mama a few minutes to recover here, and then it is *on,* Johnny Bite-Down." The thought sent a fresh wave of desire through me.

"Grace, you have sex hair!" He laughed, guiding my hand up to the back of my head, where I could feel a nest beginning to form.

"Ah well, it was worth it." I giggled, rolling on top of him and sliding down his body. "Now then, let's see what young Mr. Hamilton is up for . . . ooh, I see he is already up," I said teasingly.

"Hey, I thought you said you needed some recovery time, Crazy," he said, protesting weakly, trying to grab my shoulders.

"Hamilton, shut the fuck up and enjoy this," I commanded, using his own words against him.

He smiled and nestled his head back into the pillows, folding his arms behind his head to give him a better view of me.

"Carry on, then." He smirked.

And carry on I did.

twelve

$\mathcal{I}$ crawled down his body like a smitten kitten, intent on where I was headed. He hissed when I let my breasts brush against him, sliding up and back again with purposeful movements designed to make him come unglued. This was not my first time at the rodeo, and I knew I was quite good at this. Though he had started out smirking, his mouth had quickly turned into a perfectly shaped O as his eyes closed and he exhaled slowly.

"Grace," he whispered, drawing my name out for literally seconds. His hands returned to my hair almost instantly and brushed it back from my face. When his eyes opened again, he saw me positioned with my mouth directly above him, not moving at all.

I let my breath caress him and I watched him twitch beneath me. Then I gently took him into my mouth, just barely, and let my tongue sweep out to touch the tip of him.

He groaned.

The sound of Jack Hamilton groaning was quite possibly the most beautiful sound in the world.

I let my fingertips caress the length of him and then grasped him firmly. His hips bucked off the bed, as my own had done earlier. Turnabout was fair play; I was going to enjoy teasing him.

I took him into my mouth and pushed my hot tongue against him, making him buck again. I stroked him quickly and then slowly, alternating my grip between maddeningly gentle and perfectly tight. He let his hands loose in my hair, gripping me when he needed an anchor.

I wrapped my lips around the base of him and then gently surrounded him with my teeth. I pulled back, letting my teeth graze his skin with gentle pressure, releasing him with relish. I immediately took him in again, burying him in my mouth as I had done earlier, letting him fill me. His breath took on a husky quality, and I knew he was getting close. I couldn't let that happen.

I stopped and sat back on my heels, and his eyes sprang open. Tilting my head as I looked at him, I grinned.

"Grace, quit fucking with me," he growled thickly.

"Oh, I have only just begun to fuck with you," I whispered. Leaning down again, I took his hands and pressed them against the sides of my breasts, pushing them together. Then I took him between them, squeezing him and earning another groan of approval.

"Ah, Grace, your tits are heaven." He moaned.

"Mmm, does that feel good?"

"You have no idea," he answered roughly.

I had some idea.

I bent down and took him back into my mouth again. I knew the sight of me with him between my breasts would be more than he could handle, and when my tongue found him again, I knew he was seconds away from his release. My mouth was furious on him, pumping him in and out of me, and his groans grew steadily louder as he tried to pull away from me.

"Grace, oh God, Grace, I'm going to . . . mmmm . . . ," he stuttered, sitting up, trying to be a gentleman about this.

I paused only to say, "I know," and with one hand pushed him back onto the bed, lowering myself to him again.

I felt him starting to come before he actually did, and I kept my mouth tightly on him. I knew he wanted me to pull away but I wouldn't miss this for anything. I felt him explode in my mouth, and I continued to keep pace with him as he shook.

Watching Jack come was like nothing I had ever seen. He said my name repeatedly, loudly at first, and then quietly, almost reverently, as he began to climb back down. I watched as his face, brow furrowed and clenched in passion, began to soften, and my favorite smile crept in.

He was luminous.

He was angelic.

He was mine. Whether he knew it or not, he was mine.

I released him from my mouth, kissing him softly. I planted sweet kisses all along his belly and his chest as I crawled back up and settled into his nook, where he held me close. He continued to say my name, getting quieter with each breath he took. Then he kissed my forehead, pulling me closer to him.

"Jesus, Grace, that was amazing," he finally said.

"Mmm, I'm glad you thought so," I answered, snuggling in.

We lay quietly for a few minutes, both of us lost in our own thoughts. Only our breathing and the light humming sound he made every so often punctuated the silence.

Then I heard something else . . . a snicker, and then a thump. Then another snicker.

"Did you hear that?" he whispered.

"Yes, unfortunately I did," I whispered back, gathering the sheets and pulling them protectively around us. "You might want to prepare yourself," I said, warning him, knowing we only had seconds.

"What are you talk—"

Then the door burst open.

Holly and Nick danced into the room, laughing madly. Holly looked at the two of us tangled in the sheets and opened her mouth to say something but started giggling again as she tried to get it out.

Jack stared at them and looked at me for help.

"Wait for it," I said, quietly instructing him.

Holly took a deep breath, and as Nick sank to his knees in hysterics, she finally said, "The British are coming! The British are coming!"

She fell on the bed, laughing like a loon, and Jack looked at me again with raised eyebrows.

"I am so sorry," I said, pulling myself up into a sitting position, which he mimicked. He graciously pulled the sheets up a little higher to cover me more and, after a second thought, pulled his side higher, as well.

We let the two fools laugh until they calmed down, and then I spoke.

"Are you done now?"

"That depends. Are *you* done?" she asked, starting to laugh again. Nick was now pulling himself off the floor, and he collapsed on the bed as well.

"Holly, the British already came," Jack said, shaking his head at the crazy that was currently on display.

The two of them looked at each other and broke into a fresh round of laughter.

"There are too many people on this bed. If you're wearing pants, you have to leave, now," I announced, pushing Nick with my covered toe.

Jack's mouth was turning up at the corners and he looked as though he was suppressing his own laughter.

"Don't encourage them; they'll never leave," I said, scolding him. "And, Holly, Jack and you work together! I'm pretty sure this is crossing some kind of line into a hostile working environment."

"Do you feel hostile toward me, Jack?" she asked, turning to him.

"No, although if you had come in earlier, I wouldn't have felt too kindly toward you," he answered, taking my hand and kissing the back of it.

I smiled at him. This was insane, but we were good.

"Awww," Nick and Holly said at the same time. They looked as though they were going to start getting comfortable, and I was not having it.

"It smells like sex in here," Nick whispered loudly to Holly, and I began to blush while Jack began to chortle.

"Okay, that's it. *Out!*" I shouted, gathering the covers and starting to get up.

"No, no, we'll leave. I don't want to see any more than I need to," Holly said, finally pushing herself off the bed.

"Speak for yourself, sister. I haven't seen enough," Nick said, also dragging himself off the bed.

"Next time, we lock them out," Jack said, pulling me back to him as they made their way to the door.

"She's got sex hair," I heard Nick say as they walked out.

"Well, durr. Didn't you hear all the screaming?" she gig-gled back. "Night, kids." She closed the door behind her.

I jumped out of bed immediately, crossing to the door and quickly locking it.

"What are you doing?" Jack asked as I stood by the door for a few seconds.

I held up my hand, motioning for him to be quiet. Sure enough, not ninety seconds had gone by when I saw the knob begin to turn.

"Damn it, they locked it," I heard Holly whisper.

"I didn't think she'd take it so hard," Nick whispered back.

I looked back at Jack, still in bed.

"That's what he said!" we both yelled, and we heard them run downstairs, one of them tripping and hitting the floor with a loud smack. We both laughed.

"Sorry about that," I said, leaning against the door.

"No problem. Now get that sweet ass back into this bed before I come over there and get you," he answered.

I stared at him, his lean torso visible above the sheet, which had settled low around his hips. He was leaning back against my headboard, and he had never looked sexier.

He gazed at me with a now-familiar gleam in his eye.

"Already? Don't you need a few minutes?" I asked.

He pulled the sheets a little lower. Nope, I guess not.

"No, ma'am. I am good to go," he answered, curling his finger in a come-hither gesture.

Suddenly I loved the fact that he was only twenty-four.

thirteen

That night went down (pun intended and acknowl-
edged) in history, forever known as "Hamilton: 5/Sher-
idan: Lost Track After 17." It was probably the best night I
ever spent in a bed with a man.

And on the floor with a man.

And up against the door with a man.

And, God watch over and protect us, on the floor of the
closet with a man.

As the sun crept into the sky we were lying next to each
other, totally spent. It had been like the Oral Olympics. At
one point poor Holly had actually come to the door, begging
us to let her get some sleep. I couldn't respond, being otherwise engaged in the throes of another intense orgasm, so
Jack removed his mouth long enough to tell her to go away,
returning to me quickly. Such chivalry.

We were facing each other on our sides and he had his
arm under my head, propping me up. My leg was thrown
over his hip, my arm wrapped around his waist, and I trailed
my fingers up and down his back. We hadn't spoken for a

while, too tired to say a word. He was pressing his lips against my face, my temples, my eyelids, my lips, while softly humming a tune I didn't recognize.

I let out a groan and stretched my arms over my head, arching my back, listening as my muscles let me know they were overworked. My breasts were dangerously close to his face, and he couldn't resist placing a soft kiss on my left nipple—which responded in turn. Then his hand found my right nipple. I moaned softly, then pushed his hand away and rolled to the other side of the bed, my back to him.

"We have to stop, this is insane. I literally cannot handle any more. I think I've lost brain function. I can actually feel myself becoming stupid," I said, digging under the covers and burying my face into the pillows. He steamrolled across the bed into me, sliding his hands beneath the covers and finding my hips. He molded his body into mine, pressing his chest into my back.

"Not possible. Let's test it. What's two times two?"

"Orange?" I giggled tiredly.

"Hmm, this is worse than I thought . . . let's try another. What's my name?"

"George?" I said, puzzled.

"George? Bloody George? Grace, I'm shocked." He pressed harder into me as I laughed, and I could feel where this was going.

"Behave, George. There will be no more of that. My oonie can't handle any more." I protested on her behalf, though she was on a mission of her own. My silly body responded to him even when my brain was begging for rest.

"Settle, Sheridan. I am merely doing what all women seem to want. Spooning, is it?" He chuckled in my ear, raising the hairs on the back of my neck with his closeness.

"Well, then that's fine. Quite nice, really," I answered, giving a great yawn. "It's sleepy time now, George, and then when we wake up, we will eat." I started to drift off.

"And then . . . ?"

"Then we'll see."

He was quiet for a moment; then he laughed. "George and Gracie. It's perfect." He kissed me sweetly on the cheek, and with a final snuggle of that fine-ass body against mine, we fell asleep.

☆　☆　☆

Eleven twenty-seven A.M.

When I woke up I was still exactly where I'd fallen asleep, with Jack snuggled persistently against me. I felt his strong arms around me, hands surrounding my breasts, and I never wanted to leave this exact spot. Nevertheless, nature called.

I rolled over gently, trying not to wake him. He stirred in his sleep and I watched him drift away again, marveling at the way the light from the window danced across his face, showing the different shades of blond and strawberry in his stubbly beard. I dusted my fingertips across his lips, and in his sleep, he kissed them. Not wanting to wake him further, I wrapped myself in the sheet that was on the floor and slipped from the bed, making my way to the bathroom. I nearly groaned as my legs protested. I could barely carry my own weight. I was sore, and frankly, I had every right to be.

I avoided my reflection, taking care of business first, and then brushed my teeth. After I splashed water on my face, I finally looked.

It was terrifying.

My hair was a nightmare and there was mascara raccooned under my eyes. My lips were incredibly swollen and puffy and the area around my mouth bore the battle scars of his scruff.

"Ridden hard and put away wet" sprang to mind.

Lowering the sheet, I examined myself further, each landmark bringing back a different memory. I saw nibbles on my breast where he had bitten down a little too hard and the redness below my nipples from his scruffy stubble.

Looking lower, there was my Hamilton Brand, the tiny, but quite deliberate, bite on the inside of my thigh. Seeing this brought back a wave that settled into the pit of my stomach. It had truly been unreal.

There had been none of the awkwardness that usually accompanied the first romp with someone new. Guys usually needed a little guidance on what felt good, at least the first few times.

Not our Mr. Hamilton.

He had known exactly what I needed and when I needed it. It was as if he was put on this earth for the sole purpose of giving me pleasure. Who am I to argue with intelligent design? Or the Big Bang. And speaking of bang . . .

We never actually had intercourse. And that was, kind of . . . well . . . nice. I loved that I still had so much to look forward to with him, so much we had yet to learn about each other. And if last night was any indication—

My tummy growled. I needed sustenance.

I attempted to brush out the sex hair on the back of my head, finally giving up and sweeping the whole mess into two pigtails. I washed my face again, removing the traces of mascara, and was debating on whether to shower now or after breakfast when I finally noticed the hickey.

A mother-loving hickey! I was thirty-three, for Christ's sake!

Thirty-three and in pigtails . . .

Shut it.

The hickey on the side of my neck was the size of a quarter. I looked like I'd argued with a Hoover and the Hoover had won. Jesus. This is what you got for messing around with a twenty-four-year-old.

I opened the bathroom door, preparing to confront Jack and explain that a grown woman simply cannot go around with hickeys on her neck.

But I softened when I noticed that he was sound asleep in my bed, the sheets low on his torso, arms up behind his head, mouth slightly open.

Are they shooting an Abercrombie ad in your bedroom today?

He was so pretty.

I quickly scooped up his shirt from last night, which smelled divine, and buttoned it on. Then I grabbed a pair of panties from the dresser and quietly stepped out into the hall. I wanted to let him sleep a little longer, and I needed coffee.

Once in the hall, I was bending down to put on my panties when I heard Holly say from behind me, "That's a view I never need to see again."

I quickly pulled them on home and turned to face her with a sheepish grin. "Sorry."

She pointed at the stairs. "Kitchen. Coffee's made. I want the details that I didn't already hear myself."

You are in trouble.

I sat in the kitchen with my best friend, with the new "it boy" asleep in the room above me, and tried to explain the grand events that had taken place last night.

Holly listened as I recounted some of the sweeter moments, holding up her hand to stop me when I delved too deeply into details. She reminded me that she had heard the bulk of what had taken place, and I apologized repeatedly. She said not to worry, she and Nick had made popcorn and perched at the top of the stairs most of the night, listening.

I sat in one of her comfortable armchairs in the breakfast nook with my legs underneath me, drowning in Jack's shirt and in his scent. I was nibbling a piece of toast and nursing a cup of coffee, when I heard stirring from above.

Holly heard him as well, and as his feet slapped on the stairs, she said, "Grace, I do believe you are blushing." She smiled at me, grabbing her keys and leaving through the back door.

I sat up, then leaned back again, and then arranged myself in what felt like a natural pose. As I refined my cute sitting position, I heard, "Sheridan, do you have to pee?"

"Huh, wh-what?" I stammered, surprised to find he was already in the kitchen and looking at me strangely. He was dressed in his jeans, barefoot and bare-chested. His jeans were hanging low, and he looked like disheveled sex.

"Why are you wiggling about so?" he inquired, opening cupboards, looking for something. He picked up the coffeepot and gestured to my mug.

"Forget it," I answered, flustered. I got up to get him a mug and I found that I was nervous all of a sudden.

Maybe this was it: one-night-stand time. This was when

the awkward conversation would start, the promises to get together that would never take place. This was when the tension would begin. Damn it, I cared too much already. As I reached up to grab the mug, I felt his hand on my behind.

"Hurry up with that coffee, you little screamer, and then you can fix your man a proper breakfast," he said, giving my ass a smack and then pressing his lips to my neck.

I smiled into the cupboard. We were good.

fourteen

I made him breakfast and he watched. Eggs, scrambled. Toast, slightly burned, the way he liked it—with marmalade, like Paddington Bear. Juice *and* coffee.

While I cooked, he snuck kisses every time I walked near him. He tried to peek beneath his shirt, which I was currently wearing. I kept him away, although the toast might have been a little more burned than he would have liked, as I was fighting him off over by the Mr. Coffee.

I was famished myself, and we ate at the breakfast bar on opposite sides. I felt it was necessary to keep two feet of granite between the Brit's roving hands and me. When he finished, he groaned, patting his full belly and letting out a loud burp.

"Gross." I grimaced, placing our plates in the sink.

"Get used to it, Sheridan. I am disgusting," he said, crossing over to meet me by the dishwasher. "Piggy piggy piggy." He laughed as he pointed at himself. He was looking devious again, his fingers reaching out to touch my bare legs and migrate north.

"Seriously, Hamilton, I can't take any more. I need a shower, and I actually have things to do. Not all of us can slack full-time," I said, scolding him, backing away and finding myself in a corner.

Trapped. Damn.

"Are you really telling me you want none of this?" he said teasingly, sticking his tongue out and wiggling it at me like a cheeky schoolboy. My stomach fell out of me and ran out the front door.

"What are you, thirteen? You're disgusting." I laughed in spite of myself. "And yes, I'm telling you exactly that," I answered, my voice wavering. I was trying to put on a stern face, but he could tell I didn't have the guts to back it up. My guts, you see, having just left through the front door.

"I didn't hear you complaining last night or this morning about this very tongue," he said mischievously, moving closer. I pulled myself up onto the counter behind me, the only place I could go.

Bad idea.

"What about these?" he asked, holding up his magic hands, waving his fingers at me. "Surely you wouldn't object to these, would you?"

"Umm . . . I, hmm . . . what?" I was having trouble following the conversation.

Tell him not to call you Shirley . . .

He positioned himself between my legs and nudged them open. I stared at him. I do not have the vocabulary necessary to communicate how devastatingly handsome the man truly was. I had seen him in a suit and tie, with his scruffy hipster uniform complete, even in his own birthday suit—yet there was nothing in the world that was more excruciatingly, painfully, pinch-yourself-to-make-sure-you're-not-dreaming beautiful than the sight of Jack Hamilton, hair standing on end, shirtless and shoeless, in jeans, between my legs.

My breath caught in my throat as he slid his hands up the outsides of my thighs and hooked his thumbs around the band of my panties.

I regained a little control. "No, no, Sweet Nuts. I can't. I have calls to ret—"

His mouth interrupted me with a kiss.

"Mmm-hmm," he responded, his mouth moving down my neck, his hands slowly tugging at my panties and sliding them over my knees.

"And I have a meeting this afternoon with my contractor . . ." I tried again, noticing that my panties were now on the floor.

"Mmm-hmm. Contractor. Got it," he whispered, locking eyes with me as he spread my legs farther. He pulled me to the edge of the counter and quite deliberately bent one leg and hooked it around his waist, giving him better access to me. His fingers touched me and I struggled to keep my focus.

"And I also have to . . . oh, God . . . I have a project due that I need . . . oh, wow . . . a project that I . . . fuck, that's good . . . *Oh!*" I cried out, abandoning all reason when his fingers slipped amazingly into me.

His thumb pressed against me, and I held on to his shoulders as I almost immediately climaxed and then began another. I had always been lucky enough to be a multiples kind of gal, but never like this. He kept me close, watching my face as I came again and again in rapid succession, that sexy half grin giving way to a furrowed brow as he worked harder to keep me where I needed to be.

"Right here, Grace. Keep your eyes on me."

I came once more, our eyes locked as I screamed his

name. Then I slumped over onto him, wrapping my arms around his neck and collapsing fully.

"You're too good to me," I whispered in his ear, kissing his neck.

"I think that goes both ways, Nuts Girl."

I giggled at my nickname. "Why don't we finish this in the shower, George?" I smiled, hooking my fingers through the waistband on his jeans, giving him a firm squeeze through the fabric and pulling him toward the stairs. He snarled and chased me into the living room. I started up the stairs before him, giving him a peek at my nakedness beneath his shirt.

"Grab my panties, will you? I don't think we should push Holly any further than we already have," I fired back over my shoulder on my way upstairs. "Meet you in the shower."

I couldn't wait to have my Brit naked and wet.

After the shower, I insisted that Jack leave me alone long enough to dry my hair. Holly had come home from the market and, after banging on the door for several minutes to no avail, finally shoved a note under it saying that I had an audition at four o'clock if I could make it. I was meeting with the contractor at my new house at five thirty, so it worked out perfectly.

It was an audition for a cop show, and I was reading for the part of a crooked lawyer. After finishing with my hair, I had to shoo Jack out of the bathroom and away from my flatiron. He had gotten it in his head that he should help me get ready and would be in charge of my hair. After I vetoed that idea, I printed off my sides and was busily making notes on the character when I noticed that he was making up the bed. He seemed to be having trouble with the bottom sheet. He couldn't get it to lie smoothly.

"You never make your bed at home, do you?" I asked, watching him attempt this.

"No, no reason to. You just get back in it at the end of the day. Why bother?" He stared at the corners, trying to get them to match up.

"Take off all the pillows first, then you can see all the corners," I said, admiring the way his ass looked in his jeans.

He began taking pillows off, and then it got much quieter in the room. "Grace, do you have something to tell me?"

"Hmm?" I looked up from my notes.

Shit.

He was holding one of the magazines with the *Time* stories. He'd found my hidden stash under my bed.

Shit. Shit.

"I can't believe it. You fangirl!" he teased, pointing at me with a glint in his eye.

"No, no, I'm not really. Holly gave them to me. She made me read them! I didn't want to . . . I . . . ," I stammered, trying to figure a way out of this that wouldn't leave me looking like a total stalker.

"Grace. Don't lie to me," he said, admonishing me, looking serious.

I walked over to the corner and stood in it, facing the wall, looking like the guy at the end of *The Blair Witch Project*. "Okay, I admit it. I started reading it because I promised Holly," I said, feeling my cheeks flame.

"And then?" he asked, walking over to me.

"Ummm. Now I'm reading it because it's interesting?" I asked more than answered.

"Grace . . ." He was warning me.

"I'm reading it because I like it. I more than like it, okay! I—I freaking *love* it!" I wailed, placing my head against the wall in shame. I waited for him to tease me, but there was only silence.

Uh-oh, now he thinks you're only interested in him because he's playing Joshua.

I spun around quickly and saw him sitting on the end of the bed, laughing.

"Why are you laughing?" I asked, walking over to where he sat.

"I love that you felt so guilty that you stood in the corner!" He laughed again. "But this does mean the tryst is officially off, Grace."

"Well, technically, since I had yet to read anything when I met you, the tryst should still be on."

"You got me on a technicality, huh? All right then, tryst on. Only if you agree to never call me Joshua when we're in bed," he said.

"Agreed. But could you do something for me?" I asked sweetly, moving closer to him. In my head, I was secretly rejoicing that he talked about us in bed like it was going to be something we did a lot.

His hands came up around my waist and I leaned closer to his right ear.

"Next time, ya know, when we're together?" I whispered, planting a kiss on his neck below his ear. He smelled all soapy and warm.

"Mmm-hmm?" he answered back, his hands clutching my hips.

"And things are getting, ya know, really hot?" I said, switching to the other ear, kissing his neck there as well.

"Mmm-hmm?" he said, his hands moving to the tie that held my robe closed, starting to pull it apart. His breathing was growing heavier by the second. I had him right where I wanted him.

"Could you maybe, possibly . . ."

"Yes?" he asked, pushing open my robe and planting his mouth between my breasts, beginning to kiss me.

"Call me Penelope? You know, your woman in the first story? I've always wanted to work in a hat store . . ." I finished, then closed my eyes and waited. I was sooo going to get it for that one.

He was still for exactly four seconds, and then he started blowing raspberries all over my chest. "Grace, that is rubbish! I knew you were as insane as all the rest! C'mere!"

I squealed as he picked me up and threw me over his shoulder. I was dying, I was laughing so hard. He carried me kicking, screaming, and laughing all the way downstairs and into the kitchen. I was shouting out ideas the whole time through my laughter.

"Maybe," I wheezed, "you could be all Super-Sexy Scientist Guy. Wear a lab coat? Or maybe"—I choked—"you could explain the space-time continuum? Or maybe . . . oh, God, I am hilarious," I said before screeching, "Maybe you could just take me away in your little time machine? Ha ha ha!"

I was laughing so hard I couldn't see straight. This was fine, because I was upside down over the shoulder of an enraged Brit. But the way he was playing grab-ass the whole way down the stairs made me think he wasn't too upset.

He carried me into the kitchen, still screaming in laughter. I didn't even notice Holly sitting at the table with Nick. He went straight to the freezer, grabbed a bag of frozen Green Giant corn niblets, set me on the counter, ripped the bag open with his teeth, pulled my panties straight out like a cash drawer, and dumped them in.

I screamed, feeling the corn sprinkle everywhere. In my frenzy to get at the corn, I fell off the counter and onto the floor, landing with a loud splat. I rolled around in a frozen-corn-induced fit, trying to get up but slipping on niblets every time I got my feet underneath me. Jack was doubled over in absolute hysterics, and I saw Holly and Nick peering over the counter at me. I was still on the floor with corn everywhere.

"*You* are a *pig*!" I screamed, finally scrambling to my feet, niblets glued to my thighs and other delicate parts.

"I told you so! And your sense of humor is so corny!" he yelled back.

Holly and Nick shook their heads at us.

Nick pointed at my hoo-ha and said, "Is that what you call cornpone?"

"Hey, your favorite show is on, Grace. It's *The Corny Collins Show*!" Holly said, chiming in.

"What's your favorite Poison song, Nick?" Jack asked.

"I don't know, Jack. What's yours?" Nick answered back, vaudeville style.

"'Every Rose Has Its Corn'!" he shouted as they both waved around jazz hands.

I glared at all of them as they laughed, making my way back toward the stairs, shaking out niblets the entire time. "Whatever, Hamilton. You were an infant when that song came out."

"What's that, Sheridan?" he yelled as I walked up the stairs.

"Oh, suck it!" I yelled back. I heard them all laughing as I went in for my second shower of the day.

"Every Rose Has Its Corn" . . . funny.

After that, I refused to see Jack. I did communicate with him through a series of notes passed under the door of my bedroom. I agreed to meet him later at my new house, and then we were going out for dinner.

I was excited, as this would be our first official "date." It was weird that he had already had his mouth on my lady business before our first date, but then again, nothing was conventional about us, so why start now?

After my audition, I went straight to my new house. I was excited to see how things were coming along since I had been there last week. They were at the end of refinishing the hardwood floors and tiling the kitchen. Many of my new appliances had just been delivered and were being installed, and most of the crew had already gone for the day. I walked through with Chad, the contractor, making notes here and there on things that were still being finished.

"Hey, Sheridan, where are you?"

My heart lurched at the sound of his voice. Even though it had only been a few hours since I'd seen him, I'd missed him.

This is getting serious.

No kidding.

"In here!" I yelled, and listened to him walk toward us.

When he came around the corner, I grinned, letting my gaze travel over him. The late-afternoon California sun was streaming through the windows, making him glow. Black leather jacket, green T-shirt, black jeans, and . . . the ball cap. Damn it, the ball cap would have to go. I needed to see those curls. They were just too good. He smiled, biting down gently on his lower lip, and I nodded to him as I continued talking to Chad.

"So, the colors for the painter have been chosen and I taped the swatches up in each room. Also, there are some scuff marks on the tile in the shower that haven't been removed. Can we take care of that this weekend?"

I motioned to Jack to follow us as we finished our tour, and he tagged along. He was smiling at me with that devious grin, and I wondered what he was thinking.

As I walked around the house, making notes with the contractor on things that they were still working on, I noticed him eyeing my legs with great interest. I was still wearing my audition outfit: black pencil skirt, black turtleneck, wide red belt, and red pumps, very forties style. My hair was pulled back into a sleek ponytail, and I was still wearing my glasses. I winked at him over the rims when I was discussing the new Viking stove with Chad, and he winked back. Knowing he was watching as we walked around, I might have put a little extra sway in my hips.

By the time Chad left, the rest of the crew had disappeared, and it was just Jack and me. Most of the lights were off, and he wandered back into the house while I saw Chad out. Then I walked through the rooms, looking for him.

"Hey, Hamilton, where are you?" I called out.

"In here, Nuts Girl," he answered from my bedroom.

I walked in and saw him looking at the walls, where I had instructed the painter to test out different swatches of paint color.

"Hey," I said softly.

"Hey yourself," he answered.

We stared at each other from across the room for a moment.

"Is it crazy that I missed you, even for that short amount of time?" I asked boldly, putting it right out there.

"Is it crazy that I missed you and I almost called Holly to find out where your audition was so I could pick you up?" he answered.

"Is it crazy that I want to kiss you so badly right now, I almost can't stand it?" I retorted, walking across the room toward him.

"Is it crazy that when I saw you in that insanely sexy outfit, I wanted to ravage you on that pile of furniture pads in the other room?" he said, crossing to me and meeting me halfway.

"Is it crazy that—" I couldn't finish; his mouth was on mine.

Is it crazy that you are probably in love with this guy after only a few weeks?

Yep. Apeshit, batshit, insane crazy in love. Shit.

Just don't tell him that . . .

Don't worry.

fifteen

*W*e made out like teenagers, kissing and caressing softly as we stood in my bedroom. There wasn't the urgency of earlier, although I sensed that it could be brought to the surface within seconds. Now there was gentleness, a quietness to our exploration. I had forgotten what it felt like to simply kiss a man and have him kiss me back, echoing my pace. This was sweet, nurturing, lovely, and loving.

This was a romance that was beginning.

We kissed until the sun began to set, then he leaned my head on his shoulder, holding me close, and kissed near my ear.

He said, "Is it crazy that—"

"Let's not start that again. We agree, we are both crazy," I said, interrupting, and patted him on the backside.

"I wasn't finished, you rude girl," he said, frowning down at me.

"Oops, sorry. Please continue," I said apologetically.

"I was going to say, is it crazy that I think your tits look amazing in that turtleneck?"

I pulled back to look at him. He was gazing down at me with a twinkle in his eye.

"You have a one-track mind, Johnny Bite-Down."

"That's true, I do." He laughed.

"And the turtleneck might have something to do with the hickey you left behind!" I scolded him, pulling it down so he could see what he'd done. He just rolled his eyes and laughed.

"By the way, I'm going to make a rule, right here and now," I said, pulling out of his arms and facing him with my hands on my hips. When I saw him laughing, I jiggled my chest at him. He was mesmerized instantly. Now that I knew the girls had such power over him, I would be using them more often.

"Eyes up here, Hamilton. My rule?" I dragged his focus back.

"Yes, your rule. What is it?" he asked, moving closer to me again.

"This," I said, flicking his lower lip. "You are not allowed to bite down on that lower lip unless you're planning on spending at least an hour using it on me."

"What is with you and my lip? I don't see the big deal." He frowned, making a show of biting down aggressively.

"It's just plain hot, so knock it off! Promise me—hey, promise me!" I snapped my fingers and squeezed his face, pressing his cheeks together so that his lips were pushed out. "Promise me you'll be my Johnny Bite-Down, and mine alone, or no more slap and tickle."

"Grace, please. I do believe if I want a little of anything, you'll be begging to give it to me," he said, challenging me.

I raised my eyebrows at him and prepared to go nuclear on his ass.

He called your bluff. You will totally give him anything he wants, whenever he wants it.

Damn it.

"But, in the interest of keeping the peace ... and our dinner reservation," he said, "I will agree to restrain the biting down until I can use it on you, as much as I can help it, agreed?" He smiled that grin that he knew I couldn't resist, and I melted.

"Yes, please. Thank you." I smiled back. He kissed me softly again as I fixed his hair, and we made our way back through the house, locking it on our way out.

We decided to take my car, but he drove. We went to Yamashiro, a Japanese restaurant in the hills with amazing views of Los Angeles. He had timed dinner just right for when the sun was setting, leaving behind a lovely glow around the gardens. The restaurant was situated in a series of Japanese gardens and was a rather famous place to dine in L.A. It was also very romantic—something that wasn't lost on me. The boy did good.

We sat at a table by the windows so we could watch the sunset, and after ordering our sushi and sake, I excused myself to run to the ladies' room. I checked my reflection in the mirror, smoothing my hair, and noticed the flush in my face. Right before I had left the table Jack had mentioned what he planned to do to me later that night, and it was enough to get my blood pumping.

It may have involved his tongue.

I overheard two girls talking back and forth between the stalls, obviously discussing a celebrity who was dining there tonight.

"I saw him over by the window! Damn, he looks good. He's all dressed up. Normally when I see him out he's much grungier."

"He's fucking hot, is what he is. I wonder who he's with."

"Eh, some woman. It must be business related. Maybe it's a meeting. That's probably why he's dressed up."

The hairs on the back of my neck began to prickle. I had a pretty good idea who they were talking about. I ducked my head into my purse to hide my face, but as they exited the stalls, I took a quick look.

They were tall. They were beautiful. They were young. They stood at the counter, washing their hands and touching up their lip gloss. I suddenly felt like a fool, an old fool.

One of them—I'll call her Stunning—caught my eye in the mirror and she spun around. "Oh! You're the one who's eating with Jack Hamilton, right?" she exclaimed.

The other one, Also Stunning, took me in, eyes flickering over me, head to toe. Not considering me any kind of threat, she turned around as well with a saccharine smile.

I looked at Stunning and said, "Yes, I am. Did you want me to relay a message to him?" I asked, remembering my manners and that Holly would not want me to start a brawl over her client in a ladies' room.

"Oh no, we'll maybe stop by the table later. Will you two be meeting long? We were hoping he might want to grab a drink with us afterward," Stunning answered, as Also Stunning smiled at the thought.

Breathe, Grace . . .

The fact that they had dismissed me as competition pissed me off royally, but I kept my cool. "I really don't know how long, but you're welcome to stop by the table. Jack always enjoys meeting his fans." I took one last glance in the mirror and swiftly exited.

My heart was pounding as I headed back to the table.

What I was doing? The idea that this could work beyond a few manic sexy times was ludicrous. We were worlds apart, despite the powerful connection that we had.

I was a thirtysomething with a giant mortgage and a fledgling career. He was about to be a huge movie star and should have been with girls like Stunning and Also Stunning back there. A thousand thoughts ran through my head in the thirty seconds it took me to walk back to our table, and all but one ran back out as soon as I saw him.

He stood up when I got to my chair and pulled it out for me. His hand found the small of my back as he guided me into my seat, and then it rose up my spine and landed at the nape of my neck, his fingers sliding under the fabric of my shirt, grazing the skin underneath. It was a sweet moment, more telling than a dozen red roses or a box of chocolates or anything else he could have done.

He wants you. Why, we don't know. But he does. He wants his crazy girl, his Nuts Girl.

I caught the eye of Also Stunning as the pair walked back through the bar, and I couldn't help but plant a soft kiss on his fingertips as they moved from the back of my neck to my cheek. His hand finally settled over my own on the tabletop, clasping my fingers in clear view of everyone in the restaurant.

I saw her nudge Stunning, and the two of them stared at our entwined hands. I couldn't stop the slight smirk that flitted across my face as their eyes narrowed at me. Jack was oblivious to all of this, as most men are in the ways of snide womanly behavior.

I sipped my sake, sucked my edamame, and, in spite of the slight confidence boost, tried to ignore the quiet but persistent alarm bells that had begun to ring in my head.

After dinner I dropped Jack off at his car, and we agreed to meet at Holly's house as soon as he picked up a few things from his apartment. There was no discussion about his spending the night; it was automatically assumed that neither of us would be sleeping alone any time soon.

I pulled into Holly's driveway, thinking about our wonderful date. On two occasions girls had approached the table, and they were so young, it was sweet to watch Jack interact with them. Thankfully, the two whores stayed away. I think they knew better.

While we stood by the valet stand, waiting for the car to be pulled around, Jack held my hand while I naughtily kissed his neck. Suddenly there were flashes—there was a photographer and he'd gotten it all. I immediately dropped Jack's hand, trying to melt into the background, as Jack smiled for the camera a few times. Then the person backed off. I looked guiltily at Jack as the valet brought my car in front, and Jack walked around to open the passenger side for me.

"Don't worry about it. No harm done." He got me tucked in before tipping the valet and taking the keys.

As we pulled away from the restaurant I said, "Oh man, that's not good. Holly is going to kill me."

"Grace, if I'm not concerned, why should you be? Maybe you'll be the identified redhead soon," he said teasingly.

I smiled, but I knew she was *not* going to be pleased if that picture showed up anywhere.

Thirty minutes later, I let myself in the back door, hearing her call out my name from the living room. She was curled up on the couch watching the news.

"Hey, asshead. How was dinner?"

"It was good."

"Where's Jack? No orgy tonight?"

"He's stopping by his place to pick up a few things, and then he'll be along." I smiled, grabbing a piece of the brownie she was munching on.

"So we have a few minutes to talk?" she asked.

"Yeah, what's up?"

"Well, remember the meeting with the producers for that musical you auditioned for a few weeks ago? The one that's still being workshopped? They want to see you again."

"Seriously? That's great! When is it?"

"Tomorrow, so I wouldn't recommend any screaming tonight. Besides, I can't take another night like that."

"That's okay. I can't, either." I smiled, thinking of how much I'd enjoyed myself, then shook my head to clear it and started toward the stairs.

"Will you send him up when he gets here?" I called over my shoulder.

"Yes'm."

As I headed upstairs, my thoughts moved from my Brit to the meeting tomorrow. This musical was very exciting, exactly what I'd have loved to be doing.

"My Brit"? When did you start calling him your Brit?

Shhhh . . .

☆ ☆ ☆

I changed into my white button-down, yawning. I was still tired from last night. I slipped between the sheets and had already started on the last story in the series when I heard Jack coming up the stairs. I smiled in anticipation of seeing him again, and when he opened the door to my bedroom, his smile mirrored my own.

"Hey," I said.

"Hey yourself," he answered, bringing a duffel bag and a guitar case into the room.

"What, are you moving in?" I asked, shocked at the size of his bag.

"No, Nuts Girl. I just brought what I needed, and I usually play my guitar at night—unless I am otherwise engaged, that is." He smirked at me. "A little late-night reading?" He nodded at my reading material.

"Hey, we went through this already. I will no longer apologize for this. This series is amazing, and your candy ass should be glad you got cast," I retorted, snuggling deeper into the bed and reopening my magazine.

Jack putzed around for a few minutes, rummaging through his bag, plugging in his iPod, plugging in his phone, plugging in his laptop. Guys have so much gear. He seemed very comfortable here already, and I equally loved and hated how much I liked seeing that. When he went into the bathroom to take a quick shower before bed, I kept on reading.

Just as Joshua was coming out of the bathroom in 1920s New York to seduce Ruby the Ziegfeld Girl, Jack came out of my bathroom. I looked up quickly and then had to look again to truly appreciate what was coming toward me.

Jack's hair was wet and yet still artfully tousled . . . how did he do that? He was clean-shaven, wearing black boxer-briefs and a grin. His strawberry-blond happy trail was calling out to me.

"Did I tell you, by the way, that I love your glasses?" he asked, nodding to the frames that I was peering over to get an unobstructed view of him.

"Thanks, um, thanks . . . hi," I stammered, once again incoherent and idiotic at the sight of his seminakedness.

"I brought you something," he said, digging through his duffel and then climbing into his side of the bed.

Isn't it a little early to start assigning sides?

Shush.

"Oh, yeah? What's that?" I asked.

He slipped under the covers with his laptop and turned to me. "Shut your eyes," he said. I did what I was told. When I opened them, he had placed a new bag of Chex Mix in my hands.

"Yes! Can we have some now?"

"You can have anything you want, Gracie." He smiled, brushing my hair back from my face and kissing me lightly on the tip of my nose.

A few minutes later, we had settled into a companionable silence. There was a pile of my discarded melba toasts on the bed between us, next to a pile of Wheat Chex that he had selflessly given up to me. He answered e-mails as I read.

It was nice. I read for a little while longer and when I could feel my eyes getting droopy, I set my book on the nightstand, then turned on the TV. I found Lifetime just in time for my favorite theme song, which I began to sing along to.

"What the hell is this?" he asked, looking up from his laptop.

"Oh, come on, you don't know *The Golden Girls*?"

"Should I?"

"They're the best! I fall asleep to the Golden G's almost every night," I answered happily, burrowing under the covers next to him. He watched in spite of himself, being drawn into it against his will. Finally, he gave up the fight and shut down his laptop. He turned off the light on his nightstand as well and cuddled up to me.

We lay watching Dorothy, Rose, Blanche, and Sophia, giggling every once in a while. He seemed to be a Rose fan. I would have pegged him for a Sophia.

He was lying with his head on my breast, arms lazily around me while I played with his hair. When the show was over, I clicked the remote and the room fell into darkness.

"Good show, right?" I asked.

"Hmm, I don't know if I would go that far," he said, his fingers finding their way to the top button on my shirt.

"Hey, mister, I have a huge audition tomorrow. I'll probably have to sing. I can't be screaming tonight," I said, already growing warm as he started in on the second button.

"Grace, it's not my fault if you can't control your volume. Exercise a little self-restraint, for pity's sake."

"Right. Not possible with you."

I relaxed into it, though, as he began kissing lower with each button he popped.

"Grace?"

"Hmmm?"

"Are you wearing anything underneath this shirt?"

"What do you think?" I said teasingly.

He undid the last button and spread my shirt out.

I was bare beneath.

"Fantastic," he breathed.

His mouth immediately went to work on my left nipple, his hand coming up to knead my right breast. I moaned in spite of myself.

"Hey, quiet down there, mouthy," he said, chiding me, one hand dipping down lower, nudging my legs apart.

"If you do that, I'm not sure how quiet I can be," I said,

getting more excited by the second. I tried to distract him by turning his face up toward mine, but the boy was already on the move.

"Grace, I'll make you a promise," he said, peering back up at me, his chin resting on my tummy.

"Yes?" I asked, my voice cracking.

"If you can keep your voice down, I'll promise you that I'll only make you come once. And trust me when I say that once will be enough," he said enticingly, rubbing circles over my Hamilton Brand.

"And if I can't keep it down?" I asked naughtily.

"Then all bets are off, and I'll ravage you like I did last night. All. Night. Long."

Hell.

Grace, you have one of the most important meetings of your life tomorrow. You cannot lose your voice.

But he said he would ravage me. And having been ravaged by Mr. Hamilton before, I was anxious to ride this roller coaster again.

Grace, grow up. Let the man get you off once. It will be spectacular, obviously, and then you can get some sleep.

But I didn't know if I could keep my voice down. I tended to lose all control when his mouth was involved.

For fuck's sake, Grace, grow up. Bite down on a leather belt or something.

He was watching my inner monologue with great fascination, chuckling at me.

"Well, Crazy? What's it going to be?" he inquired, hooking my right leg over his shoulder. He leaned his head toward me, licking his lips, watching for my answer. I was shivering.

Orgasm #1 or Orgasm #2? To be fair, Orgasm #2 would

probably quickly be followed by Orgasms #3–13 and beyond . . . and no voice tomorrow.

Oh, God, this was impossible! He was blowing on me
now, his breath making me pant heavily.

Grace . . .

I grabbed a handful of duvet and bit down.

"Good girl," he whispered with a satisfied grin, and went
to work.

And it was spectacular.

sixteen

Warmth spread through my tummy as tightness began to build. I hissed as I felt a flickering, an insistent fluttering, and then a warm wet tongue sweetly lapping at me. I leaned into it, feeling the intensity as it ran through me.

Mmmmm.

I woke with a start, breathing heavily and in the middle of a moan. I clutched the sheets to me, covering my nakedness. I could still feel the pangs of my dream orgasm beating through me. It had been so real. It felt so real. I was still completely aroused.

"Thank God you're awake. I was worried that I was losing my touch," my Brit said.

I looked down, and I saw Jack between my legs.

This would now be known as the Hamiltonian Wake-up Call.

His tongue was poised just over me, ready to deliver another kind of kiss that killed.

"Oh, God. I wasn't dreaming that?" I exclaimed, nipples on point.

"Huh-uh," he whispered, pointing his tongue and placing it against me. I leaned up on my elbows and watched him. Amazing. The sight of him, spreading me with his magic fingers and pressing his tongue against me, was the best thing I had ever woken up to.

I moaned.

Then he moaned against me, the vibration of his lips making me shiver.

He buried his face in my sex, making my toes curl and my back arch. He furiously pressed his tongue into me, bringing me to a quick peak. I clutched my thighs around him, digging my heels into his shoulders, rocking back onto the bed. Before I was finished, I pulled his face away.

"Come here," I growled, and after kissing my Hamilton Brand, he obeyed. I kissed him feverishly, the taste of me all over him.

He was still gloriously naked from the night before, and gloriously hard. I grasped him firmly while his hips bucked into mine, and my name slipped from his lips as I whispered in his ear.

"Touch me again," I said, guiding his hand back to me. We stroked each other, and I was still so sensitive from just moments ago that it didn't take much.

"Oh, God, Jack! That's so good!" I cried, never taking my gaze off his, even though my eyes wanted to roll back in my head.

He growled as he watched me come again, a devilish grin on his face. I pushed him back and knelt next to him on the bed. He kept one hand between my legs, and I dedicated both of my hands to him, watching his beautiful face. He was rock hard, moaning my name, and I imagined how he would feel inside me.

He was close, and I pressed my face to his. His head was thrown back on the pillows with that look that I'd come to love on his face. It was a thing of beauty. His eyes were fiercely shut, jaw tense, brow furrowed, mouth slightly open, moaning my name. As much as it killed me to do it, I removed his hand from me. I wanted this to be about him.

"Open your eyes, Jack," I said quietly. "I need to see you."

His lids opened and the look of wonder in his eyes stunned me silent. I felt him tense as he came, and I cupped his face with my left hand, sweeping open kisses across his cheek as I watched him.

His eyes never left mine. I felt him shudder and I slowed my hand, gently taking him back down.

"Jesus, Grace," he moaned, finally shutting his eyes, pulling my forehead down to meet his own. His breath was sweet as he continued to shudder.

I wrapped my arms around him and wrapped my body around him as well. I brought him down to my breast and cuddled him to me, holding him tightly as the last few waves ran through his body.

I loved that I could make him feel like this.

"So, this meeting, is it a callback?" he asked over the sound of the water. I stepped out from underneath the showerhead, pointing it more directly on both of us.

"Kind of. I auditioned for them last week, and rather than a traditional callback, I'm going straight through to producers," I answered, sweeping my hair out of my face. "Shampoo, please," I said. He turned around in the shower stall, giving me a peek at his cute buns. I couldn't resist a little squeeze. He flexed them for me, making me giggle.

"Fuck, you have like four different shampoos. Which one do you want?" he asked, puzzled. "And why do you have so many?"

"I need them for different days. Some days you need a clarifying shampoo, some days you need a color boost . . . today we'll go with the deep conditioning, please." I pointed at the chosen shampoo.

"Huh, I usually just collect all the free ones from hotels and use whatever I have on hand."

"Maybe that's why you feel the need to wear that damn ball cap all the time," I said teasingly.

"Don't hate the cap," he stated firmly, pouring the shampoo in his hand. "Spin 'round," he said, indicating that I should face away from him. I did, and I felt him begin to wash my hair.

Well, wasn't he too cute?

"So, producers. That's great, Sheridan. What time are you meeting them?" he asked as he continued to lather. He seemed to be having great fun making swoops and swirls with my hair and all the bubbles, and I caught what looked like a pompadour in the reflection of the glass door. He had used almost two palms full of shampoo so I wasn't surprised at all the lather.

"Holly said at two P.M. What do you have going on today?"

"I have more reshoots tonight, probably pretty late. Okay, rinse," he said, guiding me under the spray.

I felt him gently rinse all the lather out of my hair, being careful not to get any in my eyes. He really was sweet.

I returned the favor, lavishing attention on his scalp since he was a fiend for it. Since he was so much taller than I was I had to stand on tiptoe, but he made sure I was steady, keeping my breasts firmly in hand.

When I raised an eyebrow at him he said, "What? I'm supporting you. I don't want you to slip and fall."

"Uh-huh," I answered, giving his head one final scratch. "Okay, rinse."

He closed his eyes and stood under the water, while I grabbed my shower gel—brown-sugar and coconut—and proceeded to wash my body. By the time he opened his eyes again, my body was covered in fragrant bubbles and my hands were slipping and sliding around on my skin, something that was not lost on Mr. Hamilton.

"Crazy, what are you trying to do to me?" He sighed, leaning against the tiles.

"Settle, George. I'm just taking a shower. Here . . . try some of this." I flipped him the bottle.

Maybe I arched my back just a little more than necessary when I swept my hands across my breasts.

"Grace . . ." He was warning me, and I could see how I was affecting him. I giggled. He examined the shower gel. "Coconuts! It's coconuts!" he exclaimed.

"What's coconuts?" I asked, turning my back to him to rinse my front.

"That's what you smell like! You smell like coconuts and clean laundry," he said proudly, as if he had cracked some code.

He might just have been the cutest thing ever. I peered over my shoulder at him. He was grinning.

"I smell like clean laundry?"

"And coconuts—don't forget the coconuts."

"No—we really shouldn't forget the coconuts," I said, turning to face him and running my hands down his torso, and even lower. His eyes widened.

I didn't forget the coconuts.

☆　☆　☆

That afternoon as I sped down Sepulveda to my meeting, I did my vocal exercises in the car. This was a brand-new musical, still in the workshop stages. They were continually rewriting the music and the lyrics, and as an actor, the chance to be the first to inhabit a role was intoxicating.

The female lead was in her thirties and a former beauty queen. The show was based around her coming to terms with her age, no longer being the ingénue, and dealing with the aftereffects of a messy divorce. It was about a second life, defining yourself all over again. It was sweet and funny, and the music I'd already heard was amazing.

This show was me. I was all over it. Now I just had to sell the director on it. I was new to show business, as far as they knew. All I really had going for me was Holly, and she'd had to sell like hell to get me the initial audition. But once I was in the door, it had been all me.

This was my first real test, my first real reentry into the industry, and I was ready. I was excited. And if I booked this job, I would be ecstatic.

When I arrived, I met with two of the New York producers and the director. I was also supposed to meet the writer, but he had just stepped out. As I chatted with them, the director asked how long I'd known Holly.

"Oh gosh, we've known each other since college! We were roommates, and then we both moved out to L.A. within a few months of each other. She's great."

"Yes, I've worked with her on several castings over the years. Holly's fantastic." He smiled and I smiled back, proud that she was so well respected within the industry.

"Ah, here's our writer! Michael, we'd like you to meet—"

"Grace? Grace Sheridan?"

The voice was familiar and he seemed to already know me. I turned around, an expectant smile on my face.

Then I saw him. Of course he knew me.

He had broken my heart thirteen years ago.

☆　☆　☆

"Seriously, Holls, what the fuck! How could you send me in there blind like that?" I yelled, swerving in and out of traffic like a crazy person. People were honking at me, and I flipped off at least three of them at once.

"Grace, calm down. I had no idea it was the same Michael O'Connell. I mean, what are the odds?"

"What are the odds, indeed," I grumbled as I cut someone else off. "Shut up!" I yelled as the man flashed his lights at me, screaming obscenities.

"Wow, settle, Grace. Hang up the phone and come to the office. Tell me here, where you can't hurt anyone."

"Don't bet on it," I said, yanking my Bluetooth out and stepping on the gas.

☆　☆　☆

When I was in college, I had a huge crush on one of my best friends. He was in drama school with Holly and me. A big group of us were all great friends, but Michael O'Connell was my favorite.

He was incredibly talented, which first drew me to him. He was the funniest guy I'd ever met: quick-witted, dry, and with an amazing sense of timing. Like a lot of comedic actors, he also had a sweet emo streak that, in dramatic pieces, made us all weep.

He always seemed to be a little interested in me. It was especially evident when I performed, particularly when I sang. As he watched me I could see the "friend" face slip away, and he became a guy watching a girl that he liked. But he always kept me at arm's length, eternally my "buddy."

It was infuriating.

At the end of junior year, he stunned us all with the news that he was transferring to a fine arts college in Boston the next September.

All summer, I knew I had to put up or shut up. I attempted to get him alone constantly, but since we all hung out in a group so much, it was tough. Consciously or not, he knew how I felt about him and he kept me away.

Not to brag, but no one said no to me back then. I dated our college quarterback, dated the president of the best fraternity on campus, and was briefly tied to a physics professor. Yet this guy, this drama geek, was dodging me. Fuck all that noise!

At a cast party in June, I got drunk and confronted him. Holly, Michael, and I were in the kitchen, knee-deep in crappy pot and Lynchburg Lemonades, when I saw him looking at me. Really looking at me, like I always caught him doing when I was onstage.

I didn't think about what I was going to do but just pushed him up against the pantry and kissed him, long and hard. I heard Holly say, "It's about time," and walk out of the kitchen. His eyes were surprised, but then he got into it. He kissed me back, both of us dropping our drinks. I finally pulled back and told him in no uncertain terms that he was coming home with me that night. He agreed.

It was amazing. We made love all night—and I usually hate the term "made love," but that's what it was. It was three years of love and lust spilling out, and the fact that we were such good friends made it even better. He told me he'd been in love with me since freshman year.

I lay awake all night, planning. He couldn't leave now; he'd said he was in love with me. And once I kissed him, I realized that I was in love with him, too. It went way beyond a crush. This was who I wanted. I couldn't wait for the next morning.

But as it turned out, it was all kinds of awkward. He wouldn't even look at me. He was out of there as fast as he could put his pants on, and when he saw me later that day backstage, he still wouldn't look me in the eye.

We limped through the rest of that summer. I slowly walled up all things Michael O'Connell, and when he left, I never saw him again. I heard about him from time to time through our alumni contacts. He'd become a writer, doing a lot of work off-Broadway and eventually achieving great success writing for TV and film.

And now that motherfucker held my career in his hands. Goddamn the luck.

☆　☆　☆

I tore through Holly's outer office, pointing Sara back into her chair when she tried to get up. I was seething mad. It didn't matter that I had nailed, and I mean freaking *nailed,* my audition. All my anger, all my angst, all the hurt that I hadn't known was still in there was channeled into my performance, and I'd only been slightly pleased when I saw Michael's reaction. He was stunned.

I was just mad.

I slammed into Holly's office, where she was on the phone. Her eyes went wide when she saw me. "Tom? I am going to have to call you back. Yes, love to Suri. Yes, okay, bye." She hung up the phone. We stared at each other like we were in a Mexican standoff.

Cue the tumbleweeds.

"Are you kidding me?" I said quietly.

"All right now, listen. I didn't know that he—"

"Are you *kidding* me?" I repeated, my voice beginning to rise.

"Look, Grace. Settle down," she responded, her pitch mimicking my own.

"*Are. You. Kidding. Me?*" I yelled. I sank into a chair, hysterical sobs breaking over me like a tsunami. All the crap from behind my Michael wall finally came out, all over her office floor.

She let me cry, handing me tissues, knowing I needed to wade through it. When my sobs began to sound pathetic rather than anguished, she began to talk.

"First, Grace, I had no idea he was the same guy. It's a common name. Second, I had no idea that you were still so upset over him. I thought you had let all that go. Third—"

I interrupted her. "*I* didn't know I was still so upset. But seeing him—"

"*Third* . . . you got the part," she said quietly.

There was silence as I digested what she'd just said.

"What?" I asked, unsure that I'd really heard her right.

She nodded. "You heard me."

Holy shit.

"What?" I asked again, a smile beginning to break through.

"You got the part," she said, a little louder.

"Say it again," I said, really smiling now.

"You got the motherfucking part!" she screamed.

"*Holy shit!*" we both screamed together.

Sara came running. We were jumping up and down, screaming, and I still had tears on my face. She backed out again quickly.

I got the part! I got the lead in a musical! I got the lead in a musical that was being workshopped on Broadway!

On Broadway!

In New York!

In . . . *New York.*

But what about J—

I pushed it away and felt the happiness.

☆　☆　☆

165

When Holly and I looked at a calendar, we were stunned to realize that I'd have to leave for New York in ten days.

Ten *days*.

We began to plan. First, I was pulled out of the showcase. We called my scene partner and explained, and being a true professional, he was happy about my new job and wished me luck. Holly knew another actor who could step in for me. No problem.

Second, I needed a place to live. Holly called a New York agent she knew well who worked a lot with stage actors and was assured that they could find me something temporary near the theater. Until then, I'd stay at a hotel.

Third, I had a house that I hadn't even moved into yet. Most of my things were in storage and the rest were at Holly's. The contractors were almost finished, and Chad had given me a move-in date of early next week. I'd move in just in time to move back out again.

Most of the new furniture had already been ordered and was due to begin arriving tomorrow. Chad agreed to sign for all deliveries, and I'd worry about placing the furniture later, as long as they were set in the right rooms.

Finally, I had to tell the Brit.

It wasn't as if we'd known each other that long, and while yes, we seemed to be getting along famously, there had been no declarations. We hadn't defined anything because there was nothing to define. We were at the very early stages of whatever this was, and there really was nothing more to say.

Sure, it's indefinable. You can't stop thinking about him for ten minutes. Even five minutes.

It was true. He had gotten inside the walls and wasn't budging. Whether or not this was too early, this was going to suck.

☆ ☆ ☆

After dinner that night Holly went out with a client, and I had the house to myself. Jack was working on his reshoots, and I had missed a call from him earlier. His voice mail was sweet. I might have listened to it three times.

"Hey, Crazy. I have no idea what time I'm going to get out of here, probably pretty late. Lane, back off . . . no, you don't know her . . . oh, piss off, will you? Sorry about that. Do you want me to come by tonight? It could be after two. Let me know. I don't want to wake you. Is it crazy that I want to see you, though? Ah, Nuts Girl . . . right then. Speak to you later . . . it's me, George, by the way." Click.

"It's me, George, by the way" . . . funny.

I did want to see him, no matter what time it was. Now that I knew I had ten days, I was desperate to see him as much as possible.

I found myself being drawn to my laptop. I still hadn't Googled the Brit, and it was time.

I started with images . . . nice. He really was so pretty. A lot of the expressions in his pictures were somewhat weird, but he also had a lot with that signature smirk, that Johnny Bite-Down face that I found impossible to resist. And why would I, really?

Then I moved on to the fan sites. There were a lot. Then I YouTubed his ass. I watched his interviews, I saw his paparazzi shots, and I saw the videos fans had made about him. I even watched interviews from when he was in *His Better Half,* the small independent film he'd shot before being cast in *Time.*

As I watched, I became more and more sad. He was so freaking great. He was exactly the same way in real life as he was in all those interviews. He was so adorable with the press. I could tell he was really nervous but very honest.

I'd had no idea he had such a fan base. I'd had no idea these magazine stories were as popular as they were. He'd had a respectable career up until then, but now that he'd been cast as Super-Sexy Scientist Guy? He was about to be huge.

What the hell was he doing with me? *Was* he with me? Did I want him to be with me?

Of course you do.

Ah, and here was Jack out on the town. Mostly he was photographed with other scruffy hipster guys, all with ball caps as well. Did I miss the memo about ball caps? Then a few pictures with a brunette . . . wait a minute, there were more than a few with this brunette, and on separate occasions.

I found one with a caption.

"Newly cast *Time* hunk Jack Hamilton and actress Marcia Williams, still refusing to acknowledge their relationship." Huh. Curious. Well, it's not as if he didn't have a past before me. I mentally pushed this tidbit away and resumed my cyberstalking.

When I finally closed the computer, it was late. I showered quickly, in case Jack did come over, and put on the T-shirt he'd left behind. It was huge on me. Then I slipped under the covers and watched *The Golden Girls,* sending him a quick text before succumbing to sleep.

Hey, George, by the way. Yes. Definitely come over.

☆ ☆ ☆

I must have fallen asleep, because the next thing I knew, I was being cradled to a warm chest and kissed.

"Hmm? What?" I asked stupidly, opening my eyes.

"Shhhh, go back to sleep, Grace. It's just me," my Brit said.

I smiled sleepily. "Hey."

"Hey yourself," he whispered, pulling me into his nook. His hands slipped under my shirt and slowly ran up and down my back, soothing me back to sleep.

"How did your reshoots—?"

"We can talk in the morning. Go back to sleep," he said, shushing me.

This time I listened. I drank in his scent, my own personal s'more, and drifted back to sleep.

The last thing I heard him say was my name, whispered with contentment.

☆ ☆ ☆

Three seventeen A.M.

A phone was vibrating on the nightstand. It was on Jack's side and he rolled toward me in his sleep, away from the offensive sound .

"Ugh," I mumbled, crawling over him to turn it off. I was lying across his chest, trying to reach the phone, and in his sleep his hands came up to my breasts and he muttered, "Fantastic."

I smiled through my own sleepy haze. I grabbed his phone and punched random buttons to turn it off. The room fell blessedly silent.

Yawning, I started to put it back on his nightstand.

His nightstand?

I was putting it back on *the* nightstand when I saw that he'd gotten a text. Angel Grace and Devil Grace fought for 1.7 seconds . . . guess who won?

I opened the text, sent from "M."

Hey, where did you go? You disappeared. I didn't get a chance to say good-bye from Marcia

seventeen

*M*y sleep that night was thin. I tossed about, not caring whether I woke him up, but he slept peacefully, totally knocked out.

I thought about what the text might have meant and went through all of the likely reasons why this girl—the same one he'd been photographed with and the nature of whose relationship with him had been publicly questioned—would be texting him at such a late hour. There were many reasons, and most of them were innocent.

I, of course, chose to focus on the not-so-innocent.

Jack had left this Marcia in a bar somewhere after she blew him in the bathroom.

Jack had left this Marcia in her bed after fucking her senseless and then telling her he was going to take a piss but never returning.

Jack had left this Marcia at a party, surrounded by all the other naked women he had schtupped that night, neglecting to say good-bye to her personally.

But in the end, I had to let it all go. He owed me nothing. We'd known each other for only weeks, and I was leaving.

Of course, what I already knew about him told me that nothing like that had happened. I didn't really honestly think that he had been with anyone else—not in that way.

Still, I would have liked to meet this Marcia. If for no other reason than to stop referring to her in my head as "this Marcia."

I looked at him, slumbering quietly next to me, his body warming *my* bed. His arms were wrapped around *my* waist. His hands were on, as was quickly becoming tradition, *my* breasts. And I knew that he didn't want to be anywhere else.

Which was troubling, because very soon, all this fantastic was going to have to end. As all true Scarletts do, I decided to think about that tomorrow. I snuggled back into his arms and tried to put it all out of my head.

☆ ☆ ☆

I was up before Jack and decided to go for a run. I left him a note:

> *George, I went for a run, be back in an hour.*
> *Coffee is downstairs. If you wait to shower, I'll*
> *join you. Then, you know, we can be all kinds*
> *of naked.*
>
> *Gracie*

I almost wrote "Love," but I changed my mind at the last minute.

Chicken shit.

As I ran, I thought about how to tell Jack I was leaving. I knew he'd be happy for me and would realize what a tremendous boost this would be for my career. Hell, this would *make* my career. And we could work something out, right? I mean, he was crazy about me . . . at least, that's what it felt like. He'd still want to see me when I was back in town. And he'd probably be doing press in New York. We could get together then, right?

Who are you trying to convince?

Then I thought about working with Michael. Shit, this was going to be a nightmare. I knew that I could handle it. I could be a professional. A professional who wanted to remove his balls and wear them as earrings.

Gross.

Obviously, there would need to be some kind of air-clearing ceremony, or at least some kind of ass kicking. But as the writer, he had some say in who was cast, and he must have been okay with working with me.

Of course he was—he wasn't the one who was left with a smashed-up mess of a heart.

I ran faster.

When I got home, I noticed that Holly's car was in the driveway. That was weird. She never came home during a workday. I let myself in the back door off the kitchen and heard her talking to someone. Jack must have been up.

I was rounding the corner, ready to start kissing on the Brit, when I saw who she was talking to.

"Hey, Grace. Good to see you again."

"Michael! Hi! Holly, look, it's Michael!" I said, surprised into the defensive.

"Yeah, I thought it would be a good idea for the two of you to talk. Ya know, hash things out," Holly said, offering me some coffee as a peace gesture.

The air-clearing ceremony would be starting earlier than I'd planned.

I took a moment to really look at Michael, since yesterday all I could see was red. He was the same guy I'd gone to school with. If anything, age had made him better looking. Curly brown hair, sweet face, deep brown eyes. I remembered those eyes.

He was looking at me expectantly. "Grace, until I talked to Holly, I didn't realize there was anything to hash out."

"Well, I'm not surprised," I said, walking forward with my finger pointed straight at him. "You left my apartment, never saying a word about what happened, and then all summer you—"

"Um, guys? Let's be constructive here. Grace, why don't you take him out on the terrace and you guys can talk there. You don't want to wake our houseguest," she said, hinting heavily, reminding me that Jack was still asleep upstairs.

"Humph. Whatever. Come on, O'Connell," I huffed, taking my coffee and the chip on my shoulder outside. He followed with a twinkle in his eye and a wink at Holly. I saw them both.

Once outside, I turned on him.

"So, let's get this out now and then not speak of it again, shall we?"

"Fair enough. Why don't you start by telling me why

you're so pissed about something that happened so many years ago?" he asked, sitting in a lawn chair. I took the seat next to him.

"I don't know. To be honest, I didn't know I was still so pissed. But when I saw you yesterday, it brought all that rejection back and it just slammed into me," I answered. It felt good to finally be able to unload this on him.

"Rejection? What are you talking about? I watched you date countless guys, most of them jerks, all through school. And then you jump me at a party, I foolishly tell you how I'd felt about you all those years, and then when I don't instantly propose the next morning, you go back to treating me like your little buddy."

"My little buddy? You were out the door before I even had the sleep wiped out of my eyes! And then you were such a dick to me the rest of that summer!" I yelled, angrily brushing a piece of hair away from my eyes.

"Grace, did it ever occur to you that when I woke up with you that morning, after wanting to be there for three years, I panicked? I mean, come on, you're Grace Sheridan! The fact that you were even interested in me was beyond the realm of possibility! And then when you invited me back to your apartment . . . oh man. That night was, well, amazing." He sighed, leaning forward with his elbows on his knees in a way that was so familiar to me.

It was like ten years faded away instantly and we were sitting in the campus quad, arguing about Brecht and Stanislavski like the pretentious theater brats we were. Or arguing about whether to use the fifteen dollars we had between us to buy the new Toad the Wet Sprocket album or keep us in pitchers and chicken wings for two nights.

"If you felt like that, why did you leave? And why did things get so weird for us?" I asked, a wave of nostalgia passing over me that was so strong I could almost smell the Drakkar.

"Because I was twenty-one. Because you were twenty-one. Who knows, who remembers? Because we were idiots." He laughed, and I felt myself begin to relax.

We stared at each other and I saw him—really saw him. I saw the boy I remembered, and now I saw the man he had become. The face was different somehow. More full, and the facial structure was stronger. It was a little careworn, and the laugh lines that had been there even in college were etched a little more deeply. His hair was still curly and the eyes full of mischief.

I thought about what he'd said. *Did* I treat him like a "little buddy" after we had sex? Maybe, out of self-preservation. And our friendship had cooled so quickly after that.

"Revisionist history . . . ," I muttered.

"What? I didn't catch that."

"Revisionist history. One event, two sides, and over the years it changes and twists into what we need it to be," I said, looking at my old friend.

"And it is history, Grace. It really is." He smiled, taking my hand.

I was quiet for a moment, taking it all in. "You know, it really is great to see you," I said shyly, remembering how much fun we'd all had together.

"You too." He smiled again. "Oh, come here," he said, and pulled me into a big bear hug.

I heard the French door open.

"Grace?" It was Jack, standing there in jeans, once again bare chested and barefoot.

I removed my arms from around Michael's neck and smiled. "Good morning, Hamilton."

☆　☆　☆

After Michael went back inside to talk to Holly, I pulled Jack to me for a close hug. He still smelled like sleep, warm and toasty. But his eyes were chilly. When he returned my hug, it felt perfunctory.

"Did you get my note? You must have, you haven't showered yet," I said teasingly, making a show of sniffing his underarm.

He gave me a compulsory smile. "Yes, I got it, and no, I didn't yet. Who's the guy?"

Wow, he went right for it. "His name is Michael, and he's an old college friend. I haven't seen him in years."

"A friend, a college friend. Okay." He nodded, his face relaxing a touch.

"And he's also a writer. In fact, he wrote the show that I had the meeting about yesterday, and I—"

"Oh, hell, Grace. I wanted to ask you about it last night, but you were so sleepy. How'd it go?" His face was animated again.

"Well, it went very well. In fact, I . . . I got the part," I answered quietly, looking at him with hesitance.

His face broke into a huge grin. "Grace, that's brilliant! Well done!" He swept me up and swung me around in a circle. "Oh, love, that's fantastic! I am so proud of you!" he exclaimed, laughing while he twirled me. Without setting me down, he crushed his lips to mine.

Love? Proud?

I smiled into his kiss, my legs kicking in the air.

He finally set me down, hands settled firmly on my ass. "Let's go get some coffee and you can tell me all about it," he said, taking my hand and walking me into the kitchen.

Shit.

Michael looked at our entwined hands and raised an eyebrow to me. He then walked over to Jack and stuck out his hand. "Hey, man. I'm Michael O'Connell."

"Jack, Jack Hamilton, nice to meet you," he answered as the two shook hands.

Michael looked him up and down and raised his eyebrows again at Jack's lack of clothing. I loved that Jack didn't feel the slightest bit embarrassed that he was considerably less dressed than all of us.

"So, are you staying here with the girls?" Michael asked, nodding at Holly and me.

"Well, I stayed with Grace last night. And Holly loves having me here, don't ya, Holls?" He laughed, ruffling her hair.

"Oh, yes, it's just one big whorehouse here, and I'm the madam." Holly chuckled. "Actually, Jack's an actor, and I represent him. He has a huge movie about to open this fall."

"Ah, so you and he work together," Michael said. "Grace, playing this one a little close to home, aren't we?" He winked at me.

Jack looked over at him and tensed a little. He pulled me even closer.

"O'Connell, shut up," I said teasingly, pulling away from Jack and crossing over to where Holly stood by the fridge. We exchanged glances and settled against the counter to watch this unfold.

"So, Michael, was it? You're a writer?"

"Yep, I've written for film and TV for years. This is my first musical, but with Grace as my lead, how can I go wrong?" he answered coolly.

"Well, Grace is amazing, that's for sure," Jack replied.

This was weird.

"How about I make us all some lunch? Who's hungry? I'm hungry!" I said, whirling around and looking in the fridge for something to make.

I made food for the four of us, although it was a little difficult with a Hamilton stuck to my hip. Honestly, he couldn't have been more obvious if he'd just peed on me.

While I bustled about making sandwiches, Michael, Holly, and I talked about old times. It really was nice to talk to him again, and he was reminding me how much fun we all used to have together. He was telling the story about how one night we all got drunk, snuck into the theater, climbed up through the fly system, and went out on the roof.

"When the cops showed up, Grace, you were white as a sheet!" He howled with laughter.

"Because I had just vomited over the side of the building." I laughed back.

Holly had tears streaming down her face. "Oh, God, I forgot about that. You really had trouble holding your liquor then." She grinned.

"You also had trouble holding on to your clothes. You were in your bra when the cops got there. Wow, all that lace," Michael sighed.

I swatted him with the dish towel I was holding. "Shut up. I was not!"

"Oh, yes, ma'am, you were. You tried to convince the

cops that it was your costume—that you had just performed in *Cabaret* and it was really a very tiny corset." He laughed.

"That's true, Grace. You were half-naked up there," Holly said in agreement.

We all laughed while I finished making lunch, and we settled in to eat. Jack was quiet most of the time, and as the meal went on, I noticed he wasn't touching me as much as he had earlier. I grabbed his hand at one point and he smiled, but it didn't quite reach his eyes.

He was watching me and Michael.

When Michael and Holly got ready to leave, Jack and I followed them to the front door.

"Grace, I'm really glad we got things straightened out. It will be so great spending time with you again. I can't wait for you to move to New York."

Shit. Shit. Shit.

I heard Jack's intake of breath, and I saw Holly's eyes flash to him. Michael leaned in to hug me good-bye, placing a peck on my cheek. Then the two of them left.

I closed the door behind them, waiting a little longer than I needed to before turning to face Jack.

His face was confused. "You're moving to New York?"

"Temporarily."

"When?"

"Nine days."

His face hardened and he spun on his heel, walking upstairs.

☆ ☆ ☆

When I got up to my room, Jack was standing by the bed, furiously making it. I watched him as he worried the sheets up, trying to make them smooth. I went to the other side and tried to help him, but he jerked them out of my hands.

"Thanks, I've got it," he snapped.

Since I couldn't smooth the sheets, I attempted to smooth this. "Wow, third morning making a bed and you've almost got it. Nice, Hamilton. Impressive," I said jokingly, retrieving a wayward pillow from the floor.

He didn't smile. He fussed about for another minute, and then he finally rounded on me.

"Explain to me why you didn't bother to tell me that this show was in New York," he said, frustration showing through.

Is it wrong that I still noticed how hot he was with no shirt on?

"It was only an audition at first, and there were so many other actresses up for the same role I didn't think I had a shot in hell. And then when I found out I was cast, I didn't . . . well, I didn't know how to tell you." I looked at the floor, suddenly really sad that I was going to be leaving him, right when things were getting amazing.

"Grace, I know we haven't known each other that long, but hell! This was a fairly big piece of information to leave out." He sighed.

Thinking about that text from last night, I almost asked him about it, when I noticed him pulling up the duvet, upside down. I smiled in spite of myself.

He was throwing a bit of a tantrum, and I was reminded of his age. He was my little emo, but the fact that he was obviously upset at the thought of my leaving touched me.

I needed to touch *him*. I climbed onto the bed, crawled across, sat on my knees in front of him, and wrapped my arms around his waist. I laid my head against his chest, and I felt his arms come up around me. That felt better.

"I know . . . I'm sorry. Is it that hard to believe that I didn't want to tell you? I'll miss you. I've kind of gotten used to you. Who will tell me my tits are fabulous?" I said into his chest, feeling his little hairs tickle my nose. I could tell I'd made him smile, even without looking up.

"Fucking Nuts Girl. Are you really leaving in nine days?" he asked, his hands skimming along the skin between my tank top and running pants.

"Yep."

"And how long will you be gone?"

"I don't know. It depends on how well the show does. I would say at least ten to twelve weeks." I pressed my face into his skin. He smelled like my bed.

He sighed and was quiet for a moment. Then he finally bent down and kissed the top of my head. "Right, then. Let's not get all dodgy about this. This is great news for you. I'm happy for you, Grace. You know that, right?" he asked seriously, tipping my face up to his.

"Yes, I know. The timing just sucks."

"I agree." We gazed at each other for a moment, then he broke the silence. "Now, I believe you requested some shower time? I have cleared my morning and am ready to attend to your washing up whenever you are so inclined." He smiled, letting me know the squall had passed.

"Yes, please. I am soooo inclined," I answered back, kissing his stomach and beginning to move south along his happy trail. His hands came up to my hair and I pulled him down onto the bed, his arms propping him up over

182

me as I struggled to undo his jeans button. I unzipped and . . .

Hello, commando.

"Hey, I just made this bed, and you're going to mess it up," he said.

I looked around at the pillows haphazardly thrown, the sheet trailing out on the side, the upside-down duvet, and smiled. "I love that you tried, but what you are an expert at in this bed has nothing at all to do with making it. Now, get down here," I said teasingly.

He mumbled, "This is why it's crap to make a bed," as he laid his full weight on me and my legs came up around him.

It was an hour before we made it to the shower.

Then at least another hour before we made it out.

☆ ☆ ☆

That afternoon he told me that he had no real plans for the rest of that week and that, if it would be all right, he would like to spend as much time with me as humanly possible. Who was I to argue?

So we cocooned. We wrapped ourselves in a little bubble of lust and railroaded right through what should have been our first twenty dates, all in four days' time.

We ate at Fatburger for lunch almost every day. He was a freak for it. I made him go running with me at Griffith Park, but only twice. He had trouble keeping up with me the first time, and the second . . . well, let's just say we went a little George Michael behind a tree.

We drove for miles up PCH. He drove while I sat back

relaxing, watching him in his sunglasses, looking sexy as all get-out. We listened to music, trading iPods back and forth, playing each other our favorites.

We watched hours of DVDs. We watched *The Office* (UK and U.S. versions) and *Flight of the Conchords*, and we spent an entire afternoon watching a Corey marathon: *The Lost Boys*, *License to Drive*, and *Stand by Me*.

We spent a morning at my new house, helping to place all my furniture. I couldn't believe how beautiful it had turned out, and I wasn't even going to get a chance to enjoy it.

We talked for hours. I told him all about my new show and how nervous I was about it. He confessed that he was getting a little worried about all the hype *Time* was creating and whether he would be painted with the same teeny-bop brush as other actors his age.

Since we were barely sleeping at night, we snuck naps in each afternoon. We cuddled in my bed, usually with me wearing one of his shirts. It was how he preferred me to be, if he couldn't have me naked.

It always started out with me on my back and Jack draped across my chest. I'd scratch his head and he'd trace little circles on my arm. Gradually his breath would get heavier—I had learned to recognize his sleep pattern. Right before he fell asleep, I'd turn on my side and he'd fit his body around mine, holding me close against his chest, his hands holding my breasts.

We stayed in and I cooked for us every night. Holly would usually join us and then retreat to her room as Jack cleaned up. He felt that he should do the dishes since I cooked, and I let him. I found that I could watch him do almost anything and be happy.

We'd usually go for a swim after dinner, and he kept a

bottle of wine on the side of the pool for us while we splashed and played. Sometimes, if I was lucky, we'd skinny-dip.

We sang songs as if we were at freaking camp. I finally got him to play guitar for me, and he was amazing. Watching those fingers all over that guitar with the same tenderness and attention that they gave to me was amazing. And hearing him sing? He had a sweet voice, but rough at the same time. A little mushy, thick, and wonderful. He was truly talented and his voice hypnotizing. He played some of his favorites and some that he had written. He played songs I knew, so I could sing along. It was nice. He would strum absently while he watched me get ready in the morning, and when I'd make the bed (I'd taken back this particular duty) he'd write me my own little action soundtrack, his playing mimicking my motions. When he thought I should be moving faster, he played faster.

We kissed constantly. We kissed for hours. Whether we were at the table, in the shower (which was now always a synchronized event), in the hallway, or on the couch, we kissed. Slow and sweet, furious and frenetic, wanting and needing, we kissed.

We touched constantly, unable to keep our hands off each other. Whether it was hands being held across the hot tub or his hand on my thigh while we were driving, we were in contact, always. He would sweetly keep his hand in the small of my back when we were walking anywhere. I'd curl my legs around him when we were watching a movie, and he'd nudge at my hand like a cat until I scratched his head.

There was virtually no part of his body that I had left unexplored, and he'd done the same for me. We were in an almost constant state of arousal. He kept my Hamilton Brand fresh each day, providing new nibbles if it was fading. A look from him made my pulse faster, and we became so good at meeting each other's needs that it almost was inconsequential that we had yet to really have . . . sex.

I needed it. And I knew he needed it. It was only a matter of time.

But we both wanted to wait for it to be special. Because in this heightened, super-sped-up, crazy world of ours, we were moving beyond whatever this had started out as.

And I found myself falling completely and totally in love with him. It was so good, it almost hurt.

This was all kinds of fucked up.

☆　☆　☆

Late one night, on the fourth day of Grace and Jack Lockdown, we were lying in my bed watching *Say Anything*. It was the part where Lloyd plays the song to Diane through the window and I sighed deeply, feeling Jack's fingers as they gently moved through my hair.

"Oh, jeez, not you, too." He laughed.

"What? Not me what?" I asked, tapping on his knee.

"You girls all love that scene. You all want the boy with the radio outside the window," he said teasingly, planting a kiss on my head.

"That's not true. I mean, I love that scene. It's iconic. And I love that song . . . my God, I love that song. But I don't need the grand gesture."

"The grand gesture?"

"Yeah, you know—he runs through the train station to bring her the flowers before she leaves. Or he drops down on one knee in front of a room full of her friends to propose and try to win her back. He says he loves her in front of a football stadium, because he never had the guts to say it when it was just them.

"I don't want all that schmaltz. It's the little things, the daily choices. That's the love." I picked at a loose thread on the blanket. It was the closest I had come to telling him how I really felt. "I tell you what, if someone ever played a Peter Gabriel song outside my window, I do believe I would lock that very window."

"Hmm, you are curious, Grace Sheridan. Just when I think I have you sorted out . . ."

"Ah, you'll never sort this out. It's a mess in here. Stay clear, Hamilton. Stay clear." I sighed, rolling back against him.

"So, no schmaltz, huh?" he asked.

"Well, a little schmaltz is fine. Every girl needs a *little* schmaltz. I do have a small romantic bone in my body."

"Heh heh, you said *bone*," he said, deadpan.

"Oh, man . . ." I laughed, snuggling back down to him.

We were quiet for a moment, watching, then he said, "Grace, do you mind if we turn this off?"

"Fuck, no. I was just waiting for you!" I cried, pouncing on him. He laughed his surprise into my mouth but then quickly turned on that Hamilton sex that I needed so badly.

We were ready for bed, so he was wearing only his underwear-campaign-worthy boxer-briefs, which still made me shake like a schoolgirl whenever I saw him walking across the room in them.

He'd started to unbutton my shirt when I pushed him back in the bed. I slowly swung a leg over him and strad- dled him. I had barely brushed him when his hands came up rough on my hips.

"Ah ah ah, love, slowly now," I said teasingly as I began to unbutton my shirt for him. I settled lower down on his lap, feeling his hardness through his thin boxers. This time I had gone commando.

I hissed at the feeling of him pressing against my skin, and I relished the idea of how he would feel when he was inside me. I rocked my hips against him slowly, purposefully, and watched as his face changed.

Slipping the last button through, I parted my shirt for him. I was naked and his eyes drank me in. His hands left my hips to come to my breasts. I moaned into his touch as he gently rolled my nipples between his talented fingers. He tugged at me, and I cried out. His eyes were wild as he watched me above him, and I rocked harder against him, feeling the indescribable friction that our bodies were creating.

"Fuck, Grace. That feels amazing," he groaned, his eyes becoming even wilder, his face almost animalistic.

I pushed him in the way that I knew only I could push him. I lowered my body onto his, pressing myself against him. I looked him in the eye and said, "What would feel amazing is that tongue of yours. All. Over. Me." I punctuated each word with a hard thrust, slamming my hips into his rock-hard Mr. Hamilton.

His eyes narrowed, and he unleashed a low growl from deep in his throat.

He lifted me off his lap with one swift movement, and I found myself with my knees on either side of his face. He grabbed at my hips, pulling me firmly down to his mouth. His tongue snaked out, and he licked me. Hard. I sucked a breath in sharply, my hips bucking as he fought to hold me still.

"No," he said, warning me, his eyes blazing hard as he stared up at me.

He licked me again. Harder.

I rocked my hips, desperate for the friction, and he growled again. He pulled me down once more, roughly, and began lapping at me, quickly, violently. His mouth closed around me, sucking greedily at me.

I came fast and hard, in his mouth, on his tongue. Before I could even recover, his teeth—oh, my God, his teeth—teased at me. He took me into his mouth again, and with his lips pressed firmly around me, his teeth nipping and his tongue darting over me, the sensations were unlike anything I had ever felt before.

Then he moaned.

He moaned and he groaned, and the vibrations rang through me. I screamed his name repeatedly as I rocked my hips back and forth. His hands dug into my hips, bruising my skin, keeping me in place, not letting me go. My screams became wordless as the series of orgasms ravaged me, making me shake violently. He was groaning under me, his tone guttural and his face furious as he watched me come down.

He was not done with me.

He flipped me over, nudging my knees apart almost carelessly. His eyes burned into me as he dragged his fingertips from my mouth, down the center of my body, between my breasts, and below. He teased me there for a moment, watching my face as I became more and more frustrated with his swirling fingers.

Just before I began to pull my hair out, he plunged two fingers deep inside of me. My back arched off the bed, hips wild at his touch. *This* was what I needed. He found that spot, his J-spot, and he stroked me intently while his other hand pressed down. He brought his face to mine and kissed me, sucking my lower lip into his mouth.

The push and the pull, the soft and the hard, the sweet and the salt of it all was too much, and I exploded again, screaming his name once more and making him smile.

I opened my eyes and saw him kneeling over me. I scrambled up, sitting up on my knees, and yanked his boxers down quickly. My head was still spinning from the intense orgasms this man had just given me, but I couldn't focus on anything other than the sight of him. Huge, hard, swollen, and perfect.

Placing one hand on him and the other on me, I watched his face as I "addressed" us both. I wanted to come with him.

His eyes traveled down to my hand on his length and then to my other hand, which was feverishly working my own sex. I switched hands, my wetness coating him, making him moan as I worked him. I could feel myself getting closer again and I slowed, wanting to wait for him.

"Come with me, Jack," I panted, almost crying with the torture of watching his perfect face as he raced toward his own orgasm. Both of his hands shot out to the back of my neck, lacing his fingers behind me. I cocked my head to one side, leaning on his arm, kissing his skin wherever my lips could reach him.

He closed his eyes, sighed my name, and came . . . with me.

Beautiful.

Minutes later, we were wrapped as closely as we could be, arms and legs entwined, skin on skin. I was running my nails through his hair while he slipped toward sleep. I kissed him softly on each eyelid, the tip of his nose, and finally his mouth.

I loved him.

Simply.

☆　☆　☆

In the morning when I woke, he was gone. On his pillow was a single piece of paper.

> *Grace, I have looping today. I should be home*
> *by 3. Out to dinner? Last night was . . . I have*
> *no words.*
>
> > *Jack*

There was a little arrow at the bottom, indicating I should turn it over.

There was one more line:

> *I'm leaving you with just a little schmaltz:*
> schmaltz

The last word was written tiny, and I laughed through my tears.

eighteen

That morning I spent putzing around, dealing with some of the stuff that had fallen behind while we were in the cocoon.

I got caught up on the freelance project I was finishing. I could work on some smaller projects from New York, but with the salary I'd be making, I could essentially stop freelancing. I was going to be able to support myself as a working actor for the first time in my life, and I almost had to pinch myself to believe it.

I also started packing, deciding what I would send ahead to New York and what I'd bring to my new house. Shit. There was still so much I had left to do and hardly any time to do it. I could feel myself beginning to panic a little.

I needed to drop the voice-over class I had just signed up for. I needed to switch my *Martha Stewart* subscription to New York. Crap, I didn't even know where I was living yet.

I needed to go shopping. I was out of deodorant, and I needed some string cheese. And I had promised the Brit I would pick up some mother-flippin' Chex Mix.

I needed . . . I needed . . .

Settle, Grace.

I needed to do laundry. I grabbed the hamper and sat on the floor, making piles around me while I took some deep, cleansing breaths. As I was sorting, I noticed that Jack had snuck some T-shirts into the hamper. Now I was doing *his* laundry? I smiled, thinking of him throwing these shirts into my hamper with a grin, knowing that I'd call him out on it later. He was so cute when he was smirking. I pressed each of the shirts to my face, inhaling his sweet scent.

I looked around my room, where we had spent so much time over the last few days.

His guitar. An errant melba toast. His jeans, thrown across the back of my chair. A *Felicity* DVD—he really was sweet to indulge my Ben Covington fetish. His stupid ball cap, which, to his credit, he had not worn in my presence.

I picked up the ball cap and stared at it, thinking of how cute he was when I took it off his head and messed up his big curls.

Why was the ball cap wet?

I was crying. Big, giant elephant tears were pouring foolishly, relentlessly down my face. I was over-the-moon happy to be moving to New York, but I was so sad to leave him that it was messing with my head . . . bad. How was it possible that I was in so deep already?

The phone broke me out of my sad-sackery. It was Holly.

"Hey," I said, sniffing up the last of my tears.

"What's wrong?"

"Nothing's wrong, why?"

"You've got that donkey voice, that's why."

"Donkey voice?"

"Yeah, when you've been crying, you sound like Eeyore."

193

Alice Clayton

I laughed aloud. I loved her so.

"Come on, meet me for coffee," she said.

"Don't you have to work, Holly?"

"Eh, all the Scientologists are on vacation. It's been a slow week."

☆ ☆ ☆

She watched me pull into the Starbucks lot, waving at me while I looked for a spot. While I was putting the top up, I saw two guys check me out and I smiled. I still wasn't used to attractive men checking me out. Once a fat girl, always a fat girl in your head. But I knew I was glowing lately. Must have been the round-the-clock orgasms. They always did wonders for a girl's complexion.

I walked up to the table where Holly was sitting outside and smiled when I saw she'd already gotten my coffee.

"Hey, dillweed, nice of you to order for me," I said, giving her a kiss on the cheek and sinking into the chair across from her.

"Yes, I thought you could use some caffeine. Are you enjoying the view? You've spent so much time horizontal lately—be careful, now."

"Who says we were only horizontal?" My face lit up at the thought of him, vertical, horizontal, or otherwise.

"I see." She laughed as I sipped my drink.

"Holly, I have to tell you, with the way it's been already, you better get some earplugs for when we finally do the deed."

"What? Wait . . . he hasn't even fucked you yet?" she asked, or rather yelled, judging by the curious faces of everyone sitting around us.

194

My face burned as brightly as my hair. "No. And Jesus, Holls."

"How the hell is that possible? All that screaming and moaning and groaning and grunting and thrashing about that you've subjected me to, and no—"

"Dick. I know. No actual dick, yet." I finished her sentence, hiding my face in my hands.

"I have newfound respect for young Master Jack. All that wall banging with no actual bang bang? So when is this momentous event going to happen?" she asked, clearly in awe that I had yet to ride the lightning.

"I don't know. I wanted to wait . . . and now I'm leaving in less than a week . . . I . . . I don't know."

"Wanted to wait? Get on the stick, woman. Literally!"

"It's not like I don't want to. I just wanted it to be special, okay?" I sank back against my chair, feeling miserable.

"Who are you? Blossom? Grace, you have a twenty-four-year-old man in your bed every single night, and you aren't letting him into the sanctuary? A man, by the way, who women all over the country are lining up to fuck the brains out of?"

"Believe me, he'll be let into the sanctuary! And thanks for reminding me about all those other women. That's a great visual for me to have when I'm walking around Manhattan. Can we please talk about something else?" I begged.

"Yes. Why were you crying earlier?" she asked, switching topics quickly.

I grimaced and took a long pull on my iced mocha. "It's just been a whirlwind the last week, and there are many different things banging around in my head. I'm so jazzed about this show, and you know I've always wanted to live in

New York, even temporarily. But I'm leaving my new house right as I was going to get to move in!"

"And?" She pushed me.

"And I backed out of the showcase. I feel terrible about that."

"And?"

"And I will miss you, of course—you're my Dirty Martini Bitch," I said, my eyes warming.

"And?" She smiled gently.

"Oh, God, and I don't want to leave my Brit. I *really* don't want to." I sighed heavily.

"And why exactly would that be?" she asked again.

I was quiet, then broke out into a huge grin. "Because I haven't gotten the dick yet?" I asked brightly.

She couldn't help but laugh. "Look, whether you want to say it out loud or not, it's obvious how you feel about him. And it's obvious to anyone with eyeballs that he feels the same way."

I fiddled with my wallet, my way of telling her this discussion was over.

"One last thing, if I may?"

"Yes?" I asked warily.

"If you don't want to tell me, at least tell him. You should, you know." She took a sip of her drink.

"I am considering all options."

We were quiet for another moment.

"So, really, all that with just his hands?" she asked with a grin.

I smiled proudly. "And his fingers. And his mouth. And his—"

"Stop it, you're making me blush."

We dissolved into giggles, to the entertainment of ev-

eryone who was at the Starbucks off La Cienega that afternoon.

☆　☆　☆

After coffee with Holly, I headed back to the house. I had
gotten a text from Jack about dinner tonight:

> Gracie, I'm meeting a friend for coffee after looping and
> then running by my place for a bit. Dinner tonight? Wear
> something sexy—not that this would ever be a problem
> for you.

His text made me smile, but I was also feeling a little blue.
The friend he was having coffee with, was it this Marcia?
You're supposed to stop saying it that way . . .
I know, I know.
I went upstairs and grabbed my iPod and headed out to
the terrace. I wanted to soak up as much California weather
as I could, although autumn in New York was truly beautiful.
I settled into a lawn chair and breathed in the sunshine.
People said L.A. was smoggy, and it was, but there are parts
of Southern California that just plain smell better than anywhere else. I could smell sun, grass, oranges, and honey-
suckle. It was late in the day, and the warm golden glow of
the sun bathed me. I felt wrapped in it. I loved L.A. I would
miss it.
I dozed off and on, and finally took out my earbuds when
I noticed that the sun was low in the sky. It was later than I
thought.

I stretched in my chair like a cat and heard the unmistakable *putta-putta* of Jack's silly little car pulling into the driveway. He called out to me as he came in through the kitchen.

"Out here, George!" I answered, bouncing in my seat, waiting to see him for the first time that day like a little schoolgirl.

He rounded the corner.

Wow.

He was dressed for the evening. White button-down, black jacket, black pants. He was clean-shaven, my favorite stubble from the last few days gone. He smiled that super-sexy grin and closed the distance between us.

"Hello," he said, placing his hands on the armrests on either side of me.

"Hello yourself," I answered, a little high from the hit of Hamilton that had just been blasted at me.

He leaned in closer . . . and hesitated just before his mouth touched mine. He was so near I could feel the energy zapping between us, but he still held his lips there for two agonizing seconds. All I could hear was his breathing—mine had stopped.

I would never get tired of kissing this man.

He pulled back when I clutched at him, and I stuck my tongue out at him. He laughed.

"Get ready for dinner, Grace."

"Dinner schminner. Let's stay in . . . ," I purred, trying to pull him between my legs.

"Ah-ah. I'm taking you out," he said, scolding me, as I did my best to ensnare him.

"Why don't you skip the *out* and just take me?" I whispered hungrily in his ear. My talk with Holly today had made me question this whole "special" thing.

I could see hesitation in his eyes as he looked at me, weighing his options. To further entice him, I placed my hand directly over the noticeable bulge in his pants.

I squeezed.

He groaned.

I was going to win this one.

He gave in, pulling me up from the chair, snaking his arms around my waist, and crushing me to his chest. He lifted me straight up off my feet, his lips planted firmly on mine, and carried me backward through the house toward the stairs. My arms were wrapped around his neck; our eyes locked like laser beams. There were no words. We both knew where this was going.

"Hi, fuckface, I'm home!"

He stopped dead on the stairs and closed his eyes in frustration, and I sighed into his shoulder.

"Holly," we said at the same time.

He put me down on the step, kissing my forehead. "Dinner?" he groaned.

"Give me twenty minutes," I moaned back, hopping up the stairs. He gave my ass a smack, and I squealed on the way to my room.

Twenty-two minutes later, I walked into the kitchen and was greeted with whistles from Jack and Holly. I had chosen well, apparently. I was wearing a deep-green swing dress with tiny straps and an empire waist. The neck dipped low enough that it was sexy but not slutty, thank you. I wore my hair down. Luckily, I had let it air-dry that morning and my natural curls were lazy and soft, exactly the way Jack liked them. I finished off with gold kitten heels and lots of sparkle.

And my boobies were definitely sparkly.

I felt gorgeous, and the way Jack was staring at me with

a dropped jaw told me I had done well. The green of my dress exactly matched the green of his eyes, something that I didn't realize until I saw him in front of me, his eyes burning as he took me in.

"Grace, wow, you are . . . ," he said in a low voice.

"Now, now, be nice," I said teasingly, anxious to hear what he would say.

"Illegally beautiful," he said, brushing my hair back to plant a soft kiss where my neck met my jaw. My toes, freshly painted with "I'm Not Really a Waitress," curled. I literally shook in my heels from that one touch of his lips.

"Ahem," Holly said, bringing me back from orbit, but only slightly since Jack was now planting baby kisses from my neck to my collarbone.

Sweet sassy molassey, he is off the charts tonight . . .

"Guys, a moment?" she asked, throwing a grape at Jack.

"Hey, bitch, don't mess with my Johnny Bite-Down. I'll kick some ass," I snapped. Jack chuckled, and we both turned to her.

"Johnny Bite-Down? Forget it, I don't want to know. What I *would* like to know is how you're gonna explain this," she said in a serious tone, pointing to her laptop screen.

Curious, I stepped behind her and looked over her shoulder.

TMZ had posted the picture of the two of us at Yamashiro with me kissing his neck, exactly the same way he'd just been kissing me. There was no way to misinterpret the intimacy of this shot, especially the way he was holding my hand. The look on his face as I kissed him implied that there was definitely something between us. The caption read: "New star Jack Hamilton dines at local L.A. eatery with unidentified redhead."

Then there was a picture of us at Fatburger—I hadn't

even seen the cameras that day. "*Time* hunk Jack Hamilton and mystery redhead."

Finally, there was a picture of us holding hands again, walking out of Whole Foods. He was laughing, and I was gazing up at him adoringly. This time there was a paragraph.

"British heartthrob Jack Hamilton has been photographed all over Los Angeles with a mystery girl. Has this Brit boy been bitten by the love bug? Or has a cougar gotten her claws into this very single guy?"

Tears prickled my eyes. *Cougar.*

As in, what the fuck was I thinking, dating this much younger man?

As in, what the fuck was he thinking, hanging out with my ancient ass?

As in, what the fuck must everyone be thinking when they see us together?

And the bitch of it was that I wasn't even old enough to be a cougar.

I shook it off, smiling through the fuckery. "Hey, you should come see these, Hamilton! You look great, although the redhead next to you clearly needs some antiaging cream!" I forced a laugh out.

"I've seen them," he said softly. "And, Grace, you're insane. I think you look lovely in those pictures."

"Well, the insane part is obviously true. Cougar, huh? You dirty boy," I said teasingly, swallowing hard on the lump in the back of my throat.

He crossed to me and took my hands. "Stop it," he said, brushing his nose to mine and clasping my hands to his chest.

I blinked back the tears furiously, bending my head so he couldn't see them.

I could hear Holly typing behind me.

"So, anything else on there I should see? Ashton and Demi make any appearances this week?" I asked, turning away from him and going back over to Holly. I heard Jack grumble behind me. I was getting some control back. I was squishing it back down.

"Nope, that's it," she said, closing her laptop. "Look, guys, no one's happier than me about this weird little thing you've got going on. I think it's great. In fact, I think it's pretty fucking fantastic."

"Holly, listen, I know that—"

She held up her finger. "That being said, I have to play the part of manager and say that being photographed like this, all over town—not a good idea." She looked at me apologetically, and I nodded to show her that I understood.

"Holly," Jack said, "I'm not going to change what I do in my personal life just because it's more media savvy. We should get that straight right now," he said, slipping an arm around my waist. I leaned into him instinctively. Though it looked like we were presenting a united front on this, I agreed with Holly.

I cut in, attempting to smooth this over. "You know what? I think we should go to dinner, and we can figure all this out later."

Jack wasn't upset, but I could see his jaw tighten. Besides, I was leaving in just a few days. It would soon be a nonissue.

Holly looked at the two of us and sighed heavily. "Jack, you know I think you're a great guy. And I obviously love my girl more than anything. But trust me when I say this is the worst time in your career for you to be perceived as unavailable.

"That's all I'm going to say for tonight. You two enjoy

yourselves." She smiled, kissing Jack on the cheek, and turned to me. "And for fuck's sake, Grace, just keep your hands off him in public."

"I hate you, fucko," I sneered.

"I hate you more. Now, scoot." She giggled, leaving the kitchen. And me alone with my Brit.

There was an awkward silence, a first for us.

"So, should we go?" I asked. I couldn't stand the silence anymore.

"Yes, let's go," he said, smiling at me and catching my hand as we walked toward the door.

He stopped me right before we went outside.

"Are we cool, Gracie?" he asked, his eyes worried.

I smoothed his hair back, his eyes relaxing with my touch. I traced my fingers down over his furrowed brow, down his cheek, and pressed my fingers into his lips, which formed into a pucker.

"We're cool, George. We're cool," I answered, smiling at him.

Liar.

This was going to break my heart.

nineteen

We were quiet as we drove, both of us lost in thought. I didn't want the night to be about the earlier conversation, but all I kept seeing when I closed my eyes were those pictures and the word *cougar* emblazoned across the insides of my eyelids. I'd known the age thing was going to come back to bite me in the ass sometime—I'd just hoped it wouldn't happen so fast, and in full view of his fans.

I usually never felt old. Thirty-three wasn't old, for Christ's sake. However, if you were dating an actor who was twenty-four and the object of young girls' affection . . . thirty-three was decrepit.

But God, those pictures! They were actually very sweet. They had captured what we were: happy and content, funny and fresh, Jack and Grace. I loved the pictures, especially the one at Fatburger. We were in line at the counter, waiting to order. He had me tucked into his side and we were both looking up at the menu. And his hand was on my ass, lovingly. Like when you were fourteen and you went to the amusement park and your boyfriend planted his hand on your butt while you walked around, looking for that slow boat ride where you could make out in the dark, hands all fumbling and frantic.

And the picture of us coming out of Whole Foods? Hell, I'd frame it and put it on my mantel, it was so cute. Our hands were swinging between us as we walked out to my car, having just been caught kissing in the frozen-food aisle. Jack was holding our grocery bags, and I was brushing his hair out of his face with the hand that wasn't held by his.

I looked over at him, driving my car, as was now habit. Usually when he drove we talked and held hands, or he played with my pant leg, trying to push it farther up my thigh. I usually pretended to try to stop him, but truth be told, I loved that he couldn't keep his hands off me.

But tonight was different. His hands were clutched tightly on the steering wheel, his jaw was tense, and I could see the worry on his face. I could fix this simply by taking his hand off the wheel and holding it in my own.

I couldn't quite bring myself to do it, though.

He sighed again, and I was sure he was wondering how to fix the tension that had built up between us. I was quiet, biting my lip and staring out the window. Every now and again, I saw him look at me out of the corner of his eye, darting his eyes back to the road when I tried to meet them. He seemed so far away.

He looked so sad, so concerned. He was as torn up about this as I was. I felt terrible, seeing him look so conflicted.

Fix this. Fix this now.

He ran his right hand through his hair again, and before he could place it back on the steering wheel, I caught it and brought it to my lips.

205

He turned quickly to look at me, his eyes surprised and . . . relieved?

"Hey," I whispered.

"Hey yourself." He smiled back, face lightening immediately, then dropped our hands to my thigh, where he immediately pushed up my skirt so he could rest them on my bare skin.

As soon as I felt his hand on my skin, I felt a sense of calm, of peace, of quiet settle over me.

I felt a sense of grace.

☆ ☆ ☆

We pulled into Geoffrey's, one of my favorite restaurants. It was in Malibu, perched on top of a beautiful cliff overlooking the Pacific. I'd never told him this was one of my favorites, but he knew. We held hands as we walked into the restaurant, and the host took us straight to one of the tables right in front, the ocean spread out before us. Both men went to pull out my chair, and I grinned when Jack won.

After tucking me in he sat across from me, and I was reminded again how truly striking this man was. We smiled for a moment, listening to the waiter finish explaining the specials. Then we picked out a bottle of wine together and settled into a good silence, watching the tide roll in below us.

"So, should we talk about it?" he asked, brushing a piece of my hair back behind my ear. He'd been watching me struggle to keep it unstuck from my lip gloss.

"We can, but it doesn't change anything. It would be great if we could walk right into a crowded Hollywood club holding hands in front of all the paparazzi, but we can't."

He curled his hand around mine. "No, I suppose we couldn't." He sighed, concern flashing through his eyes again. I was determined to not have those gorgeous green eyes look like that again.

"So, let's just cross that bridge when we come to it. Besides, I'll be far away in New York, and then you can slut it up playboy style again." I grinned, pulling my dress a little lower and exposing just enough of my breasts to pull his focus. Sure enough, like a magnet, his eyes were drawn there, and when he looked at me again the green was on fire.

The waiter brought our wine, and after we ordered, Jack raised a glass to me. "So, here's to our second meal at the beach, and may this one be seagull-shit free."

"That might be the best toast I have ever heard in my entire life," I said, clinking his glass merrily and sipping the wine.

We laughed, and then Jack leaned into the table a little, taking my hand again.

"So, I have something I'd like to propose."

"Be careful, Hamilton. The first night we met, you told me that we would engage in a tryst—and that happened, didn't it?" I thought of that magical night, when the dirty martinis had flowed as freely as the banter.

"I remember, Sheridan, and I've quite enjoyed trysting with you. But this one is different."

"Oh? Do tell." I sipped my wine, delighting in the feel of his fingers tracing circles on the inside of my palm.

Gazing down at our hands, he said, "I have to go out of town this weekend, to Santa Barbara."

I felt my face fall. I only had a few days left, and he was leaving.

Then he looked up, staring at me through his lashes. "I

want you to come with me. Will you come?" he asked, his words rushing out.

Like I would ever say no to him. Like I would ever say no to *that*.

Fantastic hotel sex! A giggle escaped before I could catch it.

"What are you thinking?" he asked, the corner of his mouth turning up in that sexy half grin that made my knees go weak.

"I was thinking, *Fantastic hotel sex*," I said, my grin now ear to ear.

Understanding dawned in his eyes, and they burned into mine. "Hmm, hotel sex. The best kind of sex." He chuckled low.

"Hotel sex, where Grace doesn't have to be quiet," I purred.

"Hotel sex, where Jack doesn't have to be quiet, either," he answered right back, making my tummy clench at the thought of Aggressive Jack making another appearance.

"Hotel sex, where we will finally have *the* sex. Is it wrong of me to want to skip dinner and drive to Santa Barbara right now?" I asked, only half-kidding.

"No, it's not wrong. I've half a mind to drive you there right now. You could use a good shagging," he answered, raising my palm to his mouth, pressing his sweet mouth to it, and then darting his tongue out to lick it lightly.

My mouth hung open. *He wants to shag me.*

Why did that sound so dirty, sexy, and all-around nasty in the best possible way? I could see the T-shirt now: *I got shagged in Santa Barbara, and all I got was this fantastic orgasm.* It had a nice ring to it. I was sooo going to get shagged.

About time.

☆ ☆ ☆

After dinner we drove back to Holly's, touching the entire time. When we paused at a stoplight his hands were unstoppable, roaming all over my legs, my arms, over my dress, under my dress.

Whenever we stopped at a stoplight, he leaned over and kissed me like someone was going to take my lips away from him and he was determined to get all that he could while he could.

I was a little free with my hands, as well. I had already unbuttoned nearly his entire shirt, his jacket long since abandoned to the backseat. When we were at a particularly long light, I had a brilliant idea.

I pressed the button that controlled the convertible top. In the middle of kissing me, he noticed the top going up and he stopped.

"Did I do that?" he asked, looking confused. "I was nowhere near the button."

"No, Sweet Nuts, but you were getting close to the button that matters. I thought we could use a little more privacy," I said teasingly, pulling my dress up high enough that he could see the white lacy boy shorts I was currently rocking.

He inhaled sharply, his eyes going dark green again. I had come to recognize the eyes going dark as a portent of good things to come.

"You're dangerous, Nuts Girl. We're still miles from the house," he groaned as I continued to tease him, showing him a little more than just my boy shorts.

"I only need a few miles to work my magic, Hamilton. Just drive the car," I said, pointing at the light, which had turned green. He smiled, placed his hand high on my thigh again, and drove on.

I pulled myself up on my knees, and then it was on. I attacked.

I was all over him. My mouth sucked hard on his neck and my tongue found his ear. I moaned into it, biting on his earlobe.

"Mmm, Jack . . . I can't wait until you're inside me," I purred crudely, knowing this would drive him out of his British mind.

He exhaled forcefully, and I saw his hands grip the steering wheel tightly.

"Grace . . . don't test me," he said, warning me as he struggled to maintain control over both himself and my car.

I leaned over, and with one hand buried in his hair and my mouth fixed on his neck, my other hand snaked into his lap and quickly unzipped him. He fumbled, trying desperately to keep me away from him, but he'd lost that battle the moment he said *shagging*. I'd been at a rolling boil since then, my oonie and me just biding our time until we could pounce.

And who could ever resist a pouncing oonie? Jack should have known by now that when my oonie wants something, she gets it.

There was also a Mr. Hamilton Junior that needed attending to. I placed my hands around him, leaned down, and took him in my mouth.

"Fuck, Grace . . . don't . . . seriously, don't . . . ahhh . . . No. No, Grace . . . Gracie, we can't . . . oh, wow . . . ahhhh . . . we really shouldn't . . . aw, fucking *hell* . . ."

He gave in.

I heard screeching tires over his little diatribe, but

mainly, I was focused on him. I licked him from base to tip, swirling my tongue around his head and then taking him in deeply to the hilt. I felt him hit the back of my throat and I moaned, sending vibrations through him. That's when I heard, "Fucking hell," and I knew he was mine.

I pulsed him in and out, using my hands to create more friction as we sped up through the canyon. It was a testament to Jack that he was able to stay on the road. One of his hands did come down briefly to tangle in my hair, and I stopped only long enough to place it safely back on the steering wheel.

I could tell he was getting close—his breathing was rough and his voice, which always chanted my name seconds before he came, was starting to get tense.

I heard a squeal and then silence. Before I knew what had happened, I was pulled out of my seat, losing a shoe in the process, and placed unceremoniously on his lap.

He had stopped me right before he came. Twenty-four-year-olds were my new favorite thing. I needed to tell Oprah to put them on her list.

But now Aggressive Jack was in the house—or rather, in the car. A car that wasn't big enough to contain him. I sat on his lap, my knees pressed into the leather behind him, as he looked at me without words. His hand stretched out to press the button that would put the top back down, and as it moved over our heads, I looked up and saw stars. I twisted around and looked over my shoulder and saw the whole of Los Angeles spread out before us.

Mulholland.

We had made it all the way to Mulholland.

We were parked, and once the engine shut off, all I could hear was my breath, his breath, and the music. The Cult's "Fire Woman" spilled out into the night.

I started to say something about the view, and his hand closed firmly over my mouth.

"No, Grace. I told you not to test me," he said darkly, his eyes almost forest by now.

His breath was still a little shaky from my recent activities, but there was no question he was in control now.

"Did I tell you how beautiful you look in this dress tonight?" he asked, slipping one finger under the strap and sliding his hand under the fabric. His other hand lifted me off his lap just enough to pull the dress out from under me, billowing it around us.

"Mmm-hmm," I answered, thinking how sweet he was.

"I want you to remember that." He grasped a handful of silk and tore it from my breast, leaving me open to the breeze and making me gasp. I was naked underneath, other than my panties, and though he continued to rip my dress off my body, he never took his eyes off mine.

Then he snarled. He fucking *snarled* at me. He scooted me up on my knees, dipping his hand underneath the band of my panties.

"And as much as I love this lace? I need to see my Grace," he said, ripping those off too. I was now completely exposed, parked on the edge of a cliff, straddling my Brit, who, by the way, was still hard as hell and pointed directly at me.

We stared at each other, our breath coming faster and faster, waiting to see which one would break first. He was breathing heavily, his nostrils almost flaring with the passion that I could feel coursing through his body and flowing into mine. His lip curled in a sneer that was beyond belief in its sexiness. He looked like an animal, an aroused and about-to-be-out-of-control animal.

The breeze raised goose bumps all over my overheated

skin. I pressed myself down against him ever so slightly, feeling his sex against mine, and then we both broke at the same time. Foreheads knocked, teeth clicked, lips smacked and probably bruised as we clawed at each other. His hands went to my breasts. He pushed them together and licked them both at the same time . . . glorious.

I buried my hands in his hair, pressing him farther against me as I began to swirl my hips . . . fantastic. He bucked up against me, his hips tilting me backward against the steering wheel and causing my elbow to hit the horn. We kissed, licked, sucked, nibbled, bit, moaned, groaned, panted, and grabbed. My wetness coated him, making us slide against each other in the most pleasing way. I could feel his hardness pressed against me, and as I rocked against him I was manipulated deliciously. I knew it wouldn't take long; this sex was on fire.

I shifted in his lap at the same time he shifted, and then . . .

I could feel him.

He could feel me.

We both stopped and stared wide eyed at each other.

He was so close, he was right there, he was almost . . . inside me.

I could feel him, right where he needed to be. The feeling made my blood boil. He gripped my hips tightly, holding us perfectly still.

"Oh, God, Jack, oh my God . . . please?" My voice shook. I couldn't wait any longer. I physically *needed* him to be inside, right now.

He remained perfectly still . . . and then I felt him push into me. Just a whisper more than he had been, still only barely inside me.

We moaned at the same time, and then he did the most unbelievable thing.

He pulled away.

I cried out at the loss. "No! No, please Jack. Come in, *please* come in." Trying to push myself down on him, I looked into his eyes for an explanation. A battle was raging across his face; he was thrilled and horrified all at the same time.

"No, Grace, not like this," he said shakily. His face was changing from lust to fear to anger and then to pure carnal frustration. Mixed with determination. Damn it.

"Not in a car, not outside, not like this. Not now," he said again, his voice cracking as he pulled away farther, away from my warmth, which was aching to envelop him. He sighed heavily and lifted me off his lap carefully, setting me back into my seat.

I was still in shock. As my heart and my body began to readjust, my brain caught up. He wanted it to be special.

We were both fools. Crazy fools.

I blushed suddenly. I was sitting in my car naked, parked on the side of a mountain, with a still-very-hard Brit next to me, both of us trying to get back in control of ourselves.

I caught his eye, and we both grinned.

"That was—wow. I can't believe how hard it was to stop myself," he said.

"No kidding. I'm impressed. And apparently a bit of a slut." I laughed, primly covering my exposed breasts with pieces of my shredded dress.

Panties? Shredded.

Pride? Slightly shredded but intact.

"Slut becomes you. And just because I'm not going to be inside you tonight doesn't mean I won't be very, very soon," he answered, twirling my panties on his finger—what was left of them.

He took off his shirt, handed it to me, then put his jacket back on. I buttoned up and leaned over to kiss his neck.

"How quick can you get us home?"

"Buckle up, Nuts Girl," he said, hand on my thigh as we tore off into the night.

☆ ☆ ☆

When we got back to Holly's we walked in giggling like teenagers, only to find Holly with a carton of Chunky Monkey. She took one look at us. I was dressed in his shirt, buttoned all cockeyed. One shoe. He was wearing his jacket, no shirt underneath . . . very *Miami Vice*. We both had bite marks on our necks. She shook her head as we went past, shaking her spoon at us.

"You'd better hope there were no photographers wherever you were, damn it!" she shouted up to us. I ran up the stairs ahead of Jack, still naked underneath his shirt, and I swear to holy Chex Mix . . . he bit me on my butt.

☆ ☆ ☆

We had a crazy night, reminiscent of our first night together. It was as if we knew that by this time tomorrow night we'd be moving beyond our little sexual frontier, and it was like a countdown of our greatest hits. He made me crazy in the bed, up against the door, in the shower, and once again . . . on the floor of the closet. His hair was a mess, my hands refusing to let go whenever he got that maniacal tongue near my lady bits.

I would like to thank whoever wrote the manual that all twentysomething men now read, because they sure love to take a taste. Not that it didn't happen when I was in my early twenties, but the quality had certainly improved. I don't know if I needed to thank Bill Clinton, or Internet porn, or *Sex and the City,* but damn.

And how the hell did a twenty-four-year-old guy know how to find a J-spot? My first boyfriend couldn't have found it with a TomTom. Truth be told, it took *me* a while, too. But my George?

And he got as good as he gave. By the time I was finished with him, he was actually begging me to let him rest—a first for him.

We were lying in bed, legs and arms tangled pleasantly and both positively glowing in our postorgasmic silence, except for Jack's Happy Sound. I did love to hear that little hum, especially when we were close like this.

I stretched, letting out a big yawn, then settled farther into the covers. Our little cocoon was so warm, and I swear that my sheets were softer when he was under them. How could that be?

He'd snuggled down so far under the covers that all that was visible was a shock of messy hair, curls askew. He was wrapped around me like a snake, with his head on my chest. His breath tickled my skin and I giggled and poked him in the ribs. The hair jumped slightly.

"Hey, are we really going to Santa Barbara tomorrow?"

"You better believe it," he said through a yawn.

"What time are we leaving? And how long will we be there?"

"We can leave as soon as we wake up. I know you'll have tons to do to get ready for New York, so we'll only be there through Sunday. Two nights."

Then I only had two nights after that before I had to leave. I quickly pushed that thought aside.

"What's happening in Santa Barbara anyway?" I asked, sliding my hand beneath the covers. I caressed his face, and his lips captured my fingers in a quick kiss.

"I have a photo shoot with some of the other cast members. You can meet them if you'd like," he said almost shyly.

"Do you want me to?" I asked. We had just been told by Holly to keep things quiet, and while Jack said he didn't care who knew we were . . . whatever we were, I knew it wasn't a smart idea. The fewer people who knew, the better.

"Well, yeah. I already told my friend Rebecca about you, and Lane—he plays Isaac in the film—heard me on the phone with you the other day. So, yes. You should meet them." He was quiet for a moment and then finished with, "If you want to."

"Yes, I want to," I answered, and felt him relax against me farther.

"Right, then. That's settled. But remember one thing, Grace."

"Yes?"

He pushed his head above the covers, looking wonderfully rumpled and sexy. "When I'm working, I'm working. You can come and meet them then. Because when I'm not working . . ." He paused and I finished for him.

"You're only going to be working *me*, George." I arched an eyebrow at him. He gazed at me and just the look in his eyes made my nipples go on point.

He noticed. His lips began to sweep kisses across my collarbone and his hands came up to my breasts.

I rolled away, to the farthest edge of the bed.

"Hey, where did you go?" he asked, surprised.

"We're going to sleep, Sweet Nuts, so tomorrow will happen faster," I answered.

He chuckled and rolled over to me, pressing his body up against me in the most comforting way. As his hands found my breasts, he whispered, "Good night, sweet girl."

I sighed happily and shut my eyes, willing myself to sleep.

Tomorrow, we'd drive.

And then?

Let the blessed shagging begin.

twenty

*W*hen I woke up, it was like Christmas morning. I was so excited that I began jumping on the bed, singing a happy tune much like "A Tisket, a Tasket": "A shagging, a shagging, I'm going to get a shagging!"

From under the covers, Jack groaned. I poked him with my toe, standing over him in a victorious pose. "Hey, get up! I thought you said the shagging would begin today," I said teasingly, using my toe to pull the covers down slowly. I revealed a creased forehead, knit-together eyebrows, glaring eyes, and a frowning mouth. As the reveal continued, however, I saw a strong chest, slim hips, my favorite trail this side of Appalachia, and . . . hello, lover! A Morning Missile. His eyes said no, but his wood said yes.

My eyes widened at the sight, and Jack arched his back as he stretched, making it poke farther at his boxers. I bit my lip. I couldn't get sidetracked, or we'd never make it to Santa Barbara.

"Hey, George, let's go! Get up!" I prodded him, humming my original shagging tune.

"Grace, stop it," he said, warning me, trying to retrieve the covers from underneath my bouncing feet.

"George. George. George," I chanted with each bounce. He glared at me again through sleepy eyes.

"Grace, I'm warning you."

"And I'm warning *you,* man. You said you'd shag me today," I repeated, bouncing harder than ever. The bed was squeaking inappropriately.

"I'm gonna *spank* you today if you keep that up," he said. "Now seriously, stop all that bouncing about. I won't tell you again."

His eyes darkened as they looked at me now fully, standing over him in my white button-down, hair messed from sleep, eyes sparkling. I started to bounce again and he moved like a cat, catching me in midair, pulling my legs out from under me so I landed flat on my back, knocking the wind out of me. He straddled me while I struggled to catch my breath between giggles.

"Grace, you need to calm down. We can't leave for Santa Barbara yet."

"Why the hell not?" I asked, trying to fight him off. He would have none of it.

"First of all, because you haven't packed," he said.

"I plan on being naked most of the time," I answered quickly.

"Secondly, the hotel won't even check us in until noon."

"We can do it in the car," I quipped, trying to get my hands free so I could grab on to him. I was more persuasive when I could touch him.

He knew this, so he kept both of my hands high above my head, pinned to the bed.

"Thirdly, has it escaped your attention that it isn't even six A.M.?"

I stopped cold. I looked at the window and noticed the sun had barely risen. The freaking birds weren't even chirping. And I was bouncing on the bed like a madwoman singing about an upcoming shag. I looked back to his face, now fully awake and glaring down at me, but not without a hint of humor.

Gulp.

"Sorry, I didn't realize how early it was. I guess I'm a little eager." I grinned, feeling a blush start to creep in.

"Crazy," he said, shaking his head at me. He pulled me up and pressed me close to him. I let my hands come up to his shoulders and hugged him tightly. We embraced for a moment, his hands tracing up and down my back. I breathed in his scent, amplified by his sleepy heat. Pipe tobacco, chocolate, and Hamilton.

"Is it crazy that I can hardly wait for tonight?" I whispered in his ear, my heart damn near beating out of my chest.

"Me either," he whispered back. He pressed his lips to my cheeks and then my lips. "Now, Grace, for the love of God, can we please get a few more hours of sleep?" He sighed, pulling me back down with him.

"You can sleep, but I need to get packing. You still need to pack, too. What time should I get you up?"

"I'm already packed. My bag is in the car." He yawned, tugging at my hair, trying to get me to lie back down next to him.

"You already packed? You mean we could have left last night?" I shrieked. He covered his ears.

"Grace, we'll leave in a few hours," he said, trying to placate me. "Pipe down, woman, and bring me those tits. You know I can't sleep without a handful." He succeeded in pulling me close enough to get ahold of me and I giggled, letting him slip his hands beneath my shirt as I tucked in next to him again.

His fingers roamed for a few moments, as was customary, sweeping across my nipples until they were sufficiently hard. He always did this until I sighed and arched into him a little before he settled in. He would sneak one arm under the pillow and me, and the other would drape under my arm, cupping me and pulling me tightly against his chest until I was in a Hamilton sandwich. His mouth would always return to mine for one last kiss, and then I usually got another one right behind my ear as his head nestled on the pillow behind mine.

There was one more gentle, contented hum, and then within a minute or two, I knew he was back to sleep. I lay quietly, surrounded by the man I hadn't even known a month ago.

I couldn't wait for that night . . .

☆ ☆ ☆

I finally got his ass in the car by ten thirty. I had lain in bed until I knew he was sound asleep again, and then I quietly packed. I went into Holly's room when I knew she'd be up and we powwowed briefly about what lingerie I should bring: slutty or sweet? I brought some of each.

I woke him precisely at nine, dragging the covers down and leaving him curled in a ball. He was a little grumpy this morning, but when I quickly flashed him a boobie, he got right up. Then he tried to get more—ahem—but I told him to conserve his energy, as he'd need it that night.

I hadn't looked forward to an event as much since the New Kids reunion concert, and that was an all-time high.

We ate a quick breakfast at the house: cold cereal and fruit. I refused to spend any time cooking when we could be on the road. He ate with agonizing slowness, chasing his Honey Nut Cheerios around with his spoon. When he started having a conversation between himself and the leftover O's, I took away his bowl and dumped it in the sink. He laughed and finally relented.

"If I didn't know better, I'd say you were stalling." I shook a finger at him while he slowly sipped his juice.

"I'm not stalling, but breakfast is the most important meal of the day, Grace," he answered, selecting his banana with uncommon diligence.

"I think you *are* stalling. Are you worried about tonight? Are you having a little performance anxiety there, big guy?" I asked, grabbing the banana and making obscene gestures with the fruit.

"I hardly think so. I'm just enjoying watching you squirm. If I didn't know better, I'd say you were a bit randy," he said teasingly, wrapping his arms around my waist.

"Hell, I'm way past that. I need to get pounded, and you're the guy who's going to do it," I said severely, pushing him toward the stairs. "I got a hole that needs fillin', a field that needs plowin', and a stocking that's aching to be stuffed."

He arched an eyebrow. "That's very crude, love," he said, chastising me, his eyes dancing with mischief.

"Now get the hell up those stairs, get in the shower, wash your kibbles and bits, and then drive my randy ass to Santa Barbara so you can make me see God," I said as I forced him backward up the stairs. He laughed the entire time and finally went into the bedroom, still shaking his head.

That little fucker was playing with me. I decided I might have to drive.

☆　☆　☆

We were driving up the coast, top down, shades on, music loud. It was another one of those perfect Southern California days: temperature in the midseventies, no clouds, and bright sun. The ocean was to our left as we drove along PCH toward Santa Barbara.

There was an open bag of Chex Mix between us and we passed Wheat Chex and melba toasts back and forth, enjoying our time together. Every so often the thought of leaving for New York would flit across my mind, but I firmly pushed it aside. We had limited time and I would spend every second of it in the here and now, loving this man next to me.

I was very skilled in the art of pushing things aside.

His right hand set up camp on my left knee. I had worn shorts for just this reason; any opportunity for his skin to touch mine was gladly accepted. I watched him as he drove, hair blowing, sunglasses on. He hadn't shaved that morning because I hadn't given him enough time to do so. I'd stood outside the shower while he was in there, threatening to flush the toilet if he didn't get a move on. He'd tried to get me to shower with him but I steadfastly refused, knowing we'd be incapable of showering together without some hanky-panky.

His profile was stunning as always: strong jaw, chiseled cheekbones, sweet lips. He caught me staring and his lip curved in that sexy smile I loved so much. "What's up, Crazy?" he asked, bringing my hand to his lips for a kiss.

"Just watching you. I'm burning this into my brain. Us, together," I answered, brushing back the hair from his face. "Jeez, I'm schmaltzy today!" I exclaimed, leaning back against the seat, tucking my legs beneath me.

"I don't think so. I've been doing a little brain-burning myself. What am I going to do without my Nuts Girl?" he asked, sounding more serious than I'd expected.

"I know! Who is going to make you watch *Golden Girls*?" I said teasingly.

"Who is going to make sure all the shampoo is washed out of your hair?" he said, teasing me right back.

"Who is going to keep you stocked up on Fatburger?"

"Who is going to dump niblets in your knickers?" he said, deadpan.

"Whose boobies are you going to hold while you sleep?"

"Who is going to listen to you snore?" He chuckled.

"Hey, I don't snore!"

"Fine, Grace, you don't snore," he said sarcastically, shaking his head.

We were both quiet for a minute.

"Seriously though, will anyone be listening to you snore? I mean, in New York? Do you think you'll . . . I dunno . . . be snoring for anyone else?" He looked nervous but was covering well.

"Will you be holding anyone else's boobies while I'm gone?" I asked quietly, immediately thinking of this Marcia.

"I asked you first," he said.

"Well, I would like to make it clear that while I officially do not snore, the answer is no: I don't plan on snoring with anyone else while I'm gone," I said, nervous now myself. This was the first time we had really discussed where this was going.

He was quiet, and I could see his jaw relax. He'd been quite tense.

"And?" I asked.

"And what?" he asked back.

"What about you? And holding boobies? Will you be . . . holding . . . anyone else's boobies?" I could barely breathe. This was a twenty-four-year-old guy who could have practically anyone he wanted. Could I really be asking him if he was planning on monkhood while I was gone?

Yes, you are, and he owes you an answer.

I waited.

"Grace, I can honestly say, with no second thoughts, that there isn't another pair of boobies on the planet that I'd rather have in my hands than yours. Sleeping or otherwise," he stated.

"Oh, baby, you say the sweetest things," I cried in a sickly sweet voice, smacking his cheek with a wet kiss.

"Blech, don't call me *baby*. You have enough nicknames for me already," he said teasingly, crisis averted.

"Oh, suck it, Sweet Nuts," I said, taunting him.

"Now, if Jessica Simpson happens to fall on me, and I have to steady her by holding on somewhere . . ."

I gave him a wet willy.

We laughed, and I hoped we could keep the promises we'd just made.

☆　☆　☆

We pulled into Santa Barbara just after noon, and as the tiny streets wound through the trees, I realized where we were staying. The Four Seasons Biltmore was a famous re-sort, and I'd stayed there once when Holly and I first moved to California. It was Spanish in its architecture, with a classic Californian open feel.

We pulled around to the front, the valet got our luggage, and when Jack checked us in, I was pleased to find that we were staying in one of the cottages right on the ocean. I raised my eyebrow when I thought about the extra privacy this would afford us, and he winked at me.

"I wanted you to be able to scream as loud as you wanted to, Crazy," he whispered, green eyes smoldering. I could feel my body warming just listening to him tease me.

"Will someone be making me scream?" I asked in my own whisper, pressing my lips to his neck, while the desk clerk coughed discreetly.

"Count on that, love," he answered, his hand sneaking down to my bum and giving it a squeeze. I giggled in antici-pation as the clerk handed over our keys.

We had just begun to make our way in the direction of the cottages, kissing deeply, when I heard a woman say, "Well, well, what have we here?"

I turned to see a pretty blonde, standing with a tall, brown-haired guy who obviously worked out a lot. They were both smiling at the two of us pawing each other in the lobby. Jack's hand gave my bum one more squeeze and then broke away. He smiled back at them, shaking the guy's hand and giving the girl a hug—one like you'd give your little sister.

"Lane, Rebecca, this is Grace," he said, pulling me back against him as I shook their hands. They seemed to be eyeing me up and down in an amused way, but it wasn't unpleasant. I immediately got the sense that they were approving, which was a nice change of pace.

"Gracie, you'd know them better as Isaac and Penelope." The other two main characters in the film. Lane, I already knew I liked. He was grinning big. Rebecca was appraising me a little more carefully, woman to woman. She played the love interest in the film, and I was curious to see what their chemistry was like off of the set.

"It's really nice to meet you. Are you staying here as well?" I asked, noticing that Lane was eyeing my chest appreciatively and giving Jack a high five.

Rebecca laughed kindly at the two of them and answered, "Yes. We have the photo shoot tomorrow, so a few of us decided to come up a day early." She smiled a bit more warmly, and I got a gut feeling I was going to really like her.

"I don't know why Hamilton was keeping you such a secret, Grace. You're hot!" Lane blurted out.

"Thanks, Lane. I do have a pretty sweet rack." I laughed as Jack blushed and shook his head at me, eyes closed. I could tell he was pleased I was getting along with his cast mates so quickly.

"So, what are your plans for the afternoon? We were just going to get some lunch. You're welcome to join us," Rebecca said.

Jack started to say, "Actually, we were going to get settled in our room—"

"We would love to come!" I interjected, smiling at both of them. It was my turn to stall now, just for fun.

We agreed to meet in the oceanfront restaurant in fifteen minutes. We said our good-byes and headed for our cottage. As we walked down the cobblestone pathway, Jack looked at me incredulously.

"What happened to not being able to wait for the shagging? I thought we were going to spend some time inside today," he said, shifting my overnight bag to his other shoulder so he could tuck me into his side as we walked.

"I want to spend some time with your friends while I can. Besides, after how much you teased me this morning about my randiness, now I'm going to make *you* beg for it," I said matter-of-factly as we walked up to the front door.

He looked at me carefully for a moment and then unlocked the door. He let me walk in before him, and I was struck by how lovely and romantic the cottage was. Fireplace, private patio, ocean view, and I could see a scrumptious king-sized bed beckoning from the bedroom. All of this I noticed in the seven seconds it took him to close the door, spin me around, lift me off my feet, and press me back up against the door.

His eyes burned into mine as he ravaged my neck with his tongue; the suddenness of his attack left me breathless. He bent his head and gently bit my earlobe.

"You want me to beg for it, Grace?" he whispered.

"Uh-huh," I managed to say, beginning to lose focus. He forced my legs to open and wrap around his waist, and I could feel him grinding hard against me. A soft moan escaped me.

"I'm begging you, Grace. I'm begging you to let me kiss your sweet tits." His tongue dragged from the top of my cleavage to the base of my neck. "I'm begging you to let me nibble on you." He ground hard against my core, eliciting a louder groan from me. "I'm begging you to let me taste you." He held me up against the door with the strength of his body alone, one hand snaking beneath my shorts and finding me instantly, pressing down hard. I gasped his name. "And I'm begging you to let me sink inside, to feel you wrap around my cock as you come over and over again," he said, bringing me to the fastest orgasm I have ever experienced. I screamed his name, still pressed up against the door. The combination of his hand and the words he'd just spoken in that damnable accent was too much, and I came again, softer but more deeply than the first.

I loved me some Hamiltonian Dirty Talk . . .

He backed away, eyes almost black, licking his fingers. "Now we'll see who's begging later." He smirked, watching my dazed expression change to one of determination. "Let's go keep that lunch date *you* insisted on, love," he said, putting his sunglasses on and grinning at me cockily.

"Gah," I managed to say, eyes crossed and legs doing the shimmy-shake. This was going to be the longest day of my life.

☆ ☆ ☆

We ate lunch with Rebecca and Lane, and I listened to stories about filming. It was interesting to see Jack with his friends. We'd spent so much time wrapped in our own little ball of bliss that it was nice to interact with others.

Jack told them with pride about my show in New York, and though his voice was tinged with a sadness only I would have noticed, he was unquestionably my biggest fan. When Lane asked how we were going to work a cross-country romance, Jack simply smiled, kissed my hand, and answered, "We'll figure it out as we go."

Rebecca obviously adored Jack and vice versa, and I felt good about leaving him with such a good friend. Lane had starred in a fairly major movie earlier in the summer, and there were already a group of women at a nearby table who'd recognized him. It didn't take long before Rebecca and Jack were recognized as well, and the women finally approached the table after much giggling. Once there, Lane showered them with hugs. He really was a natural at this. Jack was a little more reserved, as always. He really wasn't comfortable with his new fame but was taking it all in stride.

They discussed the photo shoot that was scheduled for tomorrow. It sounded like it would be good, but I wasn't sure if Jack was expecting me to tag along. I felt that Rebecca and Lane would probably be fine with it, but I didn't want to get in the way.

Jack kept his hand on my leg, on my arm, or in my hand the entire time. It was as if he hadn't heard a word Holly had said about keeping a low profile, and I loved and hated him for it. I was the one who would be crucified by the fans if there were more pictures of me. He really had no idea what an impact he had.

As the women giggled away and out the front door, I excused myself to visit the ladies' room. Lane was heading out to the lobby to take a call, so he walked me toward the front.

"So glad I got to meet you. You're a cool chick." He smiled.

"Yeah, yeah, I bet you say that to all of Jack's girls," I said, teasing him.

"Nope, you are seriously cool." He left me to blush on the way to the bathroom.

Moments later, as I headed back to the table, I saw that Jack and Rebecca were deep in conversation. Stepping deliberately behind a potted palm, I listened in. I had no shame . . .

"Twenty-six? Twenty-seven? Is she older than twenty-seven?"

He shrugged, his eyes twinkling.

"How old is she, Jack?"

"I don't actually know. She hasn't told me, and I haven't asked. I think around thirty, thirty-one maybe. I pinpointed it through all the Corey references."

"Wow, she doesn't look like she's in her thirties," Rebecca exclaimed. She was my new favorite person.

"You bet your sweet ass she doesn't." He chuckled.

"Dude, you should see your face. You're like all glowy and shit! You're such a girl!"

He laughed. "I have always been a girl—you know this."

They joked for another minute, and then he told her our story. Where we met, how we met, everything. As I listened, I watched the way his face changed when he recounted something I said or something we had done. I shouldn't have listened in, but I was glad I did. It gave me an interesting perspective into him and how he was feeling about me. I was falling more and more by the second.

"And now she got cast in this show, which is brilliant for her. But it's in New York, and she is leaving in a few days. The timing just sucks." He sighed, sitting back in his chair.

"But she won't be there forever, right? And, honey, with all the press you're about to do, you'll be in New York all the time. Stop being such a pussy, Hamilton."

He smiled at her. They seemed to be great friends.

"I know you're right. It's just, I can't tell what she wants to do about all this. I mean, I dunno, she just gets me, and I think—no, I *know* she fancies me. But she's getting ready to do this huge thing, it's so important to her and for her career."

"And you're not? Jesus, this movie is going to make you a household name! Maybe this isn't the best time for you to have a girlfriend," she said, giving voice to my concerns. He was quiet at that.

Backing away from the palm, I reentered the restaurant, making enough noise with my flip-flops to alert them to my presence. Jack immediately grasped my hand, and I brought his fingers to my lips, kissing them gently. I simply adored him.

By the time Lane rejoined us and we finished with lunch, it was well past two thirty. Jack begged off on their offer of an afternoon sail, saying he'd made other plans for us. I raised an eyebrow as I was unaware that he'd planned anything.

As we left the restaurant, Rebecca pulled me into a hug. Surprised but pleased, I hugged her back. "I'm so glad to have met you, Grace. You have no idea."

"You too. I'll see you later?" I asked.

"Definitely," she answered.

Lane wrapped me into a bear hug, and as I laughed, his hands began to travel down toward my bottom.

"Hey, man, get your hands off my girl." Jack gallantly pulled me away.

"Jack, seriously, I can't help it. That's one fine woman," Lane said teasingly, smacking me on my butt.

I jumped in surprise. "Next time you do that, I spank back," I said, pinching Lane's cheeks . . . the ones on his face. We said our good-byes and made our way through the lobby toward the spa.

"What're we doing now?" I asked, curious.

"I booked us a couple's massage. Nice, right?" he asked, nodding to the receptionist when we walked through the doors.

"Truly nice. You went all-out this weekend, Mr. Romance. But I told you, I don't need all this. All I really need is you inside me, deeply," I said in a whisper as the spa coordinator led us back to the couple's suite. She gave us instructions on what to take off and what to leave on, if we wished, and then left us to disrobe. The suite was facing the ocean and we could see and hear the waves. I breathed in the salty air as Jack began to undress.

"I'll show you mine if you show me yours, Hamilton," I joked, pulling my camisole over my head. I was wearing a new bra, one he hadn't seen yet. White, lace, lots of cleavage.

Sweet and slutty.

His eyes darkened as always when he saw me almost naked, and I delighted in performing a little striptease. I slowly peeled my shorts off, turning to toss them on the chair to show off my white, lacy boy shorts, similar to the ones he'd shredded the night before. He was in the process of taking off his shirt but stopped dead in his tracks when he saw my hands go around back and unclasp my bra.

"Now, now, we're getting massages . . . no funny stuff," I said, scolding him, then slipped the bra down and tossed it at him. It hit him in the head and fell down over his face; he looked like he was in that scene from *Weird Science*. "But, the question is, do I leave these on or go ahead and take them off? Will I want her to massage me everywhere?" I slipped my thumbs under the bands on either side of my boy shorts, pulling them almost off, but not quite. The critical bits were still covered. "Hmmm, I just don't know. What do you think, Jack?" I asked, pulling them a little lower, spinning to give him just a peek.

He quickly turned around, stripped his own clothes off down to his naughty bits, and dove under the blanket draped on his massage table. He pressed his face down into the pillow, and I could hear him groaning. I laughed, finished getting undressed, and slipped under the blanket on my table. We giggled for a few minutes, waiting for the massage therapists to come in, holding hands across the space between us.

For the next ninety minutes we relaxed, enjoying the

treatment fully. Once we'd finished up, we dressed and made our way back to the cottage. I didn't know what our plans were for the night and was happy to let Jack lead.

I felt nervous as we approached the cottage. Would we have the sex now?

Don't you want to have the sex?

Yes, yes, of course. But would I have time to change into my sweetly slutty lingerie?

Jack made up my mind for me when we got inside. "So, I'm going to leave you for a bit to get cleaned up, and then I'll be back. I made reservations for dinner tonight. How does that sound?"

"Here at the hotel, I hope," I murmured, pulling him to me for a hug.

"Yes, here at the hotel. I figured it was safer that way. If you get a little randy at dinner, we have a place close by," he said teasingly, his breath warm in my hair as he held me tight. I would miss this—the hugging, the banter, the back-and-forth that was Jack and Grace.

I pulled back a little to look him in the eyes. "Thank you," I said.

"For what?" he asked, looking puzzled.

"For this weekend. It's perfect," I answered, kissing him softly.

He kissed me back slowly, lazily, fueling the fire that was always burning between us.

"You get a shower. I'll be back for you in a little bit," he whispered.

I sighed as I watched him leave, and then I began to prepare. I would be having hot hotel sex with Jack Hamilton before this night was through.

Thank God.

In the time it took me to get ready and Jack to come back from whatever he was doing, I managed to work myself into quite a frenzy. I was excited, nervous, frantic, frazzled, twitterpated . . .

Anything else?

Horny; crazy horny.

Damn straight.

I was wearing my favorite little black dress, cut low enough to show my cleavage, enhanced by sparkle. Jack now refused to let me wear something low cut without a dusting of shimmer. I had twisted my hair up high on my head, letting a few pieces fall here and there in a carefully constructed do that said, "It's supposed to look like I just threw it up, but it really took me an hour."

As I dabbed perfume in all the right places, it struck me that I hadn't been this nervous when I lost my virginity. Tommy Jenson, eleventh grade. His parents' basement on a blanket that smelled like camp. Young MC on the radio. It was quick and painful.

Ugh.

I was a Hamilton virgin, and I couldn't wait to be deflowered.

Jack came to the bathroom door and knocked. He'd used the other one to get ready.

"Grace, you decent?"

"Pfft, like that's ever stopped you before," I said teasingly as I appraised myself in the mirror.

Hair? Nice. Makeup? Flawless. Skin? Glowing. Knockers? Up. Confidence? High.

I opened the door, and once again he did not disappoint,

wearing a gray button-down, black leather jacket, black pants, and my favorite Doc Martens. And he was biting down on his lower lip . . . in an attempt to drive me crazy? Hell yes. I sighed and he sighed back at me, our eyes traveling over each other.

"Grace, did I tell you how sexy you are today?"

"Nope, tell me."

"You are so sexy. It's all I can do not to ravage you right here. Because I want you, Nuts Girl. I want you in the most desperate way," he whispered as he pulled me to him.

"It does feel that way, doesn't it?" I shivered as he kissed my neck.

"Let's go eat the fastest dinner possible."

"We'll set a new record, George. Mark my words," I stated, pulling him toward the door.

☆ ☆ ☆

Once we were out of the cottage, I started toward the restaurant we'd had lunch in but Jack pulled me toward the waterfront.

"I arranged something a little more private for us. I hope you don't mind."

We walked across the gardens, the night perfumed thickly with jasmine and rose. We came upon a little pergola that had been set up with one table, two chairs, and a dozen candles that shone through the darkness. I could hear soft music playing, and I was delighted to see that while there was one waiter, there was no one else around. It was like our own little hideaway.

Who said romance was dead? I smiled at him, letting

him lead me the rest of the way, and it was then I realized that I would follow this man anywhere.

Once seated, he opened a bottle of champagne and poured for both of us. He raised his glass and said with a sexy grin, "Let the seduction of Miss Grace begin."

I laughed. "Love, you could seduce me with a Dr Pepper right now. There will be no playing hard to get tonight."

He laughed, smiling at me in that way only he could. "I love how funny you are, Gracie."

"I love how gorgeous you are to look at, George," I responded, sipping my champagne and crossing my eyes at him.

"I love how you call me George," he quipped, looking at me as if I was the most beautiful creature on the planet.

"I love that you let me . . ." I trailed off, suddenly emotional as I looked at him.

"I love that you've become so important to me," he added, gazing at me from under heavily lidded eyes.

"I love that you are so totally wrapped up in my life now," I answered, my heart thumping wildly. What were we saying? We both paused, and he seemed to be making a decision . . . but I wanted to say it first. I knew how I felt.

He breathed in one quick breath and then said, "Grace, I—"

The waiter returned with our menus, interrupting him. As he began to list the specials, I caught Jack's eye and winked at him. He smiled back, that perfect smile that now belonged to me. He had my heart. I might as well take that damned sexy grin.

We ate dinner, laughing and teasing and talking about anything and everything. Even though we'd both said we were going to eat fast, we were enjoying it so much that before I knew it, the candles had burned low, the champagne (both bottles) was long since gone, and we were relaxed and fully happy.

We were alone, Jack having sent the waiter away eons ago. The stars overhead were bright. The waves were like a soft drumbeat punctuating the night.

"This was perfect, Jack. Just perfect. Thank you for such a wonderful evening," I said, taking his hand.

"Now, hold on, Crazy. This night is just getting started." H stood and pulled me to him. "I, for one, am ready to head back to our cottage . . . yes? Say yes, Gracie," he said chidingly, his hand on my face, nodding my head for me.

"Yes. Yes. Yes," I chanted, each word followed with a kiss to his neck, his ear, his chin.

"Hmm, that sounds familiar," he said, winking at me. We walked back through the gardens, through the night, back to our cottage. I could see it glowing in the distance, and my skin began to warm as I thought of all the delicious things Jack would be doing to me in there, and all the things I would get to do to him, as well.

When he turned the key and unlocked the door, I gasped. There were candles everywhere, on every surface. They were all lit, and the effect was spectacular. I turned to face him as he shrugged out of his jacket.

"You wicked, wicked man. How did you do all this?"

"I'm a celebrity. We get things done in a big way, baby-cakes," he said teasingly, running his hands up and down my back. The skin heated instantly with the electricity that always flowed so freely between us.

"And a fire in the fireplace? That's impressive," I said, walking backward into the room.

"Yeah, I saw it in a book about how to woo women . . . apparently you all like to be boinked in front of a roaring fire." He laughed and I arched an eyebrow at the *boinked*.

The laughter slipped away as we really looked at each other. I kissed him chastely and whispered, "I'll be right back. Don't go anywhere."

He smiled and answered, "Nothing could drag me out of here tonight."

I shook my head to clear it and made my way to the bedroom. Once inside, I quickly grabbed my bag and went into the bathroom. I let my hair down. It was softly curled around my face. Then I looked at the two pieces of lingerie I'd brought. I never usually dressed for bed. It was pointless. For one, Jack preferred me in one of his shirts, and I agreed. Second, I was rarely dressed for very long anyway once I was in the bed, so it was almost silly.

But this night was different, and I wanted to wear something for him.

Option one: a black baby-doll nightie, which covered me just enough. Lacy and see-through, it was hot. I looked amazing in it, and I knew it would drive Jack wild.

Option two: a white silk nightgown. It had spaghetti straps and hit me just below the knee. It swept down low in the back, while the front dipped enough to give him a glance at his favorite attributes. This one would also drive Jack wild.

I made my selection, placed my hand on the door, then took a deep breath and walked out into the living room.

twenty-one

I felt like someone else was moving me; my feet weren't moving on their own. I padded softly to where he stood with his back to me, facing the fireplace. He had turned out the lights, leaving the room entirely lit by candlelight and the soft glow of the fire that crackled quietly. The stereo was playing softly in the background. This stage was set, and I felt my nervousness return.

Why are you nervous? This is your Jack...

Which was exactly why I was nervous. This *was* my Jack, and while he had explored every inch of my body with wild abandon, this was something new, something different. And it would alter the way we looked at each other from here on. This wouldn't just be sex, though I was loath to call it making love. But something would be made here tonight.

I gazed at him quietly, watching his strong hands running through his hair as he watched the flames. I took him in—his strong back, his strong arms, his strong jaw . . . his strength.

A sigh escaped me and he turned to me, his face radiant in the glow from the dancing light. His eyes took me in, sliding down my body and back up to my face. A smile crossed his face, which I answered with my own.

"Hey," I whispered.

"Hey yourself," he answered back as he admired my choice in lingerie.

My hair spilled down across my shoulders in the firelight. I knew he could see the shape of my body beneath the ivory gown that clung to me like a sheath. I felt beautiful but still nervous, shifting my weight back and forth in a way that he'd come to call Nervous Grace.

Was he nervous too?

He was biting his lip in the way that always intoxicated me so. There was hunger in his eyes, but there was also trepidation. The fact that he seemed nervous made me fall in love with him all over again.

And I *was* in love with him. There was no getting around it now. This boy, this man, had taken my heart, wrapped it up in his arms, and carried it with him. I wanted desperately to tell him, to let him know how I felt about him.

He finally spoke, breaking the silence.

"I need . . . I need to touch my Grace," he stated simply.

As he closed the few feet between us, I grew more nervous. He stopped in front of me, reaching out to gently stroke my hair back from my face.

"Grace . . . you're beautiful," he whispered, and I felt myself relax as I leaned into his hand, pressing my cheek into his palm. His other hand cupped my other cheek, and he brought his face to mine. Gently he kissed my forehead, my eyelids, my nose, my blushing cheeks, and, finally, he brought his lips to my own.

"Your lips belong to me," he whispered.

He kissed me slowly and tenderly, his lips barely brushing mine. His kiss was like our first kiss on the beach, hesitant but deliberate. I breathed in his sweet scent, remembering the first time I was aware of it. Sun, chocolate, pipe tobacco, chimney smoke, and that pure Hamilton that underlined it all.

I felt my body responding to him, and my nervousness fell away. My hands came up to his face, mimicking his own. I opened my eyes and found him staring at me in wonder. I said, "Kiss me again, please."

He smiled and obliged. My hands fell down to his waist, pulling him tighter into me. His kiss deepened and his tongue pressed against my lower lip. I opened my mouth and felt him enter me. I moaned a little at the feel of his tongue against mine, and his hands began to lose themselves in my hair.

My hands began to work on his shirt, unbuttoning it slowly. His hands slid down as we continued to kiss, my silk catching on his rough fingertips, callused by his guitar. I finished his buttons and pulled his shirt off him. He was reluctant to remove his hands from me, so his shirt hung down behind him while my hands ran the length of his torso.

The smattering of strawberry-blond hair tickled my nose as I pressed myself closer, snuggling into his chest. I reveled in the feel of my skin on his, warm and comforting. His hands roamed endlessly across my arms, my neck, my back, my sides, finally settling on my shoulders as he carefully began to push the straps of my nightgown aside. It dropped slightly, dipping low. He smiled again as his eyes followed the curve of my skin, then returned to mine, the green beginning to deepen.

His eyes belonged to me.

As my nightgown lowered, one breast was exposed. He gazed with something like awe at the little freckle that was perched just above it—his "landmark" freckle, he called it—and his fingers ghosted over my skin. It pebbled beneath his fingertips, and I heard his low intake of breath as he touched me. I could feel him responding to my arousal, and he increased the pressure on my breasts. I moaned my approval, and he lowered his head to me, stopping to kiss my collarbone and the little hollow at the base of my neck. He swept kisses down my chest, trailing a path toward my exposed breast. My hands went up to his hair, and I ran my nails up and down, encouraging him.

He captured my nipple in his mouth and I could feel it rise beneath his touch, while his hand kneaded my other breast. I moaned thickly, shifting my legs a bit with arousal. He bit down lightly, beginning to drive me a little mad. My gasp of pleasure increased the fever that was building.

Then he pulled away from me, to my dismay. His face was a little playful.

"Where do you think you're going, George?" I asked, my voice sounding husky and low.

"Oh, I love it when you call me George," he murmured, returning to my skin, his voice thick and seductive.

His voice belonged to me. He slipped an arm around my waist and scooped me up, the other arm hooking underneath my knees, cradling me to him. As he walked toward the bedroom, I kissed his neck. His eyes burned into mine as we made our way toward the bed.

"This is like a Danielle Steel novel," I said teasingly, and he rolled his eyes at me.

"Would you just let me do this my way, please?" he replied, blowing a raspberry on my neck.

I smiled bashfully at him as I saw that he had turned down the covers for us already, and then I noticed there were chocolates on the pillows.

"Candy!" I exclaimed before I could help myself.

He chuckled. "You want to eat candy now, love?" he asked, nuzzling at my ear.

"No, not right now. But it's nice to know that it's here . . . for after." I smiled.

"Yes, for after," he replied, setting me gently on the bed. He leaned over me, kissing me more deeply now. Like an undercurrent, the passion between us was now becoming more pronounced. There was a need, a hunger that would quickly consume us.

I pushed his shirt back and it finally fell off as I began to work at his zipper. He groaned when I brushed against him, and I felt his excitement under my hands. I looked back up at him and was astounded by the lust in his eyes, the green growing darker by the second. I pushed his pants down and they fell to the floor.

He was bare beneath.

I licked my lips instinctively. "Nice."

He grinned in return. "I believe you forgot yours too," he answered devilishly, touching me through the fabric of my nightgown between my legs. I hissed and he chuckled, pressing harder on my already swollen sex.

I lay back, propped up on my elbows, admiring the view of my Jack, naked between my legs. It was a sight I would never tire of—the lean lines of his torso, the muscled forearms, the tapered fingers, the lovely blond hair that led my eyes down to the heaven that was him.

245

With achingly slow precision, he slipped the straps farther down my arms and removed the silk gown. I lay before him, naked and wanting.

He breathed in heavily, almost gasping, and said, "Beautiful." His tongue crept out, licking his lower lip in anticipation.

His tongue belonged to me.

I could have stared at him for days on end and never tired of the view.

He leaned back, admiring me as well. "I love the soft curves of your breasts, the lean angles of your arms, the flush of your skin, the roundness of your hips," he purred.

I was relaxed under his gaze. Everything about him told me he loved my body, exactly the way it was.

Everything he was doing, everything he was saying, was making me ready for him, and I desperately wanted him to make me *see God*.

He leaned over me, pressing his lips against my breast, taking my nipple into his mouth again, swirling his tongue and listening to me moan.

"That is so . . . unreal," I murmured, throwing my arms above my head and arching my back so that I was pushed up like an offering. My legs came up tight around his waist as he swept kisses across from left to right, slowly building me up. I moaned almost in anguish as he dragged his tongue down across my stomach and circled my belly button.

"Oh, God," I cried as he fluttered his tongue along the length of my tummy, tasting the salt of my skin, smelling its scent.

He returned to my breasts, taking each nipple in his mouth in turn, nibbling firmly as I writhed below him. He sucked on the right one before releasing it with a pop that made me arch off the bed entirely and bury my hands in his hair. My eyes flashed open wide, my desire growing frantic.

My left hand struggled to dip below and find him, but he kept himself just out of reach.

"No, Grace, not yet. You," he said, caressing my breasts again, marveling at how they fit perfectly into his hands. "So amazing. Your breasts belong to me . . ." He moaned.

True to form, he would make sure to take care of me before himself. I had come to enjoy this aspect of his tenderness, of course, but it never failed to amaze me how much he enjoyed bringing me pleasure, putting my needs before his own.

What he was doing to me was making me crazy. My blood was boiling, and my insides were going to mush. I was moaning almost constantly; the feeling of his mouth on my breasts was beyond description. As I felt him brushing his lips lower on my body, I cried out again in anticipation, knowing where he was going.

I felt his warm hands on my thighs, nudging them apart tenderly. He gazed down at me, his eyes fixed in unapologetic worship. What had I done to deserve this man? As he settled between my legs he looked up at me once more, his eyes meeting mine. I moved my left hand down to grasp his right, holding tightly to him. He smiled at me as his lips kissed the inside of my right thigh.

"Jack . . . ," I breathed, keeping my eyes on him as he continued to sweep gentle kisses along the soft skin, moving to my other leg. He was within inches of me, yet he concentrated his mouth along the tender skin on either side, eyes always on me. He watched as I began to breathe more heavily, every pass taking him closer to where I needed him to be.

I could see the need in his eyes, the want and the lust.

"Please, Jack, please," I begged him.

His eyes spoke to me, answering my pleas. His mouth hovered over me, teasing me for what seemed like hours, but actually only seconds passed. Finally he kissed me, as only he could.

His mouth belonged to me.

No doubt he could feel me tense beneath his mouth. He knew my body so well now, understood that I was already close. He dipped his tongue into me, slowly, knowing the reaction he would get.

I rose up off the bed violently and gave a great sigh. Using his fingers, he gently parted me, sweeping his tongue up and down, back and forth, and I began to moan again.

He lapped at me more forcefully now, making swoops and swirls with his tongue. He pressed his fingers into me, curling, searching for my J-spot. He'd chuckled the first time I'd told him I'd renamed it after him, but he'd thought it fascinating . . . and flattering.

Pressing his fingers down, he fixed his mouth firmly on my other sweet spot.

My breath came fast as I began to cry out, "Oh, God, Jack . . . please . . . don't stop . . . don't stop . . . that is so good . . . oh, God." I began to rock my hips in syncopation with his tongue, his mouth, and his fingers as he stroked me from the inside. My moans became his as he struggled to keep me flush against the mattress.

He ceased for a moment, looking up at me and grinning that devilish grin.

"Your taste belongs to me."

His mouth, his tongue, his fingers, his hands, his everything were in perfect concert, and with a shiver, I came.

I came hard and strong, sweet tension surging through

my body and out of my fingertips and toes and the ends of my hair. I chanted his name over and over again like a prayer as wave after wave crashed through me. I saw light and love, and I felt another orgasm take me again.

I shuddered and shook, and he stayed with me the entire time, never stopping, keeping time with me and staying just ahead of every need I had. He knew what I wanted even before I did.

As I finally came back down, my eyes almost crossed, I felt his teeth nibbling at the inside of my thigh, refreshing my Hamilton Brand. I smiled through my orgasm haze, thinking of his wicked, wicked ways.

His wickedness belonged to me.

As he marked me as his yet again, I smiled, rose up on my elbows, and beckoned him to me with one finger. He kissed my thigh one last time, crawling up to me.

My lips crashed into his, my taste still coating his mouth, and he groaned. He groaned for what he had just given me and for what I was about to give him. He raised himself up, pushing us both back farther up onto the bed. I moved with him, still kissing him furiously.

"Your body belongs to me," he said, sliding his body against mine.

He was between my legs, and he stopped kissing me as he felt himself positioned exactly where I was aching for him to be. His eyes met mine, and with wordless communication, he asked my permission. My eyes answered yes. Yes. Yes.

Then, with a tenderness I had never experienced, he pressed into me. We both stopped breathing as he entered me, sliding divinely through me, filling me, complementing me and loving me. Our eyes never left each other, and as I felt him fill me completely, tears sprang to my eyes with the pureness of what this had become. I watched his face change from lust to pure joy as he felt me welcome him. This was perfection.

I enveloped him. I watched his face as he entered me, his eyes anchoring me as I stopped breathing. I felt the tears in my eyes as he filled me. He looked over-the-moon happy, and I couldn't move. I was overcome with the sensation of his finally being inside me, and the feeling was beyond comprehension. We both held still for a moment, lost in wonder.

Then I began to move beneath him.

Glorious.

I rocked my hips slowly, purposefully, driving him deeper into me. He let his breath out, and as I felt him penetrate me more deeply, I tightened around him, making him shudder.

"So warm, you're so warm. So . . . warm," he chanted, sinking in.

He moved with me, making me shudder in turn as our rhythm increased. I arched my back, and he pressed his lips to my breasts. He raised himself up on his arms, propping himself above so he could look down at me, and I gazed up at his sweet face, overcome with emotion as I moved with him, matching each thrust with a forcefulness that was driving me over the brink.

He pulled out almost entirely, and then he slipped back into me, driving me up higher on the bed. My hips repositioned and he drove into me deeper, filling me in a new way, creating a different sensation for us both. I wrapped my legs higher around his waist and dragged my nails down his back, eliciting a hiss from him.

"Grace, I need to see you," he groaned, withdrawing and then flipping over quickly so that he was on his back and I was above. I swung one leg over him and then straddled him.

He grasped my hands firmly as I sank down slowly, taking him in as deeply as I could.

"Oh, God, Grace, that's brilliant." He moaned as I began to rock against him. His hands released mine and he caressed my breasts, rolling my nipples between his fingertips, causing me to clench down tightly around him again, bringing another groan from him. My hands came up to my hair, getting lost in it as I felt him, so hard, inside me.

He began to say my name, slowly at first, and then as my hips sped up, his hands gripped me tightly, and he sat up. I wrapped my legs behind him, this new position causing him to penetrate me more deeply, and I began to shudder. The sensation of everything was too much, and the tears that had been in my eyes from the second he entered me now spilled over.

His words belonged to me.

I began to clench down around him, and I knew we were both close.

My mouth was right next to his ear, and I said his name repeatedly as he pushed into me. He felt amazing. I was overwhelmed with emotion and the perfection of this moment, and he lifted his head off my shoulder, urging me to meet his gaze.

"Open your eyes, Grace. Look at me," he managed to say as I dug my hands into his hair. I did what he asked, and when he saw the tears streaming down my face, his own face broke into the most beautiful smile I have ever seen.

"Oh, Grace. Gracie . . . I love . . . ," he started to say but never finished. I placed my hand over his sweet mouth and whispered through my tears, "I know."

The feeling of him inside me as I began to come, my shuddering and his shaking, drove me over the edge, and with throaty groans, we came at the same time.

I had the distinct honor of watching his angelic face as he came inside of me . . . the furrowed brow, the pursed lips, the clenched jaw, his whole face set in exquisite torture. It felt exactly right. We'd never taken our eyes off each other.

I know he'd been about to tell me he loved me. I would let him next time.

With the sexiest groan I'd ever heard, he collapsed against me, sighing sweetly, and wrapped his arms tightly around me, trying to get as close as possible. We fell back against the cool sheets, disentangling, only to tangle once more as I felt the loss of him immediately.

"Don't go . . . no," I said, wanting to keep him inside of me as long as possible. I cradled his head to my breast, running my fingers through his hair as he sighed contentedly, his breathing slowing. His hands traveled across my body, revisiting his favorite places, finally resting on my breasts.

As I heard his Happy Sound, I felt a sense of lovely exhaustion and peace. I no longer cared what would happen tomorrow, or the next day, or the day after that.

With my Jack snuggled up against me in the most delicious way, I sighed my own happy sigh and closed my eyes. I knew now, with certainty, that I belonged to him.

☆ ☆ ☆

About twenty minutes later, both of us still nestled into each other, he cleared his throat and lifted his head off my chest, where he had been contentedly drawing circles on my breasts.

"Well now, I don't know about you, but I think that was a fine bit of shagging, yes?" he asked, a glint in his eye.

"Yes, that was *damn* fine. But I do have one request," I answered.

He looked concerned. "What, love?"

"Can I eat that candy now?" I asked.

I heard him mutter, "Candy . . . pfft," and then I was whacked with a pillow. This time my tears were from laughter as I attempted to defend myself from a pillow-wielding, naked Brit.

There is really no defense against that.

twenty-two

*T*wo seventeen A.M.

I woke up with a start and felt Jack clutch me closer in his sleep. I had been dreaming bad dreams.

Sad dreams.

In the last one, Jack and I were standing on opposite sides of a busy street in a crowded city. We were trying to cross the street to each other and kept being buffeted back onto the sidewalk. Each time one of us would try to cross, another line of angry cars would rush past, making it impossible for us to reach each other. Finally, he was tired of waiting and turned from me, walking away. That was when I woke up. It didn't take a genius to figure that one out . . .

I pulled myself out of his embrace and, grabbing his shirt from the floor, went out to the sitting room. The fire had burned down to embers, glowing like rubies in the darkness. I buttoned up, running a hand through my hair, and noticed the moon over the ocean.

It was full and round and seemed to be very close to the

earth. I opened the patio door, then grabbed the throw from the couch against the cool breeze. Wrapped in soft cashmere, I let myself out into the night and stood in the quiet. The only sound was the ocean. I breathed in the salt air, letting out the tension that had come with the dreams.

Watching the moon and the sea, listening to the waves roll in and out, I thought about what had happened earlier—the absolutely indescribable feeling of him inside me. Just thinking about it brought a flush to my skin.

You had sex . . . and it was good.

That was an understatement.

I heard footsteps behind me, and I smiled as I felt his hands creep around my waist.

"What are you doing?" he asked in a stage whisper.

I shivered as he kissed my ear. "Just looking. Did I wake you?"

"Yes. I woke up because my hands were empty—you took away my favorite pillows." He swept my hair back to nuzzle the nape of my neck.

"We had *sex*," I blurted out, and I could literally feel him smiling.

"We sure did." He chuckled.

I giggled, but when he kissed my neck, my hands came up behind me and tucked into his hair. I pushed back against him slightly and felt him press into me, his arousal evident.

I sighed as I felt his hands sneak under the throw, under his shirt, and up to my breasts. When he found them, I groaned, my nipples hardening immediately beneath his talented hands.

He turned me around to face him, and I saw that he was still naked.

"Aren't you cold, Sweet Nuts?" I asked, wrapping my arms around him and sharing my blanket.

"No, actually, you have me quite warmed up," he stated, taking my hand and guiding it lower, encouraging me to grab some Hamilton.

Oh, go on, you deserve another . . .

I really did.

I wrapped my hand around him, relishing the way he moaned instantly at my touch. I urged him back inside the cottage, moving him backward toward the couch. Once there, I pushed him down and removed the throw, propping one leg up on the couch as I stood before him. Then I unbuttoned my shirt and leaned closer to him.

"How about a little more slap and tickle?" I asked in a husky voice. He just grinned that damn sexy grin at me. It made me insane when he did that.

Finished with the shirt, I let it fall to the ground. I took his hands and placed them on my hips, my leg still propped up, opening me up to him. I let one of my own hands dip below, dragging through my own sex, moaning as I did so. His deep green eyes were heavily lidded as he watched me touch myself.

He licked his lips; he was dying to taste me. I let my hand come up and extended one finger to him, running it across his lips, letting him take it into his mouth, suck enthusiastically. He groaned and tightened his grip on my hips. I leaned closer to him, placing my mouth right next to his ear.

"Now that you've made love to me, which was unbelievable, I want you to fuck me," I whispered, feeling him tense beneath me. "Hard."

His tongue darted out and licked my neck . . . hard. He grabbed my hips, leaving handprints on my skin . . . hard. His right hand came up and pulled my hair, angling my neck so that he could nibble at me . . . hard. He took my right hand and put it on his cock again . . . hard.

"You feel that? That's all you, Crazy," he said, looking at me with fire in his eyes.

He even looked at me hard. This would be the polar opposite of what had happened earlier. This would be a straight-up, old-fashioned pounding.

I placed a knee on either side of him and his arms came up to encircle my waist. Placing my hands on his shoulders, I felt him pressing against me. This time, instead of taking him in slowly, I took him in hard.

We both cried out at the suddenness of it, and I marveled again at how well we fit together. I rose back up again, almost withdrawing all the way, and then slammed my hips back down.

"Oh fuck, that's good," I moaned, and he went crazy. He gripped my hips tightly, rocking me back and forth furiously on him, grinding into me as his mouth sucked my nipples.

I arched my back and pushed my breasts farther against him, riding him as I had wanted to for so long.

Nonsensical words were pouring forth from my mouth. I no longer had the power of coherent thought. He, however, was able to say the most deliciously nasty things.

"Fuck, Grace, you feel amazing . . . Christ, Grace, I love watching you ride me . . . God, your tits are brilliant."

These were said in my ear as he pounded into me, moaning and groaning and speaking in that heavenly accent. The more into it he got, the thicker the accent got. The closer we both got, the faster and harder he fucked me. He was finally, blessedly, fucking me like it was his job.

I came hard, screaming his name loudly, and he grinned at me while I thrashed about on top of him, feeling his hard cock inside of me, stroking my J-spot over and over again.

He felt my multiples as deeply as I did, groaning each time another wave started, pumping into me firmly and holding on to my hips, anchoring me and moving me the way he knew I needed it.

I came back just long enough to say in his ear, in a sex-filled voice, "Jack, you fuck me so good." And then he came. He came with a groaning bellow that shook me to my core and made me come again.

We were covered in sweet sweat as he pulled me down onto the couch with him, sighing, grinning, stroking, touching, rubbing, and caressing. We sank into the pillows with him still inside me.

"Jesus . . . ," I said.

". . . Christ," he said, finishing for me, and we laughed.

We were quiet for a moment. Then I said, "Well, I *did* make you promise to make me see God this weekend." I chuckled, sweeping his hair back from his forehead and kissing it lightly.

"And did I?" he had the nerve to ask.

"Yes—and all the saints," I answered, grinning.

The next morning, I woke up early. It surprised me that Jack was already awake. I normally had to drag his ass up, using all manner of temptation to do so. I slipped back into his shirt again and padded out to the living room, where he was on his cell. When he saw me, he put up a finger.

"Right, then. Ten miles from here? Excellent. Right, see you then," he said, hanging up the phone.

"Who was that?" I asked, walking over to him and snuggling into his arms for a hug.

"Just making plans for the shoot later today. You hungry?" he asked, hugging me to him. He had already showered and smelled like soapy goodness.

"I'm starved. Someone made me work up an appetite last night," I purred, pressing closer into his embrace.

"Well then, let's get you some breakfast." He planted a kiss on my forehead, started pulling me toward the bathroom.

"Wait—I was thinking maybe we could order in. You know, a little room service." I winked at him, and he smiled.

"Grace, don't you think it would be nice to go out for breakfast?" He headed toward the bathroom again.

"Actually, no. I was thinking we could have a little breakfast in bed, if you know what I mean," I said teasingly, reaching out to pull him closer to me.

He laughed but still held me at arm's length. "I always know what you mean, Grace. Subtlety isn't one of your gifts. But I need to square some things away for this shoot today, and this way we can spend part of the morning together."

He patted me on the head like a child.

"Now, be a good girl and scoot. Off you go," he replied, finally succeeding in pushing me into the bathroom and closing the door.

"Good girl, my foot. You sure wanted me to be a bad girl last night," I muttered, wondering at this odd morning behavior.

"What was that, Nuts Girl?" he asked through the door.

"I said, *good girl, my foot! You sure wanted me to be a bad girl last night!*"

His response was silence . . . he really was in rare form this morning. I turned on the water, realizing this was the third solo shower in a row, and I missed my chief hair washer. Ah well, better get used to it.

As I stripped down, I heard a rustling. The little shit had shoved a note under the door. What, were we twelve?

I picked it up and read:

> *Grace,*
>
> You are my favorite girl, good or bad. But I
> must admit I'm leaning toward bad.
>
> *Johnny Bite-Down*

I laughed, wetted my fingertip, traced the shape of my hand with my middle finger pointing up, and then shoved the wet note back under the door. Even over the water, I could hear him howling.

It was so easy to crack him up.

Fifty minutes and two blocked attempts at nooky later, Jack had me seated in the restaurant and was ordering us breakfast. He was looking fine, with about two days' worth of insanely good stubble. We were both dressed casually. He was in jeans and a black T-shirt, while I went with my standard yoga pants and camisole. Since I didn't know if I'd be going to the photo shoot today, I had a backup plan to go for a run on the beach.

We talked about silly things, inane things. The amazing hotel, whether or not to go out for dinner that night, whether we would have time to do some sightseeing tomorrow before we had to head back to L.A.

My flight to New York was on Tuesday at noon, and while I was excited, I still got a little lump in my throat every time I thought about it. Jack's week was shaping up to be busy. He had three interviews on Monday and one scheduled for Tuesday.

We ate our pancakes and drank our juice, and he buttered my toast for me. I noticed at least one table that had figured out who he was, but he still showed as much affection for me as he did when we were in private. I found this both sweet and a little infuriating. It was as if he was determined to show Holly she was wrong about his fans, and I wasn't crazy about being the sacrificial lamb.

When I was finished, I stretched my arms over my head and noticed he was done as well.

"You ready to go back to the cottage? We still have a little time left before you have to leave . . . we could have some sexy times," I teased, running my fingers down his arm in a seductive way.

"Oh, Gracie, you're killing me," he said, reaching for me. "Last night, it was really great, you know?" he replied, bringing my hand up to his mouth, kissing my fingertips.

I heard a gasp from behind me, and I knew the girls who'd recognized him were either fainting or plotting my demise. I understood; I'd had the same feeling when I found out Alyssa Milano was dating Corey Haim.

I still harbored ill will toward her.

I tried to pull my hand away but he kept it tightly in his grip.

"Hey, you know what Holly said. We're not acting very smart." I smiled at him, trying to get him to understand.

"Bollocks. I say we do what we want and act how we want," he said firmly, his brow furrowed.

"I agree that it's bollocks—except that when these pictures come out, it's me that's going to have to deal with it. I'm not sure how I feel about that yet," I answered.

"Grace, how do you feel about me?" he asked, staring into my eyes.

"What? What do you mean?" I replied nervously.

"It's a simple question. How do you feel about me?" he asked again, reaching over and scooting my chair closer to him. The dragging of the chair across the tiles caused another table to look over, prompting another round of gasps.

Jesus.

"Jack, I—"

"Pardon me, but are you Jack Hamilton?" a timid voice asked.

I turned my head, grateful for the interruption, and saw a woman in her midtwenties.

As Jack began to talk to her a line began to form, and as I watched him chat with his fans, I could see his nervousness come out more and more. He was kind and sweet, and to the untrained eye, he seemed totally comfortable. But I saw how he tucked his legs closer to him, ran his hands through his hair. He made the funniest expressions with his face; it was like he was one big eyebrow. He smiled at me occasionally, and while most of the girls kept their eyes on him the entire time I could feel their eyes on me, sizing me up, trying to figure us out.

Eventually it was just us again, and we started walking

back to the cottage. We were holding hands when we both noticed some of the same girls hovering about fifty paces back, and I saw the camera phones coming out again. They'd taken plenty of pics of him in the restaurant, but shots of him holding my hand would be bad news.

I dropped his hand like a hot potato.

He grimaced but said, "For you, Grace, because I know you'll take the brunt of it. If it were up to me, I'd have you up against that tree over there." He pointed at a large Spanish oak.

"I know you would, George. I know." I laughed.

We got ready, sadly with no time for boom-boom, and headed out to the photo shoot. He promised we'd have time for boom-boom later.

We held hands on the ride there, and we talked about dinner that night. In light of the morning's outcome I firmly put my foot down when he asked if I'd like to go out for dinner again.

"Hell, no. We're eating dinner in bed, naked, stopping only to screw," I answered, bouncing on the seat in anticipation.

He laughed as we pulled into the estate where the photo shoot was taking place. "Well, after the shoot, I'm sure some of the cast will be going out for a drink. Can I at least get you drunk first?"

We had decided that I'd skip the shoot today and hook up with him later on in the evening.

"Sure—not that you'll need that to take advantage of me.

Now that I have had a little Hamiltonian Sex Machine, I don't think I can do without it," I said with a grin.

He parked the car near everyone else's and then kissed me passionately, holding my face in his hands. "Gracie, my ego can't take the thought of you saying *little* and *sex machine* in the same sentence as my name," he said seriously.

I laughed, and as I got out of the car, he swatted me on the butt.

"Damn, George, you need to watch that. I'm already bruised from the drilling you gave me last night!" I said teasingly, backing away from the car, watching him chuckle. I backed right into a wall.

A rather warm wall that was laughing.

I turned around to see Lane smiling down at me. *Nice, Grace; way to keep it quiet.* I blushed crimson and hung my head as he roared.

"Drilling? You've got a naughty girl here, Hamilton."

"Oh, man," I mumbled as Jack came up beside me.

"She is naughty, but in the best way. Now, back off, ass." He chuckled.

"Yeah, back off, ass!" I cried, pushing on Lane's well-muscled chest. He grinned at me, and I faked a punch at him.

He was cool. *I think he has a meeting with Holly next week . . . interesting.*

"See you tonight?" I asked, leaning into Jack's side as he waved Lane away.

"Yep. I'll get a ride with one of these guys when we're all done. Call you later?" he asked, kissing my forehead.

"Call me later, yes." I smiled, pulling his face down so I could kiss him a little less chastely. I could hear Lane whistling behind us, and we both rolled our eyes.

"Kick his ass for me, will ya?" I chuckled.

"Grace, have you seen the size of that guy?" he shot back as I turned to get back into the car. He watched me pull away and then headed toward the trailers with Lane, laughing like a little kid.

When I got back to the hotel, I settled in with my laptop. I had an e-mail from Holly's friend in New York, who was setting up where I'd be living for the next few weeks or months. Turned out I would be staying at the W in Times Square while they got my sublet worked out. Times Square . . . a little touristy, but I did like W properties, and it would be close to the theater.

I also had an e-mail from Michael, giving me some details about the rehearsal schedule that was due to begin on Friday. I'd have a few days to get my bearings before we did the first read on Friday morning. He'd attached some notes about the characters, as well as a new batch of rewrites. He also wanted to get together Wednesday night to go over some character outlines so that I felt ready for the first reading.

I'd executed a one eighty with Michael. He'd gone from being someone I never thought of, to someone I wanted to strangle, to someone I was glad to know again. It would be nice to have a friend in New York, and I was sure he would become a good friend again.

I filled my morning nicely with another massage and a facial at the hotel spa. I had a lovely lunch at the poolside café, then spent about an hour engaging in a mildly pornographic texting marathon with Holly back in L.A. But mainly, I was waiting for Jack to call.

When I saw his name on my phone screen, it immediately brought to mind the feeling of him inside of me the night before, and I answered the phone with a soft growl. Which may have come out like a cough.

"Are you choking?" he asked.

"No, it was my attempt to be sexy for you," I managed to say, my face turning red as I wheezed. He waited and chuckled as I got myself under control. "How's the shoot going?"

"It's good—it'll probably take most of the day, but I should be headed back to the hotel by late afternoon. What've you been up to?"

"Oh, a little of this, a little of that. I miss you."

"I miss you too, Nuts Girl. Wait a sec, hang on . . . I'm on a call! I'll be right there . . . with my girlfriend, if you must know," he told someone, and my heart jumped when he used the term *girlfriend.*

"Oh, tell Marcia I said hi!" a woman's voice chirped, then I heard a rustling as Jack covered up the phone. My heart stilled in my chest as I waited for Jack to come back.

"Grace?"

"I'm here," I said quietly.

"Sorry about that. There's some cast members here that I haven't seen for a while," he replied, his voice uneven.

"Well, I'll let you get back to your shoot. See you later."

"Right, see you later," he answered.

I hung up the phone and sat for a moment, not moving. *What did you really hear, huh?*

Someone who still thinks this Marcia is his girlfriend— that's what I heard.

I pushed the shit aside and went for a run. At some point, I'd really need to deal with all the things I'd been repressing lately. But as I began my run it all fell silent, and I concentrated on the view of the ocean and smell of the salt air. It really was pretty here.

I spent the afternoon wildly obsessing about this Marcia and how to bring her up with the Brit. Admittedly, I'd been a

tad shady when I opened that text from her, and aside from
the photos I'd seen on the Internet, I had no basis for knowing anything more than what I'd overheard some woman say
today. Her words proved that they used to be an item. But
how recently had they *stopped* being an item?

What, do you think he had no relationships before you?
No.

Do you think he came out of a box like that, just for you?
No.

You have a helluva past. Do you want to be judged on that?
NO.

*Then fucking grow a set and ask him! Or shut up about
it. You're leaving in three days. You want to spend it talking
about some ex-snatch of his?*

Wow, my inner monologues were getting decidedly
nastier.

After my run, I went for a swim, worked on a project for
a client that I was almost finished with, and watched some
reality TV. I kept busy.

About five thirty, I got a text from Jack.

Hey, up for a drink? Some of the cast and crew from the
shoot are meeting in the hotel bar. Yes? Say yes, Grace.

I texted him back.

Yes, Grace.

He quickly responded.

See you in an hour. Then, room service . . . me . . . and
all the pounding you can handle. Say yes, Grace.

I texted back.

Yes, yes, yes, please.

I wasn't *too* proud.

When he got back, he texted me and I met him downstairs. I saw Lane and Rebecca and a few other people from the shoot, including the photographer.

I went up to Jack, who was at the bar with his back to me. "Are you Joshua?" I asked in a timid voice. He turned around with a resigned look, until he saw me.

"Not funny, love." He frowned but then pulled me into a kiss so passionate it literally swept me off my feet. He actually picked me up. I heard Lane wolf-whistling behind me.

I kissed him back feverishly, pressing myself against him, letting him feel my breasts under my thin cotton shirt. I got a reaction instantly. I loved tasting the beer and the whiskey in his hot mouth.

"Get me a shot, will you?" I asked, pulling away and nodding to the bar.

"You want a shot?" He knew I rarely did shots.

"Yep," I answered, rubbing my gloss off his lips.

Lane mouthed the word *drilling* at me from behind Jack. I rolled my eyes at him and gave him an obscene expression involving my tongue and cheek. He laughed aloud.

"Okay, here ya go," Jack said, handing me a shot and taking his own in hand. I winked at him and tossed it back. It burned and I made an awful face, which almost made him spit his out.

After we found seats with the rest of his group, he introduced me to some of the other cast members, including the woman I had overheard on the phone earlier.

"So sorry about that. Jack sure was irritated with me over that little slip," she said, shaking my hand and introducing herself as Bailey. She played Joshua's sister in the film.

"No worries." I smiled evenly.

"No, really, I felt like such an ass. Although I can tell you, I've never seen Jack so worked up over a girl the way he is with you." She smiled sincerely, and my stomach unwound a bit.

Jack winked at me from across the booth, and I shamelessly blew him a kiss.

We hung out in the bar for almost two hours, laughing and talking. I thoroughly enjoyed spending time with people from Jack's other life. I really liked Rebecca. She congratulated me on the show in New York, and she promised she would do her best to keep the ladies away from him as much as possible. That chick was damn funny, and she didn't let Jack give her any shit, which I loved. He was in his element with this group, telling stories and cracking everyone up with his Brit wit.

And Lane? Well, Lane was a dear. He was funny and sweet and so pretty. He was just great—a really great guy.

One shot turned into two, and then two into three, and when you added the dirty martini that I sucked down, I was feeling no pain. The photographer was still there, and as I got tipsier, I got friendlier as well. I'd started out the evening sitting next to Jack, and by the time I noticed it was after eight o'clock, I was sitting fully in his lap, his arms wrapped around me, and I was trying to get him to suck the pimento out of the olive from my cocktail. I happened to be holding the olive between my teeth. The photographer saw this as a perfect opportunity to get some candids, and away he clicked.

Jack saw I'd had enough to drink, so he complied with my pimento request because he knew I wouldn't let it go. Once he completed this task and Rebecca and I stopped laughing, the photographer insisted on getting one of the two us, just smiling at each other. I realized that I had no pictures of the two of us that weren't on TMZ, and suddenly all I wanted was one great shot to take with me to New York.

We posed a little, making it fun, and the last click of his camera got one of us looking straight into the lens, pressed together, me still sitting on his lap.

I yawned suddenly, and he leaned in and whispered, "Hey, Nuts Girl, let's get out of here. I need some quiet time alone with you. I missed my girl today." He kissed my neck, and I shivered.

I put my mouth next to his ear and whispered, "I had a drink. I had several, in fact. Now let's go back to the room so you can fuck me six ways from Sunday."

Of course, I hadn't whispered as quietly as I thought I had, and loud giggling broke out all around.

Jack's green eyes darkened in the most wicked way, and he quickly threw a handful of cash on the table. "Night, all."

"See ya!" I said, giving a sloppy high five to Rebecca as Jack walked me quickly from the bar, leaving everyone to stare after us with amused looks.

"I freaking love her," I heard Rebecca say as we walked out.

☆ ☆ ☆

We walked through the gardens toward our cottage, tiki torches lighting our way, and at some point I decided it would be a good idea to jump on his back and make him carry me piggyback style. I was kissing his neck as we walked and squeezing him between my legs—which wasn't a good idea, because he'd just run his hands up my legs and almost under my shorts—when a group of women, about my age or maybe a little older, walked by on their way toward the restaurant. They stared at me, on the back of this very young and very hot guy, with his hands all over me, and they looked impressed.

They grinned and one actually gave me a "You rock!" and a high five as they passed, and I laughed aloud.

"You sure are giving a lot of high fives tonight, Nuts Girl," he said teasingly over his shoulder as I played with his hair. I sighed and rested my chin on his shoulder as he took out the key to let us in.

"What can I say? They love me in Santa Barbara!" I sang, Ethel Merman style.

"Wow. That was loud and right in my ear."

"Shut it, Hamilton, or you will get the entire *Oklahoma!* score tonight—and don't think I don't know all the words to every song." I laughed, ducking down as we walked inside. He kept me on his back as he put his bag down and plugged in his cell phone.

"Are you going to get down any time soon?" he asked, walking over to the patio doors and sliding them open.

"No, I like it up here," I answered promptly, and launched into a song from *Oklahoma!* "'Don't throw bouquets at me...'"

"Grace..."

271

I continued, louder, and added a tongue in his ear.

"Gracie . . ."

The song went on, an actual Oklahoma twang now making itself known.

"A few shots and I get a musical?"

"'People will say we're in love.'" I continued to sing, playful still.

"Oh man, you really *do* know all the words." He swung me around to his front and sat me on the patio railing.

I sang on, thinking about the lyrics, losing the twang and adding my heart.

He was quiet now, moving to stand between my legs, with his head cocked to one side like the dog in that stereo ad, smiling at me.

I ended the song, wrapping my legs around him and pulling him closer to me. He leaned his forehead toward mine, resting against me. We were both quiet for a minute, and then I giggled. "This is why I don't do shots. They make me go all Broadway."

"I like when you're all Broadway, sweet girl."

We were quiet for another minute, and then I pulled away.

"Let's order some dinner so we can get to the sexy times sooner," I said, breaking the spell that Rodgers and Hammerstein always cast.

I moved past him to get the room service menu, but he caught my hand. "Hey, Gracie. Where you running off to?" he asked, pulling me toward him.

"I'm not running anywhere," I answered as he wrapped his arms around my waist. Feeling emboldened, I continued. "Wanna know a secret?"

"What's that, love?" he asked, sweeping gentle kisses along my jaw.

"It's not that much of a secret, but I want you to know—"

"Hey, if you're going to say what I think you're going to say . . . wait, *are* you going to say it?" he asked, smiling down at me.

"Yes, I think so." I grinned shyly back.

"Well, then I think we should say it at the same time, yes?" he said.

"Count of three?" I asked. He nodded.

I started. "One . . ."

"Two . . . ," he said, eyes twinkling.

"Three," we said together. We both paused, smiling hugely, and then I took a deep breath.

"Jack, I love you."

"I know," he said at the same time.

"Ass!" I said, smacking him on the arm.

"That was great!" He laughed.

I turned and started to walk off the patio in a mock huff, feeling his arms grab me and not let me go. I smiled since my back was to him and he couldn't see.

"Gracie, Gracie, Gracie. You know how I feel." He chuckled, turning me around to face him.

"Say it, George. I want to hear you say it," I said teasingly, scratching his scalp the way I knew he loved.

"Well, lately I find myself quite in love with you, Sheridan," he said, tracing my mouth with his fingertips.

I kissed them and then said, "Mmm, I love you too, Hamilton. I really, really do."

He kissed me slowly and sweetly, and then pulled away a little to look at me.

"You didn't just say it because I got you drunk, right?" he asked, grinning sexily.

"No, dear, I got drunk all on my own. *Now* can we please order dinner?"

"Let's go get the menu, Nuts Girl." He laughed, taking my hand and leading me into the cottage.

"I don't need to look at the menu; just order me a grilled cheese and a chocolate shake. And ask them to bring more candy, please," I said, heading toward the bedroom to change into something more comfortable.

"Grilled cheese, shake, got it," he answered, grabbing the phone.

"And see if they have any energy drinks, something with ginseng," I called back to him from the other room.

"You want an energy drink *and* a shake?" he asked.

"No, silly. The ginseng is for you, to keep up your stamina." I laughed, changing into one of the hotel robes.

I heard him muttering about not needing help with his stamina. He was right about that.

"Oh, and, George?" I asked, poking my head around the corner just in time to see him put the phone down again, rolling his eyes slightly at me when he saw me.

"Yes, bossy?" he asked.

"I love you," I said, blowing him a kiss.

"I love you, too," he answered, catching my kiss and placing it on his cheek.

Yeah, we were pretty freaking great.

twenty-three

$\mathcal{A}$s promised, we ate our room service in bed, clad only in our hotel robes. I insisted that he be naked beneath, making it easier for me and my trusty oonie to pounce after dinner. We laughed and talked, and I even let him have a few bites of my grilled cheese. The shake I kept for myself. Grace does not share ice cream. She does, however, talk about herself in the third person.

By the time he wheeled the cart away, I was thoroughly sated and happy. I giggled and applauded when he began performing an impromptu striptease on his way back into the bedroom, and I even hummed a burlesque bump-'n'-grind tune while he danced about. I hooted and hollered, and threw a flower in appreciation of the show.

He was truly one of the funniest guys I had ever met. I hoped that as his fame increased, his fans would get to see that side of him. He wasn't just a pretty face. He was damn smart and had one of the quickest wits I'd ever encountered. What I loved about him was that he was never embarrassed. He always let go of how silly he sometimes looked and it was absolutely endearing. Who would've guessed the guy who was making women swoon across the country could engage in the silliest robe removal I had ever seen? Certainly not me.

He finally dropped the robe while I screamed in laughter, then he crawled under the covers at the foot of the bed, now humming his own tune. I watched as his truly biteable buns disappeared under the comforter, and I squealed as I felt his teeth nip at my ankles. His entire body crept under the covers, and I tracked his progress based on the bites on my calf, the side of my knee, the top of my thigh, and finally my Hamilton Brand. This was reached only after he prodded my legs apart with his nose, his hands wrapping around my hips and pulling me roughly down the bed. He continued to hum his merry little tune, and at some point, I heard it change into something that sounded like "God Save the Queen." I began to hum along with him, and I felt him smile against my skin.

Once he hit the Promised Land, however, he stopped humming, and I began to moan as he kissed me, tracing the entirety of my sex with his tongue and lips, being agonizingly gentle. I sighed, arching my back like a cat and stretching my arms over my head. Sometimes he would work me slow and long, and I could tell this was going to be one of those times.

Those nights were always un-freaking-believable.

He spread my legs wider, hooked them over his shoulders, and continued his gentle caressing. His tongue made delicate circles around me, working up and down and making me moan deeply. His fingers opened me farther, leaving me completely vulnerable to whatever he wanted to do.

He was *so* good at this. But instead of letting me have a quick release, he'd take me just to where my legs began to shake, and then he'd back off, blowing cool breath on me, making me shiver and cry out.

By the time he had made me almost-come the fourth time, I was begging for it. Just before he brought me to the place where I would finally see stars, he moved quickly up my body, poking his head out from under the covers.

He entered me slowly, deeply, and I was able to watch his face as he nudged his way inside. We both cried out as he sank in, inch by inch, taking what seemed like an hour to finally be in me. We sighed together, and I wrapped my legs around his waist tighter, desperate to have him as deeply as I could take him in. I looked up at his earnest face as he slid in and out, his blond curls hanging down all crazy and sexy, and his strong arms as he held himself over me. He sucked in his bottom lip and bit down on it with his teeth as I bucked up to meet him.

Beautiful.

"Oh, God, Jack, that is . . . oh, God." I struggled to find the words to explain how good he felt inside me, and couldn't. He continued his slow, methodical movements, designed to make me shiver and shake, as I listened to his throaty moans. He hooked my right leg up over his shoulder, and with this new angle he went even deeper, hitting my J-spot, which made me cry out instantly.

"Come for me, Gracie, please . . . I need to feel you come," he begged as he felt my walls begin to squeeze him more firmly. His brows came together as he pumped into me firmly, constantly, with no letup as I raced toward my orgasm.

This time, I came crazy quiet. Having been worked to the brink of pleasurable insanity, I shook wordlessly, totally caught up in my body, his body, and the effect he had on me. It was like a star exploding. He shouted my name as he emptied into me, releasing a deep moan.

He sank down onto me, burying his head in my neck, and

I held him tightly as he shook, my legs and my arms refusing to let him leave my body. I took all of his weight and his sighs and his shakes as he completely relaxed into me.

I ran my nails up and down his back and finally into his hair as he sighed his Jack's Happy Sound, warming my skin with his sweet breath.

We stayed like that for several minutes, then he finally lifted his head from my breast. I brushed his hair back from his forehead and kissed him softly.

"Can I tell you something?" I asked.

"Of course." He smiled.

"I love you," I replied, kissing him again.

"I love you too, Gracie." He sighed into my kisses. We cuddled for an hour, wrapped up together and eating hotel chocolate.

God Save the Hamilton.

Later on, we might have gotten some chocolate in places that it had no business being, and we decided a quick rinse-off was needed. We had yet to use the huge shower together, and it seemed to be a good time.

Firing up the rain showerhead above, we turned on all the side sprays and even the steamer for a sauna effect. I went back into the bedroom to grab one more piece of chocolate, and when I came back into the bathroom, the entire shower was filled up with steam. I couldn't see Jack but I knew he was already in there, because he had written the word *poo* on the glass door in the steam. I could hear him in there chuckling.

"Hamilton, you are such a child," I called out.

"Sheridan, get your ass in here," he said, sticking his head out and releasing a cloud of steam into the room. "The words will get progressively worse if you don't."

Mmm, I had missed seeing my Brit all naked and wet.

I slipped out of my robe as he watched me and climbed in past him. Standing under the main rain shower, I felt the water rush down over me. I could also feel the six other jets spraying different parts of my body, and that was really nice.

Almost naughty.

He grabbed my shampoo, and as he lathered me up, I let my arms snake around his waist, holding his wet body closer to mine. He was careful, as always, to keep the suds out of my eyes, and then as he tilted my head backward under the spray to rinse it clean, he leaned in and kissed the hollow of my neck.

"Mmm . . . ," I whispered. He laughed wickedly as he worked the conditioner through, paying special attention to the ends, like I'd taught him.

Now it was my turn. As I stood on my tiptoes to reach his head, he steadied me with a firm grasp on my breasts. "Grace, I really could look at your tits for hours. God, they are just fantastic . . ." He trailed off and I moaned softly as his fingers slipped over my nipples.

What is it about being wet that makes everything feel so amazing? It's as though every sense is heightened and every touch, every caress, feels more intense.

As soon as I rinsed his hair out, he took my shower gel, lathered up a sea-wool sponge, and began moving it across my body, leaving a trail of scented bubbles. I grabbed a similar sponge and proceeded to wash him as well, working my way from his chest and arms down to his stomach, skipping down to his legs and back up to his Mr. Hamilton.

He was all kinds of hard. As I slid the sponge across him he twitched, and when I looked up at him, I saw dark green burning back at me. He lowered his sponge between my legs and I planted my feet wider, giving him increased access.

I dropped my sponge, using my hands and the bubbles to stroke him firmly up and down, feeling him get even harder. He mirrored my actions, swirling his fingers through my slick, wet . . .

I moaned, feeling him twitch again as soon as he heard me.

I could feel sprays of water hitting my body everywhere and the steam was thick and hot, making my head swim.

I needed to feel his skin and I pressed myself up against him, our wet bodies sliding across each other as he pushed me against the wall. The coolness of the tile, the nozzles spraying in so many directions, and the sight of Jack standing naked under the rain shower, the water running down his face and body, made my knees go weak.

"Fuck me, please. Fuck me," I begged, pulling him still closer. He quickly picked me up, wrapped my legs around him, and was inside my warmth instantly. His body held mine in place as he pounded into me, everything slippery, hot, and wet.

His face was inches from mine as I scratched at his back, getting more and more aggressive with him. The speed with which he slammed into me and the grunts he made each time made me crazy. I crashed my body against his as he impaled me.

I could feel every inch, every thrust, every pump, and it made me out of my mind with lust. My insides were on fire;

I was loving how hard he was pressing into me, using his strength to ravage my body.

"Grace . . . Fuck, Grace!" he groaned.

"Yes, yes, fuck Grace!" I screamed, feeling his body sliding against mine.

My body's tension was building, increasing, threatening to split me in two with its ferocity. I pulled at his hair, making him slap at the tiles behind me.

We came together, with me screaming his name and him biting my neck as he burst into me. We stayed like that for a moment, panting heavily, the water still beating down. Then he finally released me, holding me close and kissing me on the cheek. The way he could be dirty and biting me one minute and sweet and loving the next is what made him so incredible.

Then he whispered, "While you're in New York, I'm having them install a shower like this in your new house. Don't even try to argue with me."

He'd get no arguments from me.

☆ ☆ ☆

That night we exhausted ourselves, staking our claim all over the cottage, and finally ended up in the one place that was oddly becoming a tradition.

"Why the hell do we always end up naked in a closet?" he asked sleepily, his hands possessively surrounding my breasts as we came down from another round of mind-blowing sexy times.

"I don't know. We're kinky, I guess," I croaked, my throat raw from a night of blissful screaming. He really had shown great foresight in choosing accommodations separate from the other guests. I certainly wouldn't have wanted to be in a room next to my loud mouth, and Jack hadn't held back at all, either.

I stood up shakily, reaching down and pulling him up, and we dodged the hangers and the ironing board and made our way back toward the bed. I slipped into his discarded shirt, and he found his boxers hanging from the TV.

I went to my side and he to his, and as we met in the middle, I said, "George, it is now sleepy time, not sexy time. I need sleep, are we clear?" I raised my eyebrows in a severe way.

"You'll get no arguments from me. You've worn me out, woman. I am officially all used up." He pulled the duvet up over us as I clicked on the TV.

"Hey, you just called sleepy time. Turn that off, Grace." He tried to grab the remote away from me.

"Wait, wait . . . aha!" I yelled triumphantly, finding Lifetime and my favorite show. The theme song from *The Golden Girls* streamed into the room.

"Bloody hell," he muttered, but by the end of the song he was humming along with me, and by the end of the first scene, he was laughing along with me.

And by the end of the episode, we were both fast asleep, all tucked in and peaceful.

☆　☆　☆

The next morning we woke up early, started the day with a bang (ahem), and were on the road back to L.A. by ten thirty. I wanted nothing more than to stay in bed with him all day, but Tuesday was getting so close, and I still had so much to do.

We drove in relative silence and listened to songs on our iPods. We held hands the whole time, reluctant to separate even when we stopped for gas. It was as if we were quietly beginning to acknowledge how little time we had left with each other, and it was getting harder to ignore.

He kept his hand on my leg the rest of the drive back to L.A., and when we finally pulled into Holly's driveway, it was already midafternoon. He needed to head back to his place for a while, and as I kissed him good-bye, I almost couldn't let him go.

He kissed me longingly and swept my hair up into a loose ponytail, holding it on the back of my neck.

"Crazy, I'll be back before you know it. You won't even have unpacked yet, I bet," he said, looking at my sad face.

"I know, I know . . . I'm being silly. You want to stay in for dinner tonight?" I didn't want to leave the house for anything. I wanted him all to myself.

"That sounds great. You can make me dinner." He smiled, tickling my ribs.

"We can cook together. You get to help me." I laughed, squirming out of his grasp.

"That's a deal. I'll be back as soon as I can, love," he replied, kissing me once more. Then he drove away.

I walked into the house, shocked at how empty I felt without him there. This wasn't the way it was supposed to happen. I was supposed to have had a little fling with a hot Hollywood piece of ass, moved to New York, and had that be the end of it.

Now I was head over heels in love with this wonderful guy, leaving in less than two days, and we hadn't even discussed what we were going to do about it.

What a fucking mess.

Holly was in the kitchen, sitting at the counter with a plate of crackers and a can of spray cheese. She didn't even try to hide the fact that she was really shooting the cheese straight into her mouth and leaving the crackers behind.

"So, how was the dick?" she asked immediately.

"The dick? It was nice." I sighed and leaned back against the fridge.

"How nice?" she inquired, pushing the cheese through her teeth and showing it to me.

"So nice, I'm amazed I'm able to walk, frankly," I said, sliding down the fridge and sitting on the floor.

She looked at me carefully and then put the top back on the can, tossing it to me. "What's wrong, Grace?" she asked, starting in on the crackers.

"Why do you think something is wrong? I had a fabulous weekend, got fucked like it was going out of style, and . . ." I trailed off.

"And?"

"He told me he loved me," I said, raising my hands to my face.

"Shut up," she breathed, eyes wide.

"And I might have said it back." I grinned, peeking at her through my fingers.

"Wow. Then what the hell is wrong?"

I thought for a minute. "I feel blue, Holly." And then the tears finally started.

I was so happy and so sad at the same time; it was bound to come out. She came and sat down next to me, putting an arm around me and letting me sob.

"Okay, you're blue because you love him and you're leaving," she stated.

"Uh-huh," I sobbed.

"And you're blue because he loves you and he'll be three thousand miles away."

"Uh-huh," I cried.

"And you're blue because he's twenty-four, and what the hell does a twenty-four-year-old movie star have in common with a thirty-three-year-old aspiring actress who's moving to New York, albeit temporarily?"

"Yes!" I wailed, clutching the can of aerosol cheese to my chest. She pried it out of my hands, replacing it with a kitchen towel.

As she patted my back soothingly, I gradually calmed down. When I finally got myself under control, I looked at her in despair.

"Hol, what am I going to do?"

Her eyes were thoughtful as she considered. "You're going to decide what you want and then talk to him about it. I knew he loved you, and I'm glad he said it. You deserve to have all the facts in front of you when you talk.

"But you need to go into this with your eyes wide open. Things are going to be difficult . . . you know this. He's going to be busy; so are you. You'll both be pulled in two totally different directions, and they'll be the opposite directions from where you'll want to be."

I blew my nose into the kitchen towel, and she grimaced but continued. "Talk to him, Grace. See what he wants to do. I know long-distance doesn't usually work that well, but in this industry, couples are separated all the time. You never know. Stranger things can happen. Who knew you would

285

even get to this place?" She squirted another shot of cheese into her mouth.

I was silent for a moment.

"What're you thinking about?" she asked.

"I'm thinking that I want some spray cheese."

She smiled and handed it over.

We sat on the floor for a while, not talking, just passing the can back and forth in the same way that we used to share a joint. Cheese, marijuana . . . same thing, really.

That night, we had a lot of fun making dinner. I made grilled salmon, roasted asparagus, saffron rice, and a salad. Jack assisted. He was allowed to heat the oven, stir the rice, set the table, and kiss my neck whenever he felt it looked lonely. This apparently was a lot.

After dinner, we went outside and shared one of the lounge chairs on the terrace. We engaged in the random chit-chat that people do, wrapped up in each other and looking at the stars. I was looking at one star in particular and wondered how I was going to leave him in less than two days. I must have sighed rather heavily, because he whispered, "What's up, Crazy?"

"What do you mean?" I asked, snuggling back against him. His legs were extended and I was perched between them, leaning back against him. His arms were wrapped solidly around me.

"You're here, but you're not really here. You want to tell me what's going on?" He prodded, nuzzling at my neck with his soft lips in a way that usually made me go all silly.

There was no silly right now.

I sighed again, turning on my side to face him. "I'm think-ing about what happens on Tuesday, when I get on a plane and leave your sorry ass."

"Ah, Tuesday. Well, what do you think should happen?" he asked, looking very serious all of a sudden.

"Hell, I don't know. I know it's probably suicide to try to make some big proclamation right before I leave, but I'm just going to miss you so damn much. These last few weeks have been pretty fucking amazing," I said, touching his face.

"I agree. Amazing. So why do you assume it won't con-tinue to be amazing? I, for one, am looking forward to all the phone sex we'll be having." He grinned, looking so hand-some I almost burst into flames just being next to him.

I smiled but then shook my head. "See, that's just it. Why would you want to have phone sex with me when you could be having actual sex with anyone you wanted here?" I asked quietly, not able to meet his eyes.

He raised my chin and made me look at him. He glow-ered at me. "I'm going to pretend you didn't just say that," he replied shortly.

"Why? You won't have to watch *Golden Girls* all the time anymore. You can go back to going out, living your hipster lifestyle, which, frankly, you should. You're twenty-four, for fuck's sake, and I've been keeping you at home every night. How the hell are you not bored? There'll be women lining up for you!" I was getting all worked up, and quickly.

"Grace, you seem to be under the impression that I tell women I love them all the time. Can I tell you how often I've said that to anyone other than my family? Twice. That's it: in my entire life, twice. Why would I fuck around on you?" he asked, getting heated.

"Hey, man, people in love fuck around all the time. It happens," I retorted, leaning up on the chair and out of his arms. "How about the next party you're at, when there's a blonde and a brunette wanting to take you home with them? What do you do?"

"I tell them about the redhead that I'm in love with, and then I tell them to piss off. Where the hell is this coming from?" he asked, getting angry.

"It's coming from the fact that we're going to be three thousand miles away from each other, and I'm scared to death about what's going to happen. Maybe I shouldn't be so involved already, but I am. And even though you probably should be involved with somebody else, I hate the idea," I said angrily, sitting up straight.

"Be with anyone else? Why don't you let *me* decide who I want to be with? Is this something I need to worry about? You seem awfully defensive. Something you want to tell me, Grace?" he asked, watching me carefully.

"Oh, please. You're the one who's going to have a pussy parade to choose from as soon as you pop back up on the grid. They'll be falling over with their legs in the air, and it can be just like before you started spending your evenings with Ma Kettle," I snapped.

He glared at me, running his hands roughly through his hair. "Grace, you are bloody insane! Are you bent on fucking this up before we really even get going? And a pussy parade? You're really pushing it," he said, the warning clear in his voice.

I shoved myself out of the chair and stalked over to the ledge, looking out at the city—the city that I was leaving. *In two days.* Why the hell was I picking a fight with him now?

I spun about fast, seeing him sitting in the chair dejectedly. He looked confused and hurt and pissed as hell.

Would you quit trying to mess this up?

I walked back over and stood in front of him. He didn't look up.

"Jack?" I asked, trying to get him to look at me. He didn't answer. I tried again. "Hey, look at me. Please?" I asked.

His eyes closed at the word *please*. "I'm pissed at you, Gracie," he said darkly, but the use of the name *Gracie* let me know he was more hurt than pissed.

"I know. I'm pissed at myself right now. Can you understand why I'm nervous, though?" I inquired, daring to reach out another hand to his hair, scratching at his scalp.

He ducked away from my hand; he wasn't going to let this slide so easily. "I get why you're nervous to leave, but I don't get why you think I'd do something like that. If this is gonna work, especially when we're apart, there needs to be some basic trust," he said, finally opening his eyes and looking at me.

Oh, man, he was better equipped at twenty-four to deal with this than I was.

"I know, love. You have to understand, I've got thirty-three years' worth of crap baggage knocking around behind me, and if you take me, you take the baggage. Old insecurities . . . they're a bitch."

"You don't think I'm nervous about this, too? The timing of this whole thing is crap. We're crazy to even try to make this work, but I think it's crazy *not* to. I don't know what's going to happen, either, Gracie. We might be totally fucked."

"I agree," I answered, frowning.

"You need to settle down, though. No more pussy parade. That was uncalled for," he said, his face serious. "And quit blaming our age difference when it's your shit that's making this weird right now."

289

I paused and took in what he'd said. He was right. This *was* all my shit.

I reached out tentatively, approaching the scalp scratch once more. This time, he let me.

"Fucking Nuts Girl." He sighed, closing his eyes again in acceptance.

"How about we just take it as it comes, and we'll see how we manage the distance thing? We don't need to decide anything tonight . . . yes?" I said.

He leaned in and pressed his face against my stomach, embracing me and pulling me into him.

"Yes," he said, his voice muffled as he hugged me. We were quiet for a minute as I played with his hair. "Grace?" he asked, still muffled.

"Mmm-hmm?"

"You're thirty-three?" he asked my tummy.

"Yep." The jig was up.

"Fuck, you're old," he said, holding me tighter. He knew to restrain me.

"Hating you right now, Hamilton," I said, seething.

"Loving you right now, Sheridan." He laughed.

Shit storm over . . . or was this just a shit squall?

I managed to get out of his grip and walk over to the hot tub and slowly slipped out of my tank top and shorts. He watched me as I removed my bra and panties and slid into the water.

"You can't love me from over there. Now, get your ass in here and make this thirty-three-year-old scream," I said, leaning back against the rim with my arms spread out, making sure my breasts bobbed just above the surface.

He was in the tub in thirty-seven seconds.

And that was the night I found out Jack Hamilton could hold his breath underwater for an obscenely long time.

☆ ☆ ☆

We slept deeply that night, pleasantly exhausted. Curled up with his hands on my breasts, I slept the sleep of the solidly fucked. And that can be taken several ways.

The next morning dawned clear and sunny—classic California for my last full day in L.A. And I would be spending it mostly alone. Jack was up early, and I watched from the bed as he changed. He had interviews all day and was taking a lunch meeting with Holly and a new director for a movie he was hoping to do in the spring. He had essentially quit working once *Time* was finished shooting, devoting his time to the upcoming media blitz that would take him halfway around the world and back again.

I sighed happily at the sight of my Jack walking around sleepily, dressed only in his jeans and no shirt. His hair was extra curly this morning, and he looked adorable. He smiled when he caught me staring and asked what I had planned for today.

"Well, I'm finishing up some last-minute packing, and then I'm having lunch with Nick to say good-bye. I've gotta go over to my house late this afternoon to sign the last few work orders, and then I'm officially moved in, just to move back out." I tossed him his shirt, which was on the floor next to my bed. I couldn't resist giving it a quick sniff.

Mmm, s'mores and sex.

"Grace, did you just sniff my shirt?" he asked, incredulous.

"Yep, I did. And after you leave, I'll probably lie on your side of the bed for a while because the pillow smells like you. I'm ridiculous when I'm in love. We're talking Hallmark here." I giggled, hugging his pillow to my chest and taking deep breaths in, flaring my nostrils and widening my eyes.

"Wow, that's not attractive." He laughed, taking in my display. I curled up on his side anyway and continued to watch him putter about.

"What time are you heading over to your house?" he asked. "Maybe I'll meet you there. I need to take a look at that master bathroom before I start sledgehammering, to make way for . . . the steam shower!" He suddenly landed on the bed next to me, wrapping my neck in a choke hold like a pro wrestler.

"Like you know how to install a steam shower, pretty boy," I said teasingly, enduring an old-school noogie smack-down.

"I would supervise, obviously. I can't let these hands get too dirty," he said seriously, admiring his hands. I rolled my eyes, and he went back to scrubbing the top of my head with his knuckles.

"I'm meeting Chad there at five."

"Perfect timing. I should be finishing up with my last interview about then. I'll swing by," he said, finally releasing me.

He finished getting ready and purposefully avoided my eyes when he snuck the ball cap into his back pocket. But he didn't put it on, so he was still honoring the agreement.

Down in the kitchen, I made him toast, slightly burned with lots of marmalade (he really was like my own Padding-ton Bear . . . he was *Hamilton* Bear) and wrapped it in a paper towel so he could eat it in the car. I put a travel mug of coffee next to his bag while he gathered up the rest of his things. He wasn't exactly packing up, but I did notice that some extra things were on their way out, like his cell charger, which had been plugged in next to mine for the last few weeks.

Grace, you don't have time to panic.

He smiled when he saw the coffee ready to go for him. "Love you, Nuts Girl."

"Love you more, Sweet Nuts," I answered back, shaking my boobies at him. He raised an eyebrow and then left, blowing a kiss over his shoulder.

"See you at five!" he shouted, and soon after, I heard his car pulling away.

Then I was alone. I went up to my room to finish packing. I looked around, starting to feel blue again . . . and saw a note on my pillow! I smiled and opened it.

> *Quit pouting and get your packing done. And you look damn good for 48 years old. Tee hee?*

My laughter broke through the stillness of the house.

twenty-four

*S*o that was it. I packed my last box, packed my last suitcase. FedEx picked up the things that I was shipping to New York. They'd be delivered to the hotel, which had agreed to hold them until my new sublet was ready. Holly's friend had found me a great one-bedroom on the Upper West Side in the sixties, relatively close to the theater district. Not knowing how long I'd be in New York, I'd wanted a nice central location in a good neighborhood, close to everything I needed.

I had briefly considered moving to New York right after college, but since Holly and I knew more people in L.A. and thought it would be a better career move, we'd ended up on the West Coast. But secretly, I always regretted not having lived in Manhattan, and I was grateful for the opportunity to live there, even if just for a few months—to experience the city as a resident and not merely a visitor. I'd traveled to the city frequently for work and always loved spending time there.

Now that I was less than twenty-four hours from actually being there, I was losing some of the nerves.

My semiargument with Jack yesterday had cleared the air a bit and I felt better. When he told me he loved me, there was a feeling inside of me that was hard to describe. It was like a tugging in my stomach and a rush through my skin, hot and cold at the same time. I felt giddy and silly and thrilled when I heard him say those words. And to see his eyes light up when I said it to him was enthralling.

The day passed by quickly, and before I knew it, I was headed over to my house on Laurel Canyon, the late-afternoon sun casting dappled light through the Italian cypress trees across the winding road. The top was down, the music loud, and my smile big as I enjoyed the ending of this day.

I'd miss my friends desperately, but Holly already had a ticket to fly out for a weekend at the end of the month. Jack's schedule was getting increasingly tight, but I knew he'd come as soon as he could. There would be plenty of movie-related visits in the upcoming months.

I pulled into my driveway just after five but didn't see Chad's truck. I hoped that I hadn't missed him . . . maybe I'd beaten him here. I unlocked the front door, pausing to take in the smell of new construction mixed with the potted lemon trees placed just outside the front door. It was strange that a house I had never spent a night in already felt more like a home than anything I'd ever had before. I loved staying with Holly, but when I got back from New York, I'd be glad to have my own home.

I set my keys down on the table that I'd placed in the entryway and listened to the *click-clack* on the smooth tile as I walked toward the living room.

As soon as I rounded the corner, I heard, "Surprise!"

"Holy shit!" I screamed as people came pouring out of rooms, from behind couches, and in from the patio.

All of my friends were there, some of Holly's other clients, Lane and Rebecca, and of course, the two ringleaders. Holly and Jack were standing in front of the fireplace, looking incredibly proud of themselves and smiling at me.

I approached them, pushing my way through the wall of people offering me congratulations and good-byes. Someone put a glass of champagne in my hand, and I noticed the sign hung over the archway: BON VOYAGE, ASSHEAD!

Jesus.

"Nice touch with the asshead." I smirked at Holly, knowing that was all her.

She laughed and raised her glass. "I thought you'd like that." She clinked her glass to mine.

I turned to smile at Jack, but his mouth was already on its way to my neck. He kissed me quickly, moving his lips up my ear.

"Are you surprised?" he asked, sucking my earlobe into his mouth and kissing it softly.

The butterflies were back in my tummy. I loved when he did that.

"I am. This is nice," I answered, leaning into him as his lips moved down my neck toward my collarbone. "That's nice, too . . ." My words trailed off as he reached my shoulder, kissing it lightly. His hands slipped around my waist, and he moved me in front of him, resting his chin on my shoulder.

This all took place in less than a minute, but the intimacy was all-encompassing. The sweet way he manipulated my body, the way he claimed me so publicly and so privately at the same time, was endearing. I clutched his hands tighter into my tummy, hugging him to me as we stood.

Our relationship had blossomed very quickly and mostly privately, so I saw a few curious glances in our direction.

Mainly, though, there were amused and kind faces smiling back at us.

Jack stayed with me as I greeted my guests, delighted to meet my friends and acquaintances. Some were new, people I'd met since I'd moved back to L.A., and some dated back to when I was there the first time.

Nick delighted in telling the story of the first night Jack and I were together, regaling the crowd with what he had seen as well as what he'd heard as he and Holly ate popcorn on the staircase like two Peeping Toms.

The night was perfect, with the people I loved most surrounding me.

☆ ☆ ☆

Everyone was so complimentary about my new home, and I showed it off like a proud mama. All the furniture had finally been delivered, and while there was still a lot to be done, it was finished enough that it had a sense of self—it felt like me. Jack was telling Nick about the closet he wanted to knock out to make room for the steam shower, and Nick pretended to look interested while he was really just staring at the pretty.

I talked to everyone, thanked them all for their well wishes for New York, and promised countless times that I'd be back.

Jack stayed with me some of the time, and other times he mingled. I watched him from across the room, talking to Rebecca and Lane, and several times he caught me staring. He always waved or winked or showed me his middle finger, a rather rude habit he seemed to have picked up from me.

God, I loved him.

Much later, Holly and I found ourselves outside as the party began to wind down. They'd strung up Christmas lights throughout the trees and hung Japanese lanterns so that the entire backyard was glowing. And by *they*, I mean the party planner Jack and Holly had hired.

We sat in the Adirondack chairs on the patio, drinking dirty martinis and toasting our successes.

"Can you believe the last party we were at, we were celebrating your new management company?" I asked, tipping my glass to her.

"Yeah, and that was the night you got asked to have a little tryst." She drained her glass.

"That's true. Tryst accomplished. Holly, I can't tell you how much I appreciate everything you've done for me. Really. I—"

"Save it for your Tony Awards acceptance speech, okay? I can't handle anything like that tonight," she said, her eyes suddenly glistening.

I looked at my best friend, who would lie down in front of a bus for me, and smiled. I thought about everything we had been through and everything we'd continue to share with each other.

"Olive juice, Holly," I said, smiling at her through the tears beginning to burn in my own eyes.

"Olive juice, too, ya little fruitcake." She smiled back, grabbing the rest of my martini and polishing it off as well. She pushed out of her chair and headed into the house.

I sat for a minute, smiling up at the stars, and then went in to say good night to the last few guests.

Jack was waiting for me and swept me into a close hug. "How soon do you think we can kick these stragglers out without seeming rude?" he whispered, biting down on his lower lip as I ran my hands through his thick curls.

"You want them gone, you just say the word," I said, feeling sassy from the two martinis and the champagne. I'd pay for this when I was stuck on a plane for over five hours tomorrow.

"I want them gone, Grace," he stated firmly, his hands sneaking down and cupping my backside. Fuck, I loved it when he took charge.

"Done," I answered, crashing my lips to his for a quick but very passionate kiss.

Then I pulled away and began a herding motion toward the front door. The last few people there, including Holly and Nick, looked at me as if I were crazy.

"Let's go, people, move it out. Have you seen this tall drink of water here? Well, Mr. Hamilton and I are going to be going at it in about seven minutes, and unless you want to see some serious good-bye fuckin', you'd best get to steppin'," I told the group, continuing to herd them toward the front door.

My friends knew better than to stay, and they laughed as they hugged and kissed me good-bye.

Jack looked on with an amused expression at my brazen room-clearing methods as I walked Rebecca and Lane to the door.

Lane gave me a monster hug. "Thanks for having us at your bon voyage party, Grace. Nice digs, by the way. We'll break this house in proper when you get back," he said, ruffling up my hair with his giant hands.

"That's a promise. I'm so glad you were here tonight." I kissed him on the cheek.

He blushed, and I heard him saying, "Aw, man . . . ," as he walked out to his car.

Rebecca turned to me. "I have to tell you, even though I know Jack is going to miss the shit out of you, I think it's awesome what you're doing. I know you'll do well. If I make it out to New York this fall, can I come see you?"

"Hell yes, you can! I expect a call any time you're anywhere near the Big Apple," I said, giving her a hug. "And, Rebecca?" I said, frowning a little.

"I'll watch out for him. Keep the skanks away," she said, reading my expression.

"Thank you. Keep 'em far back! I may be three thousand miles away, but I can still kick some ass if I need to."

"I totally believe you. Good luck in Manhattan, girl," she said, hugging me back and walking out the door.

The room was almost clear. I said good-bye to Nick, thanked Holly with a kiss on the cheek and a smack on the ass, and promised to keep it quiet when we got home later that night. She just smirked and said she'd see me in the morning.

After they left I finally walked back into the living room, where Jack was sitting on one of my big fluffy couches, and I launched myself at him. He caught me midair, laughing as I pawed at his chest like a big cat.

"I got rid of them," I chirped, settling into his lap.

"You sure did," he said, kissing my forehead.

"So, now what?" I leaned my head on his shoulder.

"Well, what do you want to do?" He snuggled me closer to him.

"Ummm, get naked and have sex in my new house?" I said, looking brightly at him.

"Hell yes, let's get after it." He laughed, picking me up and walking me toward my bedroom.

Though my new bed had been delivered, I hadn't picked out sheets or anything yet. So I was surprised when we walked into the room and I saw that someone, probably the Brit currently holding me and looking at me expectantly, had appointed the bed quite nicely. Soft white sheets, blankets, a duvet, and tons of pillows dressed the California king, and the sheets were thoughtfully turned down. There was even candy on the pillows, hotel style.

"Candy!" I exclaimed, bringing a chuckle from the Brit.

I also noticed my overnight bag, alongside my white button-down shirt on the chair by the window next to his bag. I looked at him in surprise.

"I thought it might be nice to spend at least one night in your new house," he said shyly.

"George?"

"Yes?"

"I freaking love you," I squealed, throwing my arms around his neck.

"I love you too, Gracie," he answered, and carried me into the room.

After the crazy love was through, we lay in bed. It was very late, although technically it was very early. I don't think either one of us wanted to go to sleep. We lay next to each other on our sides, sharing the same pillow. I gazed at him, this man who had taken over my heart completely. I took in everything, memorizing the way his lashes swept down low to almost graze his cheeks. The strong lines of his face, the cheekbones, the jawline, the nose. The sexy stubble. The sweet, soft lips that were curved in that perfect smile that always made my heart beat faster.

And the curls. I remembered the way they looked that day on the way to the beach, the blond glinting in the sun. And the eyes, the green perfection. They were locked on mine, staring at me in quiet reflection. I guessed that he was cataloging my features as well, the way his eyes were poring over me.

In mere weeks, Jack Hamilton had turned my world upside down. He'd made me feel things I hadn't felt in years, and I was grateful to him for it. I'd gone through years of quiet hell and had all but forgotten what it felt like to be revered so. I forgot what it felt like to be loved, which is why I think I fought this so long. He loved me thoroughly and completely, and while part of me was still looking over my shoulder to see who he was really looking at, I was coming to understand it.

I loved him that way in return. I loved him as hard as I could. The bubble we'd existed in for weeks was about to burst, but I wasn't as nervous now to see what it would be like outside our bubble.

Because this was real life. And in real life, you are tested—simple as that. We'd be tested, and we'd have to see how we did. There were still issues to be resolved, but I was determined that we'd resolve them together. That was what grown-ups did . . . and how funny that this twenty-four-year-old guy reminded me about that. I was the one with the grown-up mortgage, but the guy with the messy apartment had taught me this.

He'd also taught me how to love my body again. Post-pudge Grace certainly had enjoyed the last year's sexual freedom after such a long drought, but it was his absolute devotion to bringing me pleasure that made me love my body, flaws and all. I still saw them, but the fact that he adored me so made me grateful for how strong I truly was. And come on, the guy had practically built an altar to my cleavage. This tended to make a girl feel pretty good about herself.

I continued to stare at him, marveling still at how lucky I was to have him—and realized with surprise that he was lucky to have me, too. For whatever reason, he needed me as I needed him. And that was it.

He was the yin to my yang, the frick to my frack, the melba toast to my Chex.

We'd never stood a chance of trying to fight this—for me, he was the one.

I reached out to scratch his head and he moved closer to me, the gazing over. I cradled him to me and he stroked my breasts, nudging his head into the crook between my neck and my shoulder and wrapping his other arm around me, underneath me. He couldn't get close enough.

"God, I'm going to miss you so much, Grace," he whispered, his voice low.

I kissed his forehead, soothing him. "I know, love—me too."

"We'll be fine, right?" he asked.

He was the one who needed reassurance now, and I gave it to him. "Yes, Jack, we'll be fine," I crooned, rocking him slightly.

He let his breath out in a long, shaky sigh. "Is it terrible that there's a tiny part of me that wants your show to suck, so you can come home in just a few weeks?" he asked honestly, showing me his heart.

"It's not terrible." I chuckled softly, touched by his question. I knew without a doubt that he wanted this success for me as much as I did.

We were both quiet then, our breathing in harmony as I felt his chest rise and fall. He continued his worship of my breasts, his hands soothing me now. It wasn't sexual in nature; it was simple pleasure for us both.

"I love you, Grace," he whispered, suddenly pulling me into a bone-crushing hug.

"I love you, Jack," I answered, wrapping my legs around him to get as close as possible.

Our bodies said what we couldn't bear to say. He kissed me, I kissed him back, and then he slipped inside of me. We moved together quietly, peacefully. There was a tenderness in this night, a silent, sweet good-bye. As our bodies rose and fell in unison, our eyes filled with tears.

We sighed deeply as we came together, the union complete. He collapsed onto me and I hugged him tightly, keeping him inside as long as I could. Then we lay awake all night, neither of us wanting to close our eyes.

☆ ☆ ☆

We spent the night talking quietly, laughing and swearing, giggling and promising. When it finally became light enough that I could no longer pretend it was night, we got out of the bed and into some clothes.

After I dressed I walked through my home, already looking forward to making it lived-in. Jack packed up my things from last night and met me by the back door in the kitchen. The mood had shifted this morning; the energy was different. He was quietly resigned.

I was quietly . . . excited?

I *was* excited.

As I walked through the kitchen, I slapped a Post-it note on my new Sub-Zero fridge, where not even a jar of mustard lived yet.

"What's that for?" he asked, smiling tiredly.

I laughed, grabbing his sweet face in my hands. "I left myself a note for when I come back."

"And what did you tell yourself?" He held the door for me as we walked out toward my car.

I threw my bag into it and took the keys from him. I wouldn't get to drive in New York, so I wanted to soak up as much as I could. I dropped the top, fired up the tunes, and said, "It says, 'Welcome home, Grace.'"

twenty-five

*B*reakfast was quick. Jack made Holly and me oatmeal while I made coffee and she sliced up bananas for our bowls. We talked hurriedly about last-minute plans. I'd be leaving my car at Holly's. We figured it would be better to have it somewhere that someone actually lived. The two of them would check on my house every other week or so. There were still a few pieces being delivered, but between Jack and Holly, they had it covered.

I offered Jack the use of my car while I was gone but he declined, insisting he quite enjoyed his broken little car and saying, "Now that the car snob will be away, I'll be pleased to drive it again."

Jack and I beat a hasty path upstairs after breakfast, determined to sneak in as much time alone as we could before we needed to leave for LAX. My flight was at one, and we figured on leaving for the airport around ten.

It was already eight thirty.

We headed straight for the shower, dropping our clothes so fast, it was like someone was holding a gun to our heads, and I laughed. "It's like Dead Man Showering," I quipped as I wriggled out of my bra.

"It does have a certain finality to it, doesn't it?" Jack chuckled as I struggled with the last clasp. "Can I please help you with that?"

He stood behind me as I held my hair up, and when it was finally off, his hands slipped down to the band of my panties and began sliding them over my hips.

"I don't recall asking you to help with those, Sweet Nuts," I said, scolding him, my breath catching in my throat.

"I don't recall asking for your opinion on this matter, Nuts Girl," he growled as the panties went down. "Let's go get wet."

"Too late," I said, the lower half of my body beginning to warm as his hands began to explore.

"Is that a fact?" he asked, walking me backward into the bathroom.

"Oh, like you're not totally turned on?" Mr. Hamilton Junior was poking insistently at his boxers. My hands went up to his shoulders and I ran them down the length of his arms, while his snaked around my waist, pulling me to him.

"Why do you still have these on?" I asked, snapping the band on his boxers.

"You tell me, Crazy," he said, reaching past me to turn on the shower.

I removed the offending boxers in the time it would take to say *Hamiltonian Wake-up Call*.

We scrambled in and lathered quickly. He washed my hair, covering me in bubbles. Then, of course, he held my boobies for balance while I washed his hair. He truly never tired of playing with them. I honestly think if he'd had his own pair, I might never have heard from him again. Luckily, I never tired of his playing with them, either. He had me moaning within seconds, and then groaning a minute later. He was taking my washing up very seriously this morning, and there wasn't a place on my body he didn't attend to. He brought me to three quick, intense orgasms, and before I knew it we were out of the shower and on the floor of the bathroom, with me on top, riding him in a frenzy, getting water all over the floor.

We fucked frantically, laughing when he knocked over the tower of toiletries with his foot, making baby powder and tampons rain down on us. We laughed when the squeak of his ass against the marble became almost louder than my groaning. And we *really* laughed when we came together, tension and giggles giving way to satisfaction.

I rolled off him, landing squarely on my cold flatiron. I yelped, and when he tried to help me, he hit his head squarely on the toilet.

I looked around at the state of the bathroom—the open shower door, the Always with wings and mascara strewn about the floor, the flatiron under my bum, and Jack rubbing his head.

I laughed until tears streamed down my face, my naked body jiggling in places that I knew couldn't look good. And I didn't care.

"I . . . love you . . . so . . . much . . . ," I choked out.

"I love you too, Gracie . . . Always," he said, deadpan, holding up a maxi pad.

I laughed so hard, my stomach hurt.

Jack crawled over to me, knocking bottles left and right with his knees, and kissed me square on the lips. "You're crazy, but you're *my* Crazy. I love it."

☆ ☆ ☆

Nine fifty-seven A.M.

I stood with Holly in the driveway while Jack put my suitcases in my car. I fought down the lump in my throat. I could tell she had one, as well.

"So, you have everything, right?" she asked. "Neil is going to call you tonight to check in. You have a meeting with him on Thursday after you get settled into the hotel, right?"

"Yes, ma'am. I'm meeting him Thursday."

"And you have your cell charger, right? You call my ass the minute you land. Do you have money for a cab into the city? It will be about forty-five dollars—don't let them over-charge you."

"I got it, Mom. I've been there before, you know. Proba-bly more often than you." I laughed at her mother-henning.

"I know, I know, asshead. I guess that's it." She pressed her lips tightly together.

"Okay, dillweed. I'll call you when I land. Bye," I said, hug-ging her quickly.

She just nodded her head, hugging me back just as hard. Then she pulled away and disappeared into the house. Holly always hated good-byes.

I turned to Jack, a little teary, and he reached for my hand. "You ready to go?" he asked quietly.

"Yep—let's do this," I answered, wiping away the tears that had escaped and climbing into the passenger side.

It was one of the few mornings ever in the history of L.A. with little traffic, and all too soon we were pulling into LAX. Jack insisted on parking and walking me in, though I wanted him to just let me out at the curbside check-in. My stomach was in knots and I knew how hard it was going to be to say good-bye to him.

We parked underground, and I swear you've never seen anyone take so long to remove luggage from the trunk as he did. We held hands, walking at a turtle's pace toward the ticket counter, and I punched in my frequent-flier number, bringing up my itinerary. I was pleased to see I'd gotten an upgrade and would be in seat 3D, a window seat.

"Sheridan?" the counter agent called, and we moved forward. Jack placed my bags on the scale and we waited for her to wrap the tags around the handle.

"You're checking two bags through to LaGuardia, right?" she asked.

"Yes," I answered. My voice was rough, and my throat felt like sandpaper. I could see Jack was starting to feel it, too.

She gave me my ticket and pointed me toward the security checkpoint for my terminal.

Jack slung my carry-on bag over his shoulder, and we walked away slowly, holding hands. Right before we got to security, he pulled me over to the wall, almost hidden behind a vending machine. He set my bag down, and I kept my eyes on the floor. I literally couldn't bear to look at him.

"Grace? Come on, look at me," he said, chiding me softly, his fingers slipping under my chin and lifting my face up.

The tears that had been building finally broke, and I clutched him to me fiercely. "Damn it, George, I'm going to miss you so much!" I cried, squeezing him as tightly as I dared.

"I know, Gracie, me too," he said, not crying, but sounding like he could.

I breathed in his sweet scent and began to kiss every part of his warm skin that was exposed. His neck, his ears, his temples, his forehead, the little part of his chest that was exposed by his open collar, his cheeks, his nose, his eyelids, and finally his mouth, which was eager for my own. His hands swept across my back and my hips, his beautiful fingers spanning my waist almost completely.

I held on as tightly as I could, trying to express with sheer force how much I was going to miss him and how much it broke my heart to leave him.

"Grace? I just want you to know how glad I am that I met you. I can't imagine my life without your crazy, sexy, beautiful ass in it now," he whispered in my ear, bringing a fresh wave of tears and a smile from me.

"God, you're amazing. I'm so lucky," I whispered back, clutching him still tighter.

He was kissing my neck with a sense of urgency, burying his face in my hair and breathing deeply. When his lips found mine again we kissed until we were both breathless, his cheeks wet from my tears, and then he hugged me tightly again.

"I should go," I whispered, my hands buried in his hair.

"Yes, you should," he whispered back, beginning to let go.

I backed away, swinging my bag onto my shoulder and taking my boarding pass from his hip pocket.

"Call me when you land?" he asked, his eyes sad.

"Promise," I answered, scratching his head one last time. He closed his eyes like a puppy, leaning into it, and I was close enough that I could feel the warmth of him.

"I love you, sweet girl." He smiled, opening his eyes and leaning down for one more kiss.

"I love you too, Jack." I smiled back.

Then I walked away. I showed the TSA officer my ID and boarding pass, then got in line. I couldn't look behind me.

"Hey, Crazy!" I heard, and I turned around smiling, along with the other thirty people in line.

"Yes, Sweet Nuts?" I yelled back, to the general amusement of all around me.

"Knock their fucking socks off!" he yelled.

I laughed and lifted my hand in a good-bye. With one last sexy half grin he walked away, disappearing into the crowd. I was still smiling when I turned back to the line.

The woman in front of me smiled. "Boyfriend?"

"Yes. That was my boyfriend," I answered, enjoying the word on my tongue.

"He's cute. And that accent! Jeez, it's hot—if you don't mind my saying." She laughed.

"I don't mind—it's totally hot." I smiled again, wiped the tears away, and headed for my gate.

☆   ☆   ☆

Once I was on the plane, my tears came back. I sat quietly sniffling, watching everyone else file onto the plane. The flight attendant had already offered me a cocktail, but I wasn't ready for that yet.

One of the reasons I felt so sad was that I didn't know when I would see him again. I could be in New York indefinitely—three months, a year. It was all dependent upon how well the show did and the kind of backing it received.

I knew Jack would be out to visit, and I knew that at some point I'd be able to get back to L.A., but not knowing when made it so difficult for me. Not to mention that I hadn't slept alone in weeks, and I knew that tonight, when the lights went out and I didn't have the Brit under the covers with me, I'd miss him something fierce.

I thought of his sweet face, looking lost as I walked away from him today. I'd seen the same sadness in his eyes that was in mine and knew he would miss me. I thought of his smile and how happy I made him when I did something as simple as scratching his head, and my insides actually ached.

What would he do if he were here now and I was crying? I smiled immediately, thinking of how quickly he'd have me pressed tightly to him, making me laugh through my tears or simply letting me cry it out. And I'd do the same for him. All I wanted to do was take care of him and have him take care of me. We needed each other equally. I knew that now.

God, I should have gone shopping for him before I left! He'd eat nothing but freaking fast food for the next three months if no one got involved.

But that was enough sad-sackery. I needed a distraction.

I pulled out a magazine and laughed ruefully when I saw that he was featured in an article about faces to watch.

Yeah—no kidding.

Somewhere over Utah...

I put the magazine down after rereading the pages with my Brit several hundred times.

The flight attendant nodded toward the article as she handed me a Bloody Mary. "Did you read the article about

Jack Hamilton? I could get arrested for the thoughts I have about that kid." She grinned.

I blushed and grinned back. "He's a tall drink of water, that's for sure."

"God, yes. I can't tell you how much I'm looking forward to his new film." She leaned against the aisle seat, making the guy next to me roll his eyes. He'd attempted to engage me in conversation, which I had quickly thwarted. Now I was ready to talk, but about a heartthrob? I'm sure he thought I was nuts.

Mmm, someone I loved called me Nuts Girl.

"Yeah, it looks really good. I love me some Super-Sexy Scientist Guy," I replied.

"You must be talking about Jack Hamilton," a voice said behind me, and the woman in 4D popped her head up to participate.

"Ha! Everyone I know adores that kid," the flight attendant squealed.

"Oh, my goodness," 4D said. "Did you see his last movie? I almost died when he was in that towel . . . gah!"

"Yeah, he's pretty to look at." The flight attendant sighed, and all three of us began to giggle like schoolgirls.

And I smiled to myself, thinking of the man who'd hit his head on my toilet bowl only hours before.

☆　☆　☆

When the plane finally landed, I was exhausted. It had been an emotional day, I'd gotten no sleep the night before, and plane rides were always tiring, especially when you imbibed the free Bloody Marys.

I grabbed my bags off the carousel and made my way toward the line of cabs. When it was my turn, I gave the driver the address of the W hotel, then checked my messages. I smiled as I listened to Holly instructing me to call her as soon as I reached my hotel. I couldn't help but call Jack and was a little saddened that I got his voice mail.

"Hey, love, I'm in a cab heading into the city now. Wanted to call and let you know I made it here safe and sound. And I even met a few fans of yours on the plane! I told them I fucked you repeatedly and often, and they seemed oddly shocked by that. Kidding. Well, call me when you get this, I don't care how late. I want to talk to you before I go to sleep. I love you and miss you already, George. Okay, bye."

I sank back in the seat and looked out the window as Queens quickly went by. We crossed the bridge, and as I saw the lights of the city, I began to smile uncontrollably. It was nearly ten and the sky was fully dark. Everything was lit up, and the way the city looked as we crossed the river was magical. Absolutely magical.

We drove across town through the concrete canyons, the driver slamming on the brakes, honking back at other cabs and at the pedestrians. Hundreds of people were out, crossing the streets, sitting at cafés, pouring in and out of doorways. There was a vibrant pulse to this city, and after the laid-back charm of Southern California, my brain was hungry for the energy of Manhattan. Every time I was there, my heart beat a little faster.

As we pulled in front of the W the bellman came out to help with my bags, and I was soon whisked inside. While I was checking in, I felt a tap on my shoulder and I turned.

It was Michael.

"Hey! What are you doing here?" I exclaimed, hugging him.

"Holly told me when you were getting in, so I thought I'd buy you your first drink in New York. You're not too tired, are you? Maybe I should've given you time to settle in." He was dressed casually, like me, in loose khakis, gray T-shirt, Converse. His hair was quite curly in the humidity and framed his dark brown eyes.

"No, no. I would love that! I'm tired, but it's not even eight to me. Let me drop off my bags and then we can grab a drink. Do you mind if we have it here?" I said, gesturing to the gorgeous lobby bar.

"That sounds like a plan. Lemme help you," he said, grabbing my bags and leading me toward the elevator.

My room was on seventeen, high enough to have a great view. And since it was the W, my room was tricked out. We were setting everything down when my phone rang. I flopped across the bed to grab it, and when I saw it was Jack, I smiled hugely.

"Hey, Johnny Bite-Down! How are you?" I asked.

"Hey yourself. How was your flight?"

"It was good. Long . . . but good." I sighed.

"Sounds like me . . . long and good." He chuckled.

"Ha ha, very funny. I miss you already, you know," I said, dropping my voice a little.

"I know. I miss you, too. I'm sorry I missed your call earlier. Is it too early for phone sex?" He laughed.

Michael stuck his head out from the closet, where he had been putting my bags away. "Hey, Grace, do you want this one in the bathroom?" he asked.

"Yeah, that's fine, thanks," I called out. "So, phone sex, can it wait until later tonight? I want to be able to give you my full attention."

"Who was that?" Jack asked, his voice curious.

"Oh, Michael was here at the hotel when I got here, and we're going to grab a drink after I get settled in," I answered.

"Are you in your room?" he inquired, his voice still curious but with a slight edge to it.

"Yep, he helped me get my bags up here, and then we're heading back down to the bar," I answered, rolling my eyes.

"Uh-huh," he muttered.

How cute; he was a little jealous.

"Oh, Sweet Nuts, I really wish I could see your face right now—along with other parts." I laughed, and he loosened up.

"Well, I'll tell you what. You go have your drink and then call me later. I'm heading out soon, too. I'm actually doing an open mike tonight."

"You are? Wow, I really wish I was there for that." I'd have killed to see him sing on a stage, just him and his guitar.

"I wish you were too, love. I'll speak to you soon then, yes?" he said softly.

"Yes. I love you, George," I cooed.

"I love you, too, Gracie."

And with that, we hung up. I sat on the bed for a moment, then Michael came back in.

"I thought his name was Jack," he said.

"What?" I asked, coming out of my haze.

"You said George . . . I thought his name was Jack," he said, looking puzzled.

"It *is* Jack. The George is a long story. Let's go get that drink."

Taking a deep breath, I pushed myself off the bed and headed out of the room with Michael. As the door swung shut behind us, I saw the lights of New York twinkling beyond the window.

I was finally here—and it was time for me to shine.

alice clayton

☆　☆　☆

A few weeks later

I pulled my orange scarf more snugly around my neck and knotted it again so it tucked right under my chin. The air was cool this morning and the leaves fell around me, blown about by a blustery breeze. Sheltered from the wind, I gazed at the scene before me:

Brownstones. Concrete.

Yellow cabs. A deli advertising both pastrami and falafel.

As I sipped my coffee, I marveled at my life and where it had taken me.

I loved New York.

The last few weeks had been amazing—and difficult. It was October now, and fall had officially come to Manhattan. The air was crisp, there were pumpkins on stoops, and I was having the time of my life. I was insanely happy.

Except, I was really missing my Brit . . .